Praise for *The Book of Phoenix*

'Immense, compelling, and powerful . . . *The Book of Phoenix* isn't just well written, and it isn't just smart as hell; it's also a damn good story.'
Tor.com

'It is possible that Nnedi Okorafor has invented a new genre; not quite fantasy, not quite magical realism; not quite sci-fi; not quite speculative fiction; not quite young adult, she takes the best of these and adds something else and I can only think to call her genre – simultaneity. With a beguiling elegance she weaves danger, possibility and history into a deeply human pursuit for justice and transformation. In this new book, with this rebirth of the Phoenix, these all come together with a breathtaking ease. A rare and unique voice in a very strong book. Read it.'
Chris Abani, author of *Graceland*

'Nnedi Okorafor has made a name for herself with novels that combine politically complex science fiction and lyrical fantasy . . . Blending poetic passages with sharp observation and the occasional cadence of a story told by firelight, *The Book of Phoenix* is an assured introduction not just to her world's myths, but to the process of mythmaking.'
New York Times Review of Books

'Okorafor's inventiveness is as stunning as ever, and the ending is nothing short of spectacular.'
Chicago Tribune

'In the library of the mind, shelve Nnedi Okorafor's *The Book of Phoenix* between *The X-Men* and *Frankenstein* . . . This is a story of vengeance, a fantastic epic battle between good and evil; written as a fable for the future.'
Barnes & Noble Reads

About the Author

Nnedi Okorafor is the author of numerous novels and short stories, including *Zahrah the Windseeker*, which won the Wole Soyinka Prize for Literature, *Who Fears Death*, winner of the 2011 World Fantasy Award for Best Novel, and *Lagoon*, which Ngugi wa Thiong'o, author of *Wizard of the Crow,* calls 'a thing of magic and beauty.'

She lives in New York, where she is a professor of creative writing at the University of Buffalo, SUNY.

THE
BOOK
OF
PHOENIX

Nnedi Okorafor

HODDER

First published in Great Britain in 2015
by Hodder & Stoughton
An Hachette UK company

First published in paperback in 2016

A CIP catalogue record for this title is available from the British Library

ISBN 978 1 444 76280 8

Printed and bound by Clays Ltd, St Ives plc

Hodder & Stoughton policy is to use papers that are natural, renewable and recyclable
products and made from wood grown in sustainable forests. The logging and manufacturing
processes are expected to conform to the environmental regulations of the country of origin.

Hodder & Stoughton Ltd
Carmelite House
50 Victoria Embankment
London
EC4Y 0DZ

www.hodder.co.uk

*To the stolen girls of Chibok, Nigeria. May you awaken with
the heart of Phoenix Okore and may your powerful flames
illuminate your swift journey home.*

"Voyage through death, to life upon these shores."
—*Robert Hayden, poet* (Middle Passage)

NOBODY REALLY KNOWS WHO WROTE THE GREAT BOOK.

Oh, the religious always have answers to explain the unexplainable. Some of them like to say that the goddess Ani wrote the Great Book and made it so that ten men and women who loved stories would find copies of it at the same time. Some of them say a mere woman with ten children transcribed Ani's words over ten years. Others say some illiterate half-witted farmer wrote it in one night after Ani blessed him. Most believe that the Great Book's author was a mad yet holy, always always holy, prophet who'd taken refuge in a cave.

What *I* can tell you is that two hundred years after it all went wrong an old man named Sunuteel was out in the desert. This man was one of those who enjoyed being out there for weeks on end, close to the sun, sand, and desert creatures. The time away from his wife made their time together sweeter. Sunuteel and his wife agreed on this. They were old. They had wisdom.

"Go on," his wife said with a smile. She took his old rough hand into her equally rough old hand. She was a beautiful woman, and Sunuteel found it easy to look into her eyes. "It is good," she said. "I need the solitude."

There had been an especially powerful Ungwa storm and the old nomadic couple had barely survived the dry thundery night of lightning. A bolt had struck near their sturdy tent, setting on fire one of the three stunted palm trees they'd camped beside. His wife had been peeking out of the tent when it happened. Thankfully, she'd blinked at precisely the right moment. She said the tree looked like a woman dancing in flames. Even as Sunuteel dragged her to the center of the tent where they huddled and prayed, his wife felt a presence. She was sure it was a premonition.

The old man was used to his superstitious wife and her odd intuitions. Therefore, he knew his wife would want to be alone to think and ponder and fret. When the storm passed and she gently encouraged him to take a few days to go and see what was out there, he didn't argue. He took the rolled up goatskin tent and satchel of supplies she handed him and kissed her on the cheek. He didn't say goodbye because in his tribe "goodbyes" were a curse.

"I leave my *chi* to keep you company," he said. Each night he was away, along with her meals, she'd prepare a small plate of food for his personal god until Sunuteel returned. He clipped his portable to his hip, facing the tiny device inside his pocket. After one last, far more prolonged kiss, he walked away from his wife. Did she think an angel was coming to visit her? His wife's descendants were from the Islamic portion of Old Naija. She said that her father used to tell her all sorts of stories about angels and djinn. She'd passed these magical stories on to their own children as they grew up.

Minutes after leaving, Sunuteel brought out his portable and laughing to himself, called up the virtual screen and typed, "Hussaina, greet *her* for me when you see her, whether she's an angel or djinni." Moments later, his wife Hussaina's reply popped up on the screen saying what she always said when Sunuteel went off, "And you make sure you bring me back a good story."

Two days later, Sunuteel came upon a cave full of computers. A tomb of old old technology from the Black Days, the Times of the Dark People, the Era of the Okeke. This was one of those caves into which panicked Okeke packed thousands of computers just before Ani turned her attention back to the earth. These computers were supposedly used to store huge amounts of information separate from digital repositories called virtual spaces. Little good this did; virtual or physical, it was all dead, forgotten, rotten.

"What am I seeing?" he whispered. "Can this be?"

He pressed a shaky hand to his chest, feeling the strong heartbeat of his strong heart. Standing here, he didn't feel so old. No, not old at all. This place made him feel young as a babe. Sunuteel, who was Okeke and therefore a descendant of the evil that caused the goddess Ani to bring the deserts, knew of the poisonous Black Days and their most poisonous genius gadgetry. However, he had always wanted to see these ancient computers with his own eyes.

So, he went in.

The cave was cool and it smelled of dust, mineral oil, plastic, wires, and metal. There were ghosts here and Sunuteel shivered from the thought of them. Still, he approached these old machines. *This* was a story to tell his wife. The third computer that he touched sparked with life. Terrified, he snatched his hand from the "on" pad he'd accidently brushed against and stumbled back. The grey hand-sized box, softly hummed. Then it spoke to the portable clipped inside the pocket of his dusty pants. The portable pinged softly as it wirelessly received a large file from the computer. Sunuteel blinked and then fled from the cave, sure a ghost had touched him.

When he made it back to his small goatskin tent beside a baobab tree, only then did he dare look at his portable. He held the coin-sized device in his palm and brought it to his face, for his eyesight was poor. He squinted at the tiny screen. Next to the file that contained messages from his wife was a black icon in the shape of a bird that seemed to be looking over its shoulder. He tapped it with the tip of his finger and a deep male voice began to speak in . . . English!

It was an audio file. Sunuteel sat back in his tent, grinning with delight. *My goodness*, he thought. *How strange. What are the chances?!* He *knew* this dead language, albeit the accent was very odd, indeed. He brought up the virtual screen. The visual words that appeared as the audio file played were tinted red instead of the usual green. He put the portable on the blanket before him. Then he watched and listened.

The voice read a table of contents as it digitally projected the words on the virtual screen in front of him:

"Section one, mythology. Section two, legend. Section three, mechanics. Section four, news . . ."

He frowned as it read on and on. After a while, he decided to click on "Section thirty-eight, memory extracts" because the phrase rung a distant bell from when he was a child. In school, the teacher had spoken about the dark times hundreds of years ago, when human beings were obsessed with the pursuit of immortality. They had even found a way to pull out and capture people's memories right from their minds so they could preserve them forever. "Just like a capture station sucking condensation from the sky to make drinking water," his schoolteacher had said.

Sunuteel had been fascinated and quietly proud of just how *far* human beings had gotten in their technological pursuit. Nevertheless, his schoolteacher had discouraged him from further research. "Sunuteel," she said. "This was what led us to receiving Ani's wrath."

And so the young Sunuteel turned away from the past and looked mostly toward the future. He loved language, words and stories. He'd gone on to become one of his village's most valued recorders and reciters. He could recite the most beautiful poetry in five different dialects of flawless Okeke, but also in the language and various dialects of the majestic and mighty Nuru people and the common language of Sipo. And most amazingly, one of the prominent village elders had been able to teach him English, too.

As far as Sunuteel knew, this elder, an old-timer in Sunuteel's village who'd always been called The Seed, was the only person who knew the language. The Seed was also the only light-skinned person in his village who was not albino. This man refused to call himself Nuru, insisting that he was "Arab," a term that had long become more an insult than an ethnic description of the Nuru people. The Seed preferred to live amongst the Okeke, the dark-skinned woolly-haired people. He'd built a house in front of one of the pyramids because it reminded him of home. When Sunuteel was a teen, The Seed looked no older than fifty, but Sunuteel's mother said he was actually much older.

"He looked the exact same when I was a little girl," she'd told him. She was right. Even now that Sunuteel was an old old man, The Seed still looked no older than fifty. Sunuteel was of a people who understood that the world was full of mystery. Thus, a seemingly immortal man living in the village didn't bother anyone. The Seed had an amazing command of the English language and though he was moody and reclusive at times, he turned out to be a wonderful teacher.

Sunuteel went on to read the only two English texts in the entire region, both of which were owned by the Seed. One was an anthropology book titled *Virulent Diseases of the Mars Colonies*, the other a book about igneous rock sediments. Despite the dryness of the subjects, Sunuteel loved the rhythm of English. It was a liquid sounding language, due to the way the words ran together.

"Memory Extracts," the voice announced in English. But then it began speaking another list and each item on it was in a different language, none of which he understood. Annoyed, Sunuteel listened for a while and was about to go back to the main menu when the male voice clearly said, "Extract number 5, *The Book of Phoenix*" in English.

He clicked on it.

At first there was a long pause and the bird icon popped on the screen. It rotated counter-clockwise. He counted thirteen rotations and when it kept going, he looked up at the sky. Blue. Clear. A large hawk-like bird flew overhead, soaring high in the sky, probably seeing him perfectly with its sharp eyes. *I will return to Hussaina in two days*, he thought. *That's enough alone time for her to stop thinking about premonitions and angels.* He smiled to himself. She would excitedly cook him a spicy meal of doro wat when he told her he had "a big big tale to tell." She loved a good story, and good stories were best told on a full stomach.

"Memory Extract Number 5," the male voice suddenly announced, making Sunuteel jump. "Title: *The Book of Phoenix*. Location Number 578."

And then a woman began feverishly speaking. Her soft breathy voice was like a powerful incantation, for as she spoke, it seemed that the old man's eyesight, which dimmed more and more every year, began to brighten. His wife would have recognized what was happening. However, Sunuteel was a man less open to such things.

Still, as he sat in his tent, gazing through the red virtual words before him and the open tent flap just beyond the words, outside into the desert, he realized he could see for miles and miles. Sweat prickled on his forehead and between the coarse hairs of his armpits. He listened. And the very first person to hear one of the many many entries from *The Great Book* was awed by the story he heard.

"There is no book about me," the voice said. *"Well, not yet. No matter. I shall create it myself; it's better that way. To tell my tale, I will use the old African tools of story: Spoken words. They are worthier of my trust and they'll last longer. And during shadowy times, spoken words carry farther than words typed, imaged, or written. My beginnings were in the dark. We all dwelled in the dark, mad scientist and speciMen, alike. A dear friend of mine would say that this time was when 'the goddess Ani still slept'. I call my story* The Book of Phoenix. *It is reliable and short, because it was accelerated . . ."*

Chapter 1

SpeciMen

I'D NEVER KNOWN ANY OTHER PLACE. The 28th floor of Tower 7 was my home. Yesterday, I realized it was a prison, too. I probably should have suspected something. The two-hundred-year-old marble skyscraper had many dark sides to its existence and I knew most of them. There were 39 floors, and on almost every one was an abomination. I was an abomination. I'd read many books and this was clear to me. However, this building was still my home.

Home: a. One's place of residence. Yes, it was my home.

They gave me all the 3D movies I could watch, but it was the plethora of books that did it for me. A year ago, they gave me an e-reader packed with 700,000 books of all kinds. No matter the topic, I consumed those books voraciously, working my way through over half of them. When it came to information, I was given access to anything I requested. That was part of their research. I didn't know it then, but I know it now.

Research. This was what all The Towers were about. There were seven, all in American cities, yet they were not part of the American government.

Not technically. If you dug for information, you would not find one governmental connection on file.

I had access to information about all the towers, and I read extensively. However, Tower 7 was where I lived, so I studied this tower the most. They gave me many "top-secret" files on Tower 7. As I said, I was always given what I asked for; this was part of the research. But also, they did not see me as a threat, not to them. I was a perfectly contained classified "speciMen." And for a speciMen, knowledge wasn't power.

Tower 7 was located in Times Square on the island of Manhattan, United States of America. Much of Manhattan was underwater, but geologists were sure this part of it was stable enough for Tower 7. It was in the perfect position for top surveillance and security. I'd read about each floor and some of the types of abominations found on them. I'd listened to audios of the spiritual tellings of long-dead African and Native American shamans, sorcerers and wizards. I'd read the Tanakh, the Bible, and the Koran. I studied the Buddha and meditated until I saw Krishna. And I read countless books on the sciences of the world. Carrying all this in my head, I understood abomination. I understood the purpose of Tower 7. Until yesterday.

Each tower had . . . specializations. In Tower 7, it was advanced and aggressive genetic manipulation and cloning. In Tower 7, people and creatures were invented, altered, or both. Some were deformed, some were mentally ill, some were just plain dangerous, and none were flawless. Yes, some of us were dangerous. I was dangerous.

Then there was the tower's lobby on the ground floor that projected a completely different picture. I'd never been down there but my books described it as an earthly wonderland, full of creeping vines covering the walls and small trees growing from artistically crafted holes in the floor. In the center was the main attraction. Here grew the thing that brought people from all over the world to see the famous Tower 7 Lobby (*only* the lobby; there were no tours of the rest of the building).

A hundred years ago, one of the landscapers planted a new tree in the lobby's center. On a lark, some Tower 4 scientists who were there to visit the greenhouse on the ninth floor emptied an experimental solution into the tree's pot of soil. The substance was for enhancing and speeding up arboreal growth. The tree grew and grew. In a place where people thought like normal human beings, they would have uprooted the amazing tree and placed it outdoors.

However, this was Tower 7 where boundaries were both contained and pushed. The tree grew ravenously and in a matter of weeks it reached the lobby's high ceiling. Tower 7 carpenters constructed a large hole so that it could grow through the second floor. They did the same for the third, fourth, fifth. The great tree eventually earned the name of "The Backbone" because it grew through all thirty-nine of Tower 7's floors.

My name is Phoenix. I was mixed, grown and finally birthed here on the 28th floor. One of my doctors said my name came from the birthplace of my egg's donor. I've looked that up; Phoenix, Arizona is the full name of the place. There's no tower there, so that's good.

However, from what I've read about the way they did things there, even the scientists who forced my existence don't know the names of donors. So, I doubt this. I think they named me Phoenix because of something else.

I was an "accelerated organism," born two years ago. Yet I looked and physically felt like a forty-year-old woman. My doctors said the acceleration had stopped now that I was "matured." They said I would always look about forty, even if I lived to be five hundred. To them, I was like a plant they grew for the sake of harvesting.

Who do I mean by "them," you must wonder. *All* of THEM, the "Big Eye"— the Tower 7 scientists, lab assistants, lab technicians, doctors, administrative workers, guards, and police. We speciMen of the tower called them "Big Eye" because they watched us. All the time, they watched us, though not closely enough to realize their great error and not closely enough to prevent the inevitable.

I could read a 500-page book in two minutes. My brain absorbed the information and stories like a sponge. Up until two weeks ago, aside from mealtimes, gazing out the window, running on my treadmill, and meetings with doctors, I spent my days with my e-reader. I'd sit in my room for hours consuming words upon words that became images upon images in my head. Now they gave me paper-made books, removing the books when

I finished them. I liked the e-reader more. It took up less space, I could reread things when I wanted, there was a lot more to read and the e-pages didn't smell so old and moldy.

I stared out the window watching the cars and trucks below and the other skyscrapers across from me as I touched a leaf of my hoya plant. They'd given the plant to me five days ago and already it was growing so wildly that it was creeping across my windowsill and had wrapped around the chair I'd put there. It had grown two feet overnight. I didn't think they'd noticed. No one ever said anything about it. I was so naïve then. Of course, they'd noticed. The plant was not a gesture of kindness; it was just part of the research. They'd never cared about me. But Saeed cared about me.

Saeed is dead, Saeed is dead, Saeed is dead, I thought over and over, as I caressed one of my plant's leaves. I yanked, breaking the leaf off. *Saeed, my love, my only friend.* I crumpled the leaf in my restless hand; its green earthy smell might as well have been blood.

Yesterday, Saeed had seen something terrible. Not long afterwards, he'd sat across from me during dinner-hour with eyes wide like boiled eggs, unable to eat. He couldn't give me any details. He said no words could describe it. He'd only held my hand, pulling at his short dark brown beard with his other.

"What does your heart tell you about this place?" he'd earnestly asked.

I'd only shrugged, frustrated with him for not telling me what he'd seen that was so awful.

"*Behiima hamagi. Xara,*" he muttered, glaring at one of the Big Eye. He always spoke Arabic when he was angry. He leaned forward, lowering his voice. "You read all those books . . . why don't you feel rebellion in your heart? Don't you ever dream of getting out of here? Away from all the Big Eye?"

"Rebellion against whom?" I whispered, confused.

"I'd even settle for being a mild speciMen," he muttered. "They are fucked up, but not *that* fucked up. At least the Big Eye let them go out and live normal lives like normal people."

"Mild speciMen aren't special," I said. "That's why the Big Eye release them out there. I'd never want that, I like who I am."

He laughed bitterly, touched my cheek and lightly kissed me, looking deep into my eyes. Then he sat back and said, "Eat your jollof rice, Phoenix."

I tried to get him to eat his crushed glass. This was his favorite meal and it bothered me to see him push his plate away. But he wouldn't touch it.

"I can live without it," he said.

Before we returned to our separate quarters, he asked for my apple. I assumed he wanted to paint it; he always painted when he was depressed. I'd given it to him without a thought, and he'd slipped it into his pocket. The Big Eye allowed it, though they frowned upon taking food from the dining hall, even if you didn't plan to eat it.

His words didn't touch me until nighttime when I lay in my bed. Yes, somewhere deep deep in my psyche I *did* wish to get out of the tower and see the world, be away from the Big Eye. I *did* want to see those things that I saw in all the books I read. "Rebellion," I whispered to myself. And the word bloomed from my lips like a flower.

They told me the news in the morning, during breakfast-hour. I'd been sitting alone looking around for Saeed. The others, the woman with the twisted spine who could turn her head around like an owl, the man with long-eyelashed expressive eyes who never spoke with his mouth but always had people speaking to him, the three women who all looked and sounded alike, the green-eyed idiok baboons who spoke using complex sign language, the woman whose sweater did not hide her four large breasts, the two men joined at the hip who were always randomly laughing, the woman with the lion claws and teeth, these people spoke to each other and never to me. Only Saeed, the one who was *not* of African descent (aside from the lion lady, who was Caucasian), spoke to me. Well, even the lion lady was part-African because her genes had been combined with those of a lion.

One of my doctors slid into the seat facing me. The African-looking one who wore the shiny black wig made of synthetic hair, Bumi. They always had her deal with me when I had to experience physical pain, so I guess it made sense for them to send her to break upsetting news to me, too. My entire body tightened. She touched my hand, and I pulled it away. Then she smiled sympathetically and told me a terrible thing. Saeed hadn't drawn the apple. He'd eaten it. And it killed him. My mind went to one of my books. The Bible. I was Eve and he was Adam.

I could not eat. I could not drink. I would not cry. Not in the dining hall.

Hours later, I was in my room lying on my bed, eyes wet, mind reeling. Saeed was dead. I had skipped lunch and dinner, but I still wasn't hungry. I was hot. The scanner on my wall would start to beep soon. Then they would come get me. For tests. I shut my eyes, squeezing out tears. They evaporated as they rolled down my hot cheeks, leaving the skin itchy with salt. "Oh God," I moaned. The pain of losing him burned in my chest. "Saeed. What did you see?"

Saeed was human. More human than I. I'd met him the first day they allowed me into the dining hall with the others. I was one year old; I must have looked twenty. He was sitting alone and about to do something insane. There were many others in the room who caught my eye. The two conjoined men were laughing hard at the sight of me. The idiok baboons were jumping up and down while rapidly signing to the woman with lion claws and teeth. However, Saeed had a spoon in his hand and a bowl full of broken glass before him. I stood there staring at him as others stared at me. He dug the spoon into the chunks of glass, scooped out a spoonful and put it in his mouth. I could hear him crunching from where I stood. He smiled to himself, obviously enjoying it.

Driven by sheer curiosity, I walked over and sat across from him with my plate of spicy doro wat. He eyed me with suspicion, but he didn't seem angry or mean, at least not to the best of my limited social knowledge. I leaned forward and asked what was on my mind, "What's it like to eat that?"

He blinked, surprised. " 'What', she asks. Not 'Why'." He grinned. His teeth were perfect—white, shiny, and shaped like the teeth in drawings and doctored pictures in magazines. Had they removed his original teeth and replaced them with ones made of a more durable stuff? "The taste is soft and delicate as the texture is crunchy. I'm not in pain, only pleasure," he said in a voice accented in a way that I'd never heard. But then again, the only accents I'd ever heard were from the Big Eye doctors and guards.

"Tell me more," I said. "I like your voice."

He'd looked at me for a long time, then he smiled and said, "Sit."

After that, Saeed and I became close. I loved words, and he needed to spill them. He could not read, so I would tell him about what I read, at least in the hours of breakfast, lunch, and dinner. Sometimes, he grumbled with annoyance when the current series of books I was reading were romance novels or what he called "woman tales," but he couldn't have disliked them that much because he always demanded to hear these stories from beginning to end as well. "I like the sound of your voice," he said, when I asked him why. He may have, but I believe he liked the stories, too.

Saeed was from Cairo, Egypt, where he had been an orphan who never went hungry because he could always find something to eat. He ate rotten rice, date pits, even the wooden skewer sticks of *kebabs*; he had a stomach like a goat. They brought him to the tower when he was thirteen, six years ago. He never told me exactly how or why they made him the way he was. It didn't matter. What mattered was that we were who we were, and we were there.

Saeed told me of places I had never seen with my own eyes. He used the words of a poet who used his tongue to see. Saeed was an artist with his hands, too. He had the skill of the great painters I read about in my books. He most loved to draw those foods he could no longer eat. Human food. Portraits of loaves of bread. Bowls of thick egusi soup and balls of fufu. Bouquets of smoked lamb and beef kebabs. Oniony fried eggs with white cheese. Plates of chickpeas. Pitchers of fresh-squeezed orange juice. Piles of roasted yellow corn. They allowed him to bring the paintings to mealtime for everyone to view. I guess even we deserved the pleasures of art.

Saeed could survive on glass, metal shavings, crumbles of rust, sand, dirt, those things that would be left behind if human beings finally blew themselves up. They tasted delicious to him. Nevertheless, eating a piece of bread would kill him as eating a giant bowl filled with sharp pieces of glass would kill the average human being.

The first time he kissed me, we were sitting together at dinnertime. I'd just finished my own meal of fried chicken curried rice. I was telling him the chemical makeup of the flakes of rust he was eating and speculating on how green rust would probably taste different to him. "I think you will find green rust tastier because it's more variable and complex." We were sitting close, a habit we'd gotten into when we'd realized that my natural body temperature was usually warm and his was cool.

He took a deep gulp of water from his full glass, turned to me, cupped my chin and kissed me. All thought of iron oxide and corrosion fled my mind, replacing it with nothing but amazed shock and the soft coolness of his lips.

"No affected behavior," we heard one of the nearby Big Eye bark and immediately we pulled away from each other. I couldn't help the smile on my face. I had read and watched many stories where people kissed, this was nothing like what I imagined. And I'd never thought it would happen to me. Saeed took my hand under the table and my smile grew bigger. I heard him snicker beside me. And I snickered, too.

Everyone in the dining hall stared at us. I remember specially the idiok baboons pointing at Saeed and me, and then signing energetically to each other. "They're just jealous," Saeed whispered, squeezing my hand. I grinned, my stomach full of unusual flutters, and my lips felt hot. Even if it were from within, it was the first time that I had ever laughed at the Big Eye.

Now, I couldn't stop thinking about what had happened. *He took my apple and he ate it. He took my apple and he ate it. He took my apple and he ate it.* The Big Eye explained that then his stomach and intestines hemorrhaged and Saeed was dead before morning. I couldn't stop stressing about the fact that I never got to tell him what was happening to me. I was sure that it would have given him hope; it would have reminded him that things would change. I wiped a tear. I loved Saeed.

As grief overwhelmed me for the first time in my life, I pressed a hand against the thick glass of my window and longingly looked down at the green roof of the much shorter building right beside Tower 7; one of the trees growing there was in full bloom with red flowers. I'd never been outside. I wanted to go outside. Saeed had escaped by dying. I wanted to escape, too. If he wasn't happy here, then neither was I.

I wiped hot sweat from my brow. My room's scanner began to beep as my body's temperature soared. The doctors would be here soon.

When it first started to happen two weeks ago, only I noticed it. My hair started to fall out. I am an African by genetics, I had the facial features, my skin was very dark and my hair was very coily. They kept my hair shaved low because neither they nor I knew what to do with it when it grew out. I could never find anything in my books to help. They didn't care for style in Tower 7, anyway, although the lion lady down the hall had very long, silky, white hair and Big Eye lab assistants came by every two days to help her brush and braid it. And they did this despite the fact that the woman had the teeth and claws of a lion.

I was sitting on my bed, looking out the window, when I suddenly grew very hot. For the last few days, my skin had been dry and chapped no matter how much super-hydrated water they gave me to drink. Doctor Bumi brought me a large jar of shea butter, and applying it soothed my skin to no end. However, this day, hot and feverish, my skin seemed to dry as if I were in a desert.

I felt beads of sweat on my head and when I rubbed my short short hair, it wiped right off, hair and sweat alike. I ran to my bathroom, quickly showered, washing my head thoroughly, toweled off and stood before the large mirror. I'd lost my eyebrows, too. But this wasn't the worst of it. I rubbed the shea butter into my skin to give myself something to do. If I stopped moving, I'd start crying with panic.

I don't know why they gave me such a large mirror in my bathroom. High and round, it stretched from wall to wall. Therefore, I saw myself in full glory. As I slathered the thick, yellow, nutty smelling cream onto my drying skin, it was as if I was harboring a sun deep within my body and that sun wanted to come out. Under the dark brown of my flesh, I was glowing. I was light.

I pulsed, feeling a wave of heat and slight vibration within me. "What is this?" I whispered, scurrying back to my bed where my e-reader lay. I wanted to look up the phenomena. In all my reading, I had never read a thing about a human being, accelerated or normal, heating up and glowing like a firefly's behind. The moment I picked up the e-reader, it made a soft pinging sound. Then the screen went black and began to smoke. I threw it on the floor and the screen cracked, as it gently burned. My room's smoke alarm went off.

Psss! The hissing sound was soft and accompanied by a pain in my left thumbnail. It felt as if someone had just stuck a pin into it. "Ah!" I cried, instinctively pressing on my thumb. As I held my hand up to my eyes, I felt myself pulse again.

There was a splotch of black in the center of my thumbnail like old blood, but blacker. Burned flesh. Every speciMen, creature, creation in the building had a diagnostics chip implanted beneath his, her, or its fingernail, claw, talon, or horn. I'd just gone off the grid. I gasped.

Not twenty seconds passed before they came bursting into my room with guns and syringes, all aimed at me as if I were a rabid beast destroying all that they had built. Bumi looked insane with stress, but only she knew to not get too close.

"Get down! DOWN!" she shouted, her voice quivering. She held a portable in her hand and her other hand was in the pocket of her lab coat. When I just stood there confused, one of the male Big Eye guards grabbed my arm, probably with the intent of throwing me on the bed so he could cuff me. He screamed, staring at his burned, still-smoking hand. The room suddenly smelled like cooked meat. "You're not going anywhere," Bumi muttered, pulling a gun from her pocket. Without hesitation, she shot me right in the leg. It felt as if someone kicked me with a metal foot and I grunted. I sunk to the floor, pain washing over me like a second layer of more intense heat. I would have been done for if someone else had not shouted for the others to hold their fire.

Thankfully, I healed fast and the bullet had gone straight through my leg. Bumi said she'd shot me there knowing the bullet would do that; I believed her. If the bullet hadn't gone straight through and remained in my flesh, I don't know what would have happened with my extreme body temperature. Bumi knew this more than anyone.

One minute I was staring with shock at the blood oozing from my leg. Then the next, I blacked out. I woke in a bed, my body cool, my leg bandaged. When they returned me to my room, the scanner was in place to monitor me, since I could not hold an implant. They replaced my bed sheets with heavy heat-resistant ones similar in material to my new clothes. The carpet was gone, too. For the first time, I saw that the floor beneath the carpet was solid whitish marble.

Bumi took me to one of the labs soon after that. This would be my first but not last encounter with the cubed room with walls that looked like glass. Maybe they were thick clear plastic. Maybe they were made of crystal. Or maybe they were made of some alien substance that they were keeping top secret. I knew nothing. I didn't even know what the machine was called. They simply put me in it, and it heated up like a furnace. I felt as if I were on fire and when I started screaming, Bumi's voice filtered in, smooth like okra soup, sweet like mango juice, but distant like the outside world.

"Phoenix, hold still," she said. "We are just getting information about you."

I believed her. Even through the pain. I always believed everything they told me. The space was just large enough for me to sit with my long legs stretched before me, my back straight, my palms flat to the surface. The smooth transparent walls warmed to red and orange and yellow, so it was like being inside the evening sun I watched set every day.

"Does it have to hurt?" I cried. "I'm burning! My skin is burning!" It did not get so hot that my flesh caught fire, but the parts of me that touched the walls—especially my legs—received first-degree burns.

"Nothing great comes without pain," she said. "Just relax."

I closed my eyes and tried to retreat into myself. But the memory of the sound of Bumi's gun firing was still ricocheting in my head. I hadn't been fighting. I wasn't as dangerous as some of the other speciMen became when in some kind of distress. I wasn't doing anything but standing there in confusion thinking about the fact that I was off the grid. Yet, she'd shot me.

I couldn't help my legs flexing and twitching whenever the pain hit. My legs ran, like a separate part of my body.

"Relax," Bumi said.

Relax. How could I relax? I frowned. I couldn't stop thinking about it. It was as if my thoughts had become tangible and were bouncing off the walls, getting faster and faster, like a heated atom. Maybe thoughts were just atoms made of a different type of material for which even the Big Eye lacked tools to study.

"I am trying," I said.

"Do you want to hear a story?"

For the first time, I was able to pull back from the sound of the gun firing and the kernel of whatever I was feeling deep in my chest. "Yes," I said, looking up. All I saw was the machine's artificial burning sun.

"Ok," Bumi said. She paused. I listened. "You read so much, so I know that you know my country, Nigeria."

"Official name is the Federal Republic of Nigeria. Capital is Abuja. Most known city is Lagos, the second largest city in the world. West Africa. One of the world's top producers of streaming films, crude oil, and fine literature," I whispered.

I heard her chuckle. "You know my country better than I do." She paused. "But to really know it, you must go there. I was born and raised in the metropolis of Lagos. My parents lived on Victoria Island in one of the high-security gated communities. Big big houses with columns, porches, marble and huge winding staircases. Manicured palm trees and colorful sweet smelling flowers. Even the houseboys and house girls dressed like movie stars. Paved roads. Security cameras. Well-dressed Africans with perfect wigs, suits, jewelry and flashy cars. Can you see it?"

I nodded.

"Good. So, I was born in that house. I was the first of five children. My mother was alone when she went into labor. My father was on a brief business trip in Ghana. The two house girls had gone to the village to visit their families before coming to stay in the house until I was born. She only had a virtual doctor to guide her through it all. She'd never had to use one before then. They could afford to have an actual doctor come to check on her and they'd hired a midwife. But she went into labor with me ten days early and the midwife got stuck in go-slow, Lagos traffic. My mother said it was like being instructed by a ghost."

"I was born healthy and plump in my mother's bedroom. She'd shut the windows and turned on the air purifier, so my first breath was not Lagos air. It was air delivered from the Himalayas." She laughed. "My mother took me outside for the first time three weeks later. I took one breath of the Lagos air and vomited from coughing so hard. Then I was ok."

I had my eyes closed. Though I could smell my skin slowly baking as the heat increased in the tiny room, I was strolling down the black paved road of Lagos beside Bumi's mother who was dark-skinned, pretty and short, like Bumi. She was pushing a light-weight stroller with baby Bumi in it, coughing and cooing.

"When I think of my youth in Nigeria, I know that I can never be fully American, even when I am a citizen."

"So you are not American?" I asked. "But you live here. You work here. You—"

"I'm legal, but not a citizen. Not yet. I will be. My work with you will earn me the pull I need." She paused. "Do you want to know about how you were when you were a baby?"

I frowned. I remembered life from when I was about a month old; I was like a three year old.

"Do you know when I was a baby?" I asked.

"I was there when they brought you," she said. "You were so small. Like a preemie. But strong, very very strong. You never needed an incubator or antibiotics or special formula. You took easily to life."

The lights in the machine went off and something beeped. I breathed a sigh of relief. "Time's up. Let's get you to your room," Bumi said. She didn't say any more about first meeting me, as we walked back to my room, following the red lines. I was curious, but Bumi always had a set look on her face when she had switched back to her Big Eye self. I knew not to ask for more of my own story.

When we arrived at my room, it was evening.

"May the day break," Bumi said. This was how she liked to say good-night to me every night. She said she'd once heard it in a Nigerian movie she'd watched. She only said it to me and usually when she said it, I laughed and smiled.

Tonight, I was in too much pain to smile, but I responded as always, "May it break."

My body ached from the burns, but by the time I entered my room, removed my clothes and inspected myself, there wasn't a mark left on my body. But I remembered the pain. You never forget the smell or the pain. I took a long cool shower.

As the days progressed, I learned that when I grew hot and luminous like this, electronics died or exploded in my hands, except that cubed room. This was why they started giving me paper books, despite the risk of me setting them afire. These paper books were limited, old and difficult to read, as I couldn't turn the pages as quickly as I could with the e-reader. And they could now easily monitor what I was reading. Although now I realize that, with the e-reader, they were probably monitoring my choices, too.

I didn't tell Saeed about the heating and glowing because at the time I didn't want to worry him. I enjoyed our talks so much. I wish I had told him.

The door slid open and my doctors came in, Debbie and Bumi. I took a deep breath to calm myself. Though the heat did not go away, it decreased, as did the glow.

"How do you feel?" Bumi asked, as she took my wrist to check my pulse. She hissed, dropping it.

"Hot," I flatly said.

She glared at me and I glared back thinking something I had not thought until Saeed was dead—*You should have asked first.*

"Open," Debbie said. She placed the heavy-duty thermometer into my mouth.

"She's not glowing that brightly," Bumi said, typing something onto her portable. I resisted the urge to grab it and hold it in my hands until it exploded. Saeed was dead because of these people. I steadied myself, thinking of the cool places sometimes described in the novels I read. I once read a brief story about a man who froze to death in a forest. How nice it would have been to be in that cold place at that moment.

"It might just be menopause approaching," Bumi said. "I believe the two factors are correlated."

I tuned out their talk and focused on my own thoughts. *Escape. How? What would they do to me? What did Saeed see?* My internal temperature was 130 degrees, but the temperature of my skin was 220. They couldn't take my blood pressure because the equipment would melt.

"We need to get her to the lab," Debbie said.

Bumi nodded. "As soon as the scanner says she's reached 300 degrees. We don't want her any higher or things around her will start to ignite. Maybe by morning." She looked at me and smiled. "May the day break."

"May it break," I responded.

They left. I paced the room. Restless. Angry. Distraught. They would be back soon.

How am I going to get out of here? I wondered. As if to answer my question, Mmuo walked into my room. He came through the wall across from my bed. My heart nearly jumped from my chest. "Mmuo, good evening," I said. He'd scared me, but I was glad to see him. Without Saeed, Mmuo was my only other friend now.

"Did you hear?" he asked, sitting on my bed. He spoke quietly, his low voice like distant thunder.

I blinked, feeling the rush of sadness all over again. He was Saeed's friend, too. "Yes," I said.

"I'm sorry, Phoenix."

My face was wet and drying with sweat. "I'm getting out of here," I declared.

Mmuo softly laughed. "You?"

"Will you help me?" I asked. "You once did things against the Big Eye in Nigeria. Can't you . . . ?"

"You get it *wrong*. I went up against Nigeria's government, but the Big Eye . . . I know better than anyone what the Big Eye will do when you cross them."

"What? What will they do?"

He waved a dismissive hand. "I'm not telling you that," he snapped.

"Then help me get out of here," I begged. "Please."

He frowned. "What is wrong with you? I can feel you from here."

I sighed. "I think it has something to do with how they made me. It's been happening for two weeks and it's getting worse."

We looked at each other, silent. I knew we were thinking the same thing, but neither he nor I wanted to speak it. If we spoke of my name, I didn't think I'd be able to move, let alone run.

"Yes, that would make sense," he said.

He called himself Mmuo, which meant spirit in a Nigerian language. He was a hero to all those who were created or altered in Tower 7. Like Saeed, Mmuo had been taken from Africa. He said he was from "the jungles of Nigeria," the same country as my doctor Bumi. I didn't believe he was from any jungle. He spoke like a man who had known skyscrapers, office buildings, and streaming movies. He knew how to disable the security on several of the floors and was known for causing trouble throughout the building. Not that he really needed to do so to get around the tower; Mmuo could walk through walls. The only walls he could not pass through were the walls that would get him out of Tower 7. Mmuo could not escape; obviously, his abilities were created by Tower 7 scientists.

He was a tall, thin man with skin the color of, and as shiny as, crude oil. He never wore clothes, for clothes could not pass through the walls with him. He was so proud and frank in his nakedness that I didn't even notice it any more. Mmuo stole what food he needed from the kitchens. He was the only person/creature who'd successfully escaped the Big Eye's clutches.

Why Tower 7's Big Eye tolerated him, I do not know. My theory is that they simply could not catch him. And since he was contained, they accepted the trouble he occasionally stirred up. Most of those in the tower were too isolated and damaged to be much trouble if freed, anyway.

"It looks like your skin is nothing but a veil over something greater," he mused, after an appraising look. It was something Saeed would have said, and the thought made my heart ache again.

"Can you open the door?" I finally asked. I paused and then pushed my request out of my mouth. "I want to see what is down the hall, near Saeed's room."

Mmuo met my gaze and held it.

"What did Saeed see, Mmuo?"

He shook his head and looked away.

"Show me, then," I said, suddenly wanting to sob. "And help me. Help me escape."

"Saeed and I, we had plans," he said. "He always said that it was right beneath your skin," he said with a slight smile.

"That what was?"

"Your taste for freedom."

He moved close to me, and I was sure he was going to hug me.

"Don't touch me," I said. "You'll . . ."

He raised a hand up and made to slap me across the face. "Don't move," he said. His hand passed right through my head. I felt only the slightest moment of pressure and there was a sucking sound.

"Wha . . . ?"

"Can you hear me?" I heard him loudly say through what sounded like a microphone. I looked around.

"Shhh! They'll hear you!" I hissed. I frowned. His lips hadn't moved.

"No," he said. He held his finger to his lips for me to quiet down and grinned, his yellow-white teeth and black skin shining in my glow. *"They won't. You are hearing this in your head."*

"Not even the Big Eye know I can do this," he said aloud, but lowering his voice as before. "Whatever they did to enhance my abilities, I can pass it into people, and they can hear me until the tiny nanomites are sweated from their skin.

"I did this to a little Tanzanian boy on the fifth floor. He had a contagious cancer, so they kept him in isolation for tests. Hearing me talk to him from wherever I was, kept him sane. At least, until he died."

His disease could have killed you, though, I thought.

He started to descend through the floor. *"Fifteen minutes,"* he said in my head, then he was gone.

I whipped off my pants and t-shirt and threw on a white dress they'd recently given me made of heat resistant thin plastic. The dress was long but light, and it allowed me to move freely. I didn't bother with shoes. Too heavy.

For a moment, I had a brief flash in my mind of actually stepping outside. Into the naked sunlight, under the open sky, no ceiling above me. I could do it. Mmuo would help me. He and I would *both* escape. I felt a rush of hope, then a rush of heat. The scanner on my wall beeped. I had reached over 300 degrees.

Just before the door slid open, I had the sense to spread some shea butter on my skin. Then I ran out of my room.

"If you want to see, turn right and then go straight. Do it quickly, they will soon know you are missing. I can't delay it long."

I was working hard not to look at the floor. I'd never left my room without instruction from the floor. Usually a yellow line appeared that told me where to go. There was none now. With nothing to guide me, I felt like I was free-falling into the heavens; like if I didn't fly, I'd die; I just had to figure out how to do it.

I jogged, my feet slapping the cool marble floor. The hallway was quiet and empty, and soon I was in a section of my floor that I had never graced. This was where they kept Saeed. *His prison*, I thought.

I crossed a doorway and the floor here was carpeted, plush and red. I paused, looking down. I had never seen red carpet. How could a "guiding line" show through a carpeted floor? Before they took it out, the carpet in my quarters had been black, thin and flat. I wanted to kneel down and run my hands over the redness. I knew it would feel so soft and fluffy. I also knew that I wasn't supposed to be here.

"*See what you must but you have to make it to the elevator in two minutes,*" Mmuo's voice suddenly said into my head. "*Go down the hall and turn left. You will see it. Hurry. Do not press any buttons when you get in.*"

"Ok," I said aloud. But he could not hear me. One-way communication. I ran down the red hallway. Through glass windows and doors, I could see lab assistants and scientists in labs. Each large room was partitioned by a thick wall. There was bulky equipment in most of them. If I were careful, no one would notice me. After sneaking past three labs, I saw the one that Saeed saw. It had to be. I stopped, staring and moaning deep in my throat. This lab was much bigger than the others and ten black cameras hung from its high white ceiling.

There were two wall-sized sleek grey machines on both sides of the room. I could hear them humming powerfully. Between them, the world fell away to another world where it was daytime, and all that was happening was perfectly bluntly brutally visible. There were old vehicles, trucks from long, long ago, boxy, ineffective and weak. But strong enough to carry huge loads of cargo to dump into a deep pit. And that cargo consisted of human bodies. Hundreds and hundreds of them. Dead. Not Africans. These dead people had pinkish pale skin and thin straight-ish hair like most of the Big Eye and the lion woman. When was this? Where was this? Why were the Big Eye scientists just *standing* there watching with their clipboards and ever-observing eyes?

It was not like watching a 3D movie. Even the best ones could never look this . . . true. Bodies. And I could *smell* them. The whole hallway reeked with their rot and blood and feces and bile and the smoke of the trucks. My brain went to my books and recalled where I had seen this before. "Holocaust," I whispered, fighting the urge to turn to the side and vomit. I shut my watering eyes for a moment and took a deep breath. I nearly gagged on the stench. I opened my eyes.

This genocide happened during one of the early world wars. The Germans killed many of these people because they were sure that they were inferior or a threat or both. The book I read spoke as if wiping them out was the right thing to do. It certainly looked wrong to me. Were these Big Eye looking through time? Is this all they could do? Look? I whimpered. Why this time period? Why this nasty moment? Couldn't they stop it? For a moment, the portal disappeared and there was lots of scrambling, adjusting machines, pushing buttons, cursing. And then the portal reappeared showing the same activities, in the same time period in the same place. Happening.

The surge of heat in my body was like a deep heartbeat of crimson flames. I shuddered and felt it ripple over every surface of my skin. I couldn't move. Saeed had probably stood here just like this, too. Acrid smoke stung my eyes. My feet were burning the red carpet. A fire alarm sounded.

Finally, I ran.

The elevator was open. It was empty. I got in and it quickly closed behind me. I wished Mmuo would say something. If it went up, I was caught. If it went nowhere, I was caught. If it went down, I might be caught, but I might escape, too. I shut my eyes and whispered, "Go down, go down, *please,* go down. Have to get out!" Sweat beaded and evaporated all over my confused body and the elevator quickly grew humid.

If I hadn't rubbed all that shea butter on my skin at the last minute, I'd have been in horrible pain, my skin drying and probably cracking. I was hot like the sun, there was a ringing in my ears, as if my own body had an alarm and it was going off, too. I looked at my hands. They were glowing a soft yellow. My entire body was glowing through my dress.

The elevator jerked upward. I grabbed the railing, pure terror shooting through me. At least, I would make it outside. I could take two breaths before they caught me. I sank to the floor. Saeed was dead, and I was still trapped. Tears dribbled from the corners of my eyes and hissed as they evaporated down my cheeks.

The elevator jerked again. "*Sorry about that,*" I heard Mmuo say in my head. He sounded distant. The elevator started moving down. I jumped up. I still had a chance. I watched the numbers decrease, 28, 27, 26. A louder alarm started to go off. They'd realized I was missing. "*I can get you to nine,*" he said. His voice was fading, and I had to strain to hear it. "*Two stairways in there. Run to the emergency one on the other side of the greenhouse, straight ahead when the doors open. You'll be on the side of the greenhouse. Just go straight ahead! Do NOT go near the center! There's . . .*" His voice faded to nothing.

Had my heat burned away his nanomites? Probably. As the elevator flew down, my feet began to burn the elevator floor. 12, 11, 10, 9. The elevator came to a sudden stop and the doors opened. The blare of the Tower 7 alarm assaulted my ears but the most beautiful sight I'd ever seen caressed my eyes. An expansive room full of trees, bushes, flowers, vines. In pots, on shelves, tangled within each other. A contained jungle that reminded me of the green roof of the building next door. I could see the city through the windows on my left. The sky was the deep rose of evening. I started quickly walking down the narrow path before me. Moss grew on the sides of trees. The humid air smelled green, fragrant, soily, I had never smelled anything like it.

I heard a rush of footsteps from amongst the plants to my right. Between the foliage, I could see them. Big Eye guards. In tough black armor with shields, with guns.

"Phoenix!" one of them yelled, spotting me. The voice pierced me, and I gasped, my eyes wide. I'd been hearing this voice all my short life. All their guns went up. "Put your hands up. We will not hurt you." It was Bumi. Now I could see her clearly. My legs felt weak.

Behind me I could hear the elevator rumbling. I still didn't move. Saeed was dead. There was nothing for me here. I was two years old, and I was forty years old. The marble beneath my feet absorbed my heat.

"*Please*, put your hands up," Bumi pleaded. "You know what you are.

We can stabilize you." She paused, obviously considering how much to tell me. I knew enough, though. Saeed was dead, and I wanted to be free.

"You're a weapon," Bumi admitted. "If you wanted to know, now you do. My job has always been to help you, to keep you *alive*. This wasn't supposed to happen, you being like this. Please, let us help you. *I* can help you."

She is lying, I thought. I shocked myself. Why did her voice sound so different to my ears now? She'd always been lying. I heard the elevator beep then the doors open just as I felt the light burst from me. There was warmth that started at my feet. It rolled up to my chest and pulsed out with a wave of heat. My shoulders jerked back, and I stumbled to the side, getting a glimpse behind me. If I had blinked I still wouldn't have missed it. My skin prickled as my glow became a light green shine. The light steadily radiated from me. It bathed every plant in the room.

The guards behind me in the elevator and on the far right side of the room all ducked down and for a moment it was quiet enough that you could hear it. All the plants were growing. Snapping, pulling, unfurling, creeping. Thick vines and even tree roots quickly crept, stretched and blocked the elevator door. Leaves, branches and stems grew so thick around the guards to my right that they were blocked from view. This was something they didn't know I could do. This was not something they had created.

The entire greenhouse swelled and flooded with foliage. Except a few steps ahead to my right. There was what I could only call a tunnel through the plants. It diagonally passed the cowering Big Eye. I ran into it just as the guards behind and to my right began to shoot toward where I'd initially been. "Phoenix!" I heard Bumi scream. "You can't do this to me! Stop!!"

I didn't stop. Were they shooting through the plants or shooting at me, I do not know. And in many ways these two things were one and the same.

Mmuo had said to go forward to find the doorway. But I lost all sense of direction. So when I ended up standing before the giant glass dome I didn't know which way to run. My first thought was of the same book that spoke of the treacherous apple of knowledge. The Bible. Except that the man with enormous wings was not held up by any wooden cross. He was suspended in mid-air with his arms out and his legs tied together. His eyes were closed. His brown-feathered wings were stretched wide.

He was naked, his ebony-skinned body, muscled and very very tall, at least compared to my six feet. He had deep African facial features and a crown of wooly hair. He was magnificent. Behind the glass dome was a rough wooden wall. The trunk of The Backbone.

Behind me, I could hear them coming. Hacking through the plants and calling my name. I wasn't going to get out. I walked up to the glass and placed a hot hand on it. The glass was thick and very cool. Was there even air in there? Was that how they held him? Was it like being in outer space? What was space like for a creature made to fly?

His eyes opened. I gasped and jumped back. They were brown, soft, kind, eyes.

"Oh my God, Phoenix! Please! Step BACK!" one of the guards screamed, shoving aside a bush. I noticed the guard did not point his gun. Nor did the others who emerged beside him. I looked back at the man with wings. He was looking right at me, no expression on his face. I was surrounded by guards, all begging me to step away, pleading that this creature was "unique and dangerous." However, none of them came to capture me. I didn't move. Bumi appeared beside the guard. When she saw me, her eyes nearly popped out of her head. She reached for me with an outstretched hand but then brought the hand to her mouth. She was afraid to speak, to make too much noise. She recoiled, behind the guard.

Seeing the Big Eye cower, seeing their fear and raw horror had a strange effect on me. I felt powerful. I felt lethal. I felt hopeful, though all was hopeless. I turned to the caged winged man and my hope evolved into rage. Even *he* was a prisoner here. I vowed that if I didn't get out, at least *he* would.

This time, I did it voluntarily. I was already so hot and I grew hotter when I reached into myself, into all that I was, all that I had been and all that I would be, I reached in and drew from my source. Then I turned to a nearby tree and let loose a pulse of light. I sighed as it left me, feeling relief. Immediately the tree's roots began to buckle and creep toward the glass cage.

CRASH! They easily forced their way through and the rest of the dome cracked in several places. The Big Eye turned and ran for their lives. I didn't bother running. There was no better way to die. He burst through, knocking me aside with the intensity of his wake. Into the now dense foliage of the greenhouse. I saw none of what happened, but I heard and smelled it. Wet tearing sounds, screams, ripping, snapping, choking, not one gun was fired. The air smelled like torn leaves and blood. Was Bumi's shed blood causing some of the smell? It was still happening when I spotted the stairway between the plants and ran into it. I fled down and down flights and came to a heavy open door and entered the lobby.

For a moment, even after all that I had seen, I forgot what I was doing. Again, a sight took my breath away. Tower 7's lobby was more spectacular than I'd ever imagined. No words could make up for actually seeing this place. This *space*. The ceiling was so high and the marble walls were draped with gorgeous flowering vines, the small trees and plants growing through the soil-filled holes in the floor. I fought not to fall to my knees. *There* was the base of The Backbone. Its trunk had to be over thirty feet in diameter.

I was dizzy. I was burning up. I was amazed. I was exhausted. There was a freed angel beast massacring its captors nine floors above. I could hear more Big Eye guards coming down the stairwell. The alarm was blaring and the lobby was empty . . . except for a lone figure standing near the exit doors. He was grinning. He'd been trying to get to this very spot unnoticed for nine years and my escape gave him the chance.

"Hurry," Mmuo cried. "Phoenix, MOVE!" I heard them burst through the stairway. I was running. I dodged small trees, scrambled around benches and leapt over plants. The door was yards away. I was going to make it. Outside, people walking by stopped to look.

Then I saw the guards come running onto the tower's wide plaza. They seemed to come from all directions. They shoved gaping people aside. They pulled up people who were sitting on benches enjoying the lovely evening. Then they formed a line blocking the exit and stood there, guns to their chests. I ran to Mmuo and would have given him a hug, if it weren't for my heat. We'd both almost made it.

"Go," I told him.

"I'm sorry," he said.

"For what?" I was having trouble thinking straight and I could smell the floor burning beneath me. I didn't know marble could burn. "Saeed would have been proud. I am proud. I set an angel free."

His eyebrows went up. "You . . ."

"Go!" I shouted, looking at the approaching Big Eye coming from the stairwell. They were flooding from doorways and were coming down an escalator on the other side of the lobby. "Don't ever let them catch you!" I said.

He sank through the floor and was gone.

I stood tall. There were hundreds of them. Men and women armed with the guns I had seen them carry all my short life. No Big Eye guard went anywhere in the tower without them. I knew how they sounded. Nearly silent. I had been hearing shots fired all my life. For a multitude of reasons but always with the same result. Something or someone who'd gotten out of control was dead or severely injured. "Protect the scientist from the subject." "Observe and learn." "We will all be better for it." "For the Research." I was taking all the pieces I had read and finally putting them together. The Big Eye crowded around me, nervous with anticipation as if I were evil. After all I had done, to them, I guess I was evil. Or crazy.

I held up my hands, feeling myself shining. The light bloomed from my body. The release felt glorious and I moaned with relief. Then more sighing than speaking, I said, "I give . . ."

"No don't! Hold your fire!" someone shouted. Bumi. There she was, a few yards to my right. The right side of her lab coat was red with blood and her cheek was shredded into wet ribbons. I could see the white of her twitchy eyes. Dragging her left leg, she limped toward me, stepping in front of three Big Eye guards, putting herself between me and their pointed guns. She coughed and said, "We don't know . . ."

But someone couldn't stop his or her trigger finger. First one shot and then several more opened fire. "WAIT!" I heard Bumi scream. No one waited.

It was as if I were punched with steel fists in every part of my body—chest, neck, legs, arms, abdomen, face. I was blown toward the door and my vision went red-yellow. I lay on my back. Everything was wet, the smell of smoke in the one nostril I had left. Smoke, but also the perfume of The Backbone. I was looking at it, gazing at how it reached, up, up, up, through the high marble ceiling, through the 39 floors above. Into the sky. Reaching for the sky.

I felt the radiance burst from me, warm, yellow, light, plucked from the sun and placed inside me like a seed until it was ready to bloom. It bloomed now and the entire lobby was washed. The Big Eye covered their faces and dropped their guns. A few ran to the stairwell, others to the far side of the lobby. Most of them ran past my mangled body and out of the building. Those ones must have known what would happen next.

I knew. I was burning as the light pulsated and pulsated from me there on the floor. My body convulsed with it as my clothes burned and then my flesh. There was no pain. My nerves had burned already.

My light shined on the plants and tiny trees of the lobby and they began to grow wildly, stirred and amazed with life. Vines strained, lengthened, thickened. Flowers twisted open. Pollen puffed the air sweet. Leaves unfolded and widened. The stone floors were covered with green yellow white brown black, the strongest roots cracking its foundation.

My light shined on the great tree that was The Backbone. Its roots groaned as they shifted, coiled, expanded, and caused the entire portion of the floor around its roots to buckle and fall apart. The tree's colossal trunk twisted this way and that, shrugging off the building that was its shackle. Chunks of the floors above began to crash down around me. I was ashes being scattered by vines and roots when Tower 7 fell.

The Backbone stood tall, stretching its branches and opening its enormous leaves over buildings and streets. At its base, a small lush jungle sprang from the rubble of Tower 7 like a wild miniature Central Park. Helicopters hovered, news crews streamed footage live, people gaped from afar. When the debris settled, there was a moment where my brilliant light shone into the now dark night time. The news cameras recorded the winged man flying out of the rubble, but not much else lived, except the man who could walk through walls. Mmuo walked out of The Backbone's trunk and stood before it. "This is what you all deserve!" he shouted, shaking his fist at the eyes of the hovering cameras. Then he sunk into the ground and was gone.

No one in the city would approach what was left of Tower 7. So those ruins sat for seven days, a pile of those things Saeed used to eat: rubble, glass, metal and . . . ash. And then I realized the meaning of my name.

CHAPTER 2

Beacon

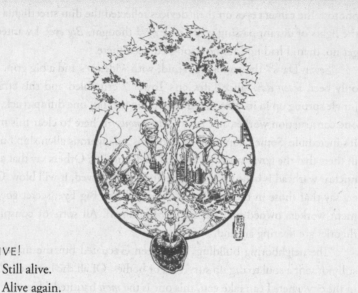

ALIVE!

Still alive.

Alive again.

I lay in a heap of rubbish in a jungle, and people were looking at me. What must they have seen? I did not move. It was night and the air was warm. I could *feel* it. The breeze blew and, despite my situation, I closed my eyes and let it wash over my face. It felt like silk. It smelled of sweet blooming flowers, stems and leaves, at first. Then there was an after-smell of dust and crushed rubble, disintegrated marble. Then it stank of raw gas, smoky rubbing alcohol, it smelled like suicide—this must have been the refuse of vehicles in the streets. This was the smell of car and truck exhaust.

I'd smelled this only once in my life. The smell had been mixed with the stench of dead bodies as I stared through a porthole in time. I pushed the memory of the Holocaust away and inhaled the air of the outside world. I was free of Tower 7. I was like the soft sweet flesh that falls out of the cracked hard shell of a walnut.

"We'll be quick," a young man in black pants and a black jacket told an anxious-looking group of about ten people. "They don't like anyone lingering here. So for this leg of the tour, no digi-cams with flashes or cam-lights. Use night-vision or don't take any photos at all." His back was to me, and I could clearly see that on his jacket, it said, "Haunted City Tours."

His audience members held all kinds of devices that could capture photos. The camera eyes on their devices reflected the dim streetlights and the lights of distant passing vehicles. *Eyes*, I thought. *Big eyes*. I wanted to get up, then. I had no idea how long I'd been there.

"Seven Days!" the young man said, with wide eyes and a big grin. "It's only been *seven days* since LifeGen's Tower 7 crumbled and this strange jungle sprung up in its place. And as you can see, not one dump truck, not one construction worker, not even a *lawnmower* is here to clear this mess. It's incredible. Some people say that there is a dangerous alien ship buried in there that the government is terrified of disturbing. Others say that a live nuclear warhead is beneath the jungle and if it is moved, it will blow. Others say that those in the building were called The Big Eye, secret government workers owned and led by the Illuminati. All sorts of conspiracy theories are floating around.

"The neighboring buildings have been evacuated but the mayor has still not sent a soul to dig up survivors or bodies. Of all the haunted places in the city where I can take you, this one is the *most* haunted." He chuckled knowingly. "Well, for now. Who knows what else the Rotten Apple has up its sleeve. Be proud to be only the third tourist group we've brought here. You're likely the last. The city can't possibly leave things this way much longer." He looked around and then said, "And be glad to be the second group that has managed to sneak here without being quickly detected."

All the people started whispering excitedly as they held their hand devices. I assumed the things stole light somehow to make photos or re-cordings. Again, I wondered what they were seeing. No one pointed at me and screamed that there was a woman lying in the rubble.

"People used to come from all around the world to see the building with the giant tree growing through its center called The Backbone." He cocked his head and winked. "Now, you don't have to go inside Tower 7 to see its magnificence. The Backbone is all that stands. Look up. You can't see its top. Since the Tower fell, scientists say that the tree has grown another five hundred feet. Even before the tower fell, it was said that it grew at night and sometimes you could hear it groaning as it grew. Its noise would shake all of New York City like a minor earthquake. I have heard this noise a few times, myself. It is not a myth. It sounds like a giant monster."

"What will they do with this place?!" an old man suddenly asked. He was the only one not holding out a device. He had an accent that was strange to me. It was not African, Arab or American. "They can't just leave it like this! It's a great big rubbish heap in the middle of the goddamn city! How is this even logical?"

The tour guide turned toward me and looked over the area. He was smirking mysteriously, as if the old man was adding to the guide's obvious act. He turned back to his captivated audience and said, "That's the mystery, sir."

The tour guide stood back as the others took more photos and stared blankly at me and the heap that used to be Tower 7. Then the tour guide said, "Shall we move on?"

Looking relieved, everyone nodded or said "Yes," or "Please." The old man was all frowns. There were no children in the group. I'd have loved to see children. I'd never seen them in real life.

I was alone now and I was glad. Every part of my body was shrieking. With life. Fresh fresh life. I was alive. I was awake. I was intact. I could move. My temples throbbed a different kind of pain. It felt like pieces of glass grinding in my head, and my vision went blurry for a moment.

I curled my body and some of the rubble that had buried me fell away. Chunks of white marble, chips of concrete, broken beams of steel, shattered glass. It was all heavy, but it did not crush me. I pushed it off. I tore off vines that had grown over me. There was no one around to hear the tinkle, crunch, and scrape of debris tumbling, sliding off my body. I got up. My vision blurred again and I stumbled. My balance felt off. Like the world around me was tilted to one side. I took a step and crushed more glass and some tiny white flowers with my tough feet. I took another and my heel ground into a piece of piping making me stumble again. Then it seemed everything settled—my vision, the way I related to the world around me. *Ok*, I thought.

I stood tall, stretching my arms, back, and legs. I felt a little odd. Like I was me, but who was me? I looked at myself. I was naked and covered in dust; I must have looked like a ghost. But I was alive. After I'd died. I vividly remembered dying. *My name is Phoenix*, I thought. *I don't know who named me, but I am named well.* I stood up straighter.

I licked my wrist. Then I smiled. My skin was still brown as the ripe shell of coconut. I was me. Tall. Lean. Full breasts. Strong legs. Long feet. Did I still have the dark brown spot on my left eyeball? The birthmark on my thigh? Did I still have the scar on my belly from when they'd taken a hipbone sample? The burn mark under the nail of my left thumb?

I frantically started swiping the dust from my skin. I swiped and swiped. My arms. Legs. Belly. Backside. Chest. There was so much dust that a cloud rose up around me. Then I stood still. The warm breeze caressing my body and blowing away the dust.

The birthmark on my thigh was there. The burn mark under my thumb was gone. I laughed as I looked up. The night sky was indigo with a hint of red; the way the night sky had always looked to me. Except now I was seeing it with my naked eye, through no window. I had never been outdoors until now. I had never seen the stars, either. I would. I would get out of the city. Away from its light pollution.

"Ok," I whispered. My voice was the same, too. I was working up to answering a most troubling question. If I was still me, was I still *me*? I stilled myself, shut my eyes and took a deep breath. Immediately, I could see it. Right through my eyelids. The soft yellow green glow that emanated from my skin. *Beacon*, I thought. *I am a beacon.*

When I attempted to escape from Tower 7, they had surrounded and riddled me with bullets as I burned to ash. My powerful light woke the plants, especially The Backbone. Then The Backbone had brought it all down, killing almost everyone and every freakish thing inside. Now I'd woken up in the ruins. I was reborn. I still glowed. I was still a phoenix. I let out a breath, a tear rolling down my cheek. It wasn't over. Silly of me to think it was.

When I opened my eyes, they fell on something white and blowing in the strong breeze a few yards away. A dress hanging on a piece of piping sticking out of a jumble of thick green shoots. Only two people would have cared enough to leave it for me. Only two people really understood what I was. There was Saeed. How I loved Saeed. But Saeed was dead. And Mmuo, who'd also been a prisoner in Tower 7 and managed to escape when it all came down. Mmuo who could walk through walls. Mmuo who had opened the door for me. He'd most likely left the dress.

I walked over to it. With each step, I felt more like myself. It was cotton, stained a little from the dust, but long. It would fit perfectly. I liked long dresses, but I hoped the cotton wouldn't burn. As I put the dress on, it felt odd on my back. I frowned. My back felt odd, now that I thought of it. Achy, as if I'd been injured there. But yet, when I touched my shoulder blade, I didn't feel the touch as much as I should have. I smoothed out the dress on my body and then touched my back again. There was a swelling there or a sort of hump.

I bent forward without a problem. Only the aching. A flare of heat flew through my body. Then I was cool again. "Wish I had a mirror," I whispered.

There was a deep groaning, and I froze. Then it came again. From behind me. I turned around. The sight took my breath away. You could not see the end of it. Surrounded by smaller trees and bushes, its great trunk was the diameter of two cars. Its rough rich brown bark was now covered with large sharp thorns. No human in his or her right mind would attempt to climb it even if the tree were at rest. Which it was not. You could sense it even from yards away. If it wanted to, it could call its roots together, pull them out of the ground and walk away. Maybe it eventually would. Stranger things certainly had happened in the last seven days.

Its leaves were broad and oval shaped and you could see them happily waving with the wind, high high high into the sky. Until you could see no more. The leaves of The Backbone were slightly luminescent, just like me. And it had bloomed large fiery red flowers that grew high up. What happened at its very top? One would need a helicopter to find out.

The groaning came again and all the sounds of the city—vehicles driving on roads, the breeze moving around the skyscrapers, the creak of crickets, the sound of people talking—it all stopped. There was only dead silence. The building across the street was dark and deserted but on the second floor, if I squinted hard, I could see a pigeon was frozen in midflight.

"Wha- ?" I startled myself. My voice felt as if it were coming from within and outside of me at the same time. "What is this?"

The grassy ground beneath my feet vibrated and then domed the slightest bit. I stumbled forward and the ground here also domed, and I was forced forward again. The Backbone wanted me close. And it must have had a hell of a secret to tell me because it had stopped time so that it could do so. At least this was my theory. Amongst the thousands of books I had read in Tower 7, one included an African myth, or was it Arab, that spoke of a tree so old that it had learned to stop time. Hadn't that tree been covered with spikes, too? My memory said it had. When I was mere feet from its lethal looking trunk, the bare ground before me began to churn.

If it weren't for the forceful sagacious presence of the tree, I'd have run. I touched the hump on my back and rubbed at it. It felt so achy. The ground before the tree was rich red soil, different from the rest, which was brown. Had the Big Eye done exactly that? Brought in special soil for it from somewhere after they'd soaked it in the special growth formula? The history of its official planting in the base of Tower 7, the exact nature of the experimental solution poured over it and subsequent care were all kept top secret. It was even omitted from the classified books and files they let me read about the history of Tower 7.

"What is that?" I whispered as something began to push up beneath the churning soil. A tan powerful thin root whipped through. Then another, then another. Then a larger root must have pushed it from below, for the wooden box rose from the soil like a gift presented by a God, held up by a kneeling slave. It rose slowly, carefully, dare I say dramatically.

It was for me. I've never questioned that.

I picked it up and the tree groaned softly. Then I tensed, all my new flesh, muscles and sinews, tightening for the first time. My body flashed a brilliant green. I was blinded for a moment, though I kept my eyes open. It wasn't hot, however, for my dress remained intact. I felt more gather in my chest. Then it burst from me, violently rustling The Backbone's leaves and the twigs, leaf stems, vines, and flowers of all those plants that grew around the great tree. The Backbone shivered.

The flap of pigeon wings behind me. I turned around and watched the pigeon finish flying to the next building. The sound of vehicles moving, vomiting plumes of exhaust. The sound of far off voices. The movement of the breeze around the concrete jungle.

Then a different kind of rumbling began. There was enough light from the street and the buildings around the area to show me exactly what was happening. It was the building across the deserted street. Where the pigeon had landed. The building was called the Axis Building because according to satellite maps, it sat in the exact center of the city. The rumbling became a great roar and the concrete building started to collapse on itself. Crush, crash, beams buckled, buttresses splintered. The destruction plumed out dust, papers, and rubble. I stared in awe. I had been looking down at this building all my life. It stood right outside my window. It was one of the buildings the city designated to house a lush roof garden full of potted trees, bushes and flowers.

I'd looked down on the false jungle and dreamed and hoped and never touched, smelled, stood within. I loved the sight of it from afar, but now I realized an unconscious part of me loathed its existence. It had been unattainable. It was not part of my world. Over eight days ago, this never would have been so clear to me, but now I was outside. Now it was. As the building collapsed, I felt joy. Most likely, there was not a soul inside it. The building would have been evacuated days ago. They had to have known it was unstable. But I loved the fact that it was I who gave it the push that finally brought it down.

Good.

The box, I held. There was no lock or latch. The wood was not heavy but it was solid. And a rich brown like the tree's trunk. Its edges were worn smooth. *Do I open it?* There was definitely something heavy inside. When I moved it this way and that, whatever was in it slid heavily this way and that. It was one thing.

I had been created in Tower 7 two years ago from the DNA of an African woman possibly born in Phoenix, Arizona. Or maybe what I was was the origin of my name. Standing out there watching the building fall, I took the idea further. *Maybe my DNA was brought directly from Africa and had nothing to do with Arizona.* I frowned as what I had been seeing all my life clicked into clearer focus. So many of those created, manipulated, enhanced, deformed, crippled people with me in Tower 7 were from parts of Africa. I'd known this by looking at people but now I wondered, *Why?*

I sighed, looking at my feet. "Fully unraveling my origins is a lost cause," I muttered.

But one thing I had learned was that, despite my origins and the sinister reasons for creating me, my light brought life. Though I burned, I was a positive force. It had been my light that had brought this jungle that grew in the debris. It was my light that had given The Backbone the strength to shake Tower 7 from its great body.

And now The Backbone was offering me a strange gift. I opened the box.

My hands went numb. My eyes watered. The scent of leaves packed my nose. The taste of mud flooded my mouth and my entire body began to glow. The grass pushed up beneath my feet, and tiny flowers blossomed from the blade tips. The Backbone softly twisted, shedding bits of bark as it stretched further toward the stars. I heard it snapping and creaking, but I was looking at the object in the box.

"It's a nut," I whispered.

Round and about the shape and size of a garden egg, it looked made of a tougher heavier wood than that of the box and the tree. Etched deep into it were mazes of lines that made circles, squiggles and geometric shapes. The black lines ran and repeated close to each other but they never touched. The designs moved in a slow dance, undulated like bizarre insects.

Heat. It coursed through me like water, rushing up from my feet, up my entire body to my head. The heat again. Seven days ago, I had heated until I burned to ash. Now here I was again. However, my clothes still did not burn. I shined brighter through my brown skin and reached into the box and picked up the strange nut.

Blackness.

Pure. Quiet. Then pricks of tiny white, blue, and yellow lights. I was seeing stars for the first time. Billions and billions of stars. As I flew through space smooth and gentle. In a vastness that made me want to weep. But I had no eyes with which to shed tears. No body with which to shudder. No nose with which to leak.

I was traveling. I would know where to land when I saw it. My direction was clear. The pull was strong. The small blue planet. Earth. I was hope sent from afar. A beacon. Deep in the red soil. Until the right time.

"They dug you up?" I said aloud, as I stared down at the nut. "They dug you up with the red soil and brought you here." That is why The Backbone knows itself, I thought. Alien seed. Alien seed in the soil of Tower 7 where scientists, lab assistants, lab technicians, doctors, administrative workers, guards and police and the mutations, monsters and mistakes they made dwelled. I laughed hard.

The world went white. I nearly dropped the box as I shielded my face. The light was harsh to my unaccustomed eyes. My heart sank as I understood I had been so focused on the nut that I hadn't noticed the chopping sound.

"Do not run," a voice blared. "Stay where you are!"

The helicopter's searchlight nearly blinded me. I had seen them many times while I was growing up in Tower 7, where the windows were thick glass. Their chopping noise was always muted. I'd never imagined they were so loud, their blades chopping the air like a cleaver on a chopping block. As my eyes adjusted, I could see that on the side of the helicopter was the logo I'd been seeing in Tower 7 all my short life: A hand grasping spears of lightning. Those of us in Tower 7 had always called the organization represented by that logo the Big Eye (the lightning represented speciMen). We never used the Big Eye's official name.

They probably thought that I had purposely brought down the Axis building. In a way I had. But shouldn't they also have been expecting me? They made me. I was their weapon. To be used for nuclear warfare or biological warfare, I did not know. But I hadn't matured in the way they had wanted or expected. I was a failed project, a rogue prisoner. Still, they had to know that I would show up again. Maybe that is why they had not begun to clear the incredible amount of debris. Maybe. Maybe not.

I shut the box, tucked it under my arm and took off. If they knew nothing else, they'd know not to shoot.

My lean legs were strong. My back flexed. Every muscle in my body was working in perfect harmony. I was made to run. I was like the finest horse. First and foremost, they'd been trying to create a human weapon. A human bomb that self-regenerated to blow up another day. One who could run fast was a plus. I'd only gotten to run on a treadmill, during my time in Tower 7. Now I got to sprint out in the open. It was absolute joy, even with the Big Eye pursuing me.

One foot, then the next. Digging into the ground and launching me forth. I felt like I could fly. Like nothing could touch me. My healthy fresh lungs expanded and drew in hearty breaths. I ran faster. Faster. FASTER. There were cars on the street, and I kept up with them as I dodged the few pedestrians on the sidewalk.

It was night and I'd always thought people retreated indoors at this time. I'd read a lot about the crime rate here. The shootings, gang violence, muggings, car crashes. But people walked the streets, men and women. In groups and a few alone. They all carried thin glowing screens and coin-like portables. Some spoke to them; others watched probably the very same shows they could watch on the sides of buildings.

I passed a group of people standing outside a restaurant. They looked confused and bewildered and were pointing toward the ruins. They'd probably heard the building fall. Did these people even *see* me? They did, but not for long. Above, the Big Eye followed, shining their searchlight, confusing the people on the sidewalks and streets even more.

So this was New York. Palm trees grew beside roads. Mango trees. Iroko. Rosewood. Mahogany. The tall buildings were adorned with lights that showed large screens with dancing people, prime time TV shows, and flashy commercials. All the buildings were draped in those sweet smelling vines the mayor said would help keep the city's air clean. Those vines had been engineered in Tower 4, which was on the US Virgin Islands, but few people knew that. Even fewer cared.

Some of the roads were smooth, and I ran on them, keeping to the side. But I got to a few that were full of potholes. The news reports I had read all year were not exaggerating. The city had a water drainage problem, and the year's heavy rainy season had exacerbated it. The vehicles on the road were fast and dented. I'd never seen one up close and I'd always wanted to drive one. The acrid smell of their exhaust was greater here.

Suddenly, I saw huge versions of myself on the buildings. In some of them I was running. Others were old photos of me not smiling, peering into the camera. These photos were from before I had been what I was now. People looked up from their portable screens, to the big ones on the buildings and then back at their screens. Fantasy meeting fantasy. How confused some must have felt when they then saw me run by.

As I ran, the hump on my back ached worse than ever. I grunted from the pain, but I kept running. They would not get their hands on the box. It was *mine*. The Backbone gave it to *me*. And it had told me where to take it. And they certainly would not have me. Never again.

I ran beneath a railway and watched the searchlight pass overhead. Then I ran along the sidewalk beneath the railway. I could see the helicopter trying to change direction, but it was too late. How would they know which way I'd gone? Or if I ran anywhere at all? I could have just stopped right there and waited. They chose to go in the opposite direction. For the moment, I'd lost them. But my face was everywhere. Someone would recognize me any moment and report my whereabouts. I slowed to a walk as I tried to figure out my next move. I passed a jewelry shop and a currency exchange. Both were closed.

As I walked, I sniffed. There was a spicy smell in the air. Tomato, onion, garlic, lemon. A perfumy aroma. A familiar one. When I came to the open door, I looked up. Ethiopian Sunrise. I walked into the restaurant.

"We're closed!" a slim brown-skinned man with granite black curly hair said. His accent reminded me a bit of my lost love Saeed. *Saeed*, I thought. Saeed was dead. They made him want to die and that was what made me want to live.

"I'm sorry," I said. "I'll leave."

"You!" he said, pointing at and striding up to me. "You're the terrorist who they are saying just brought down the Axis Building!" His eyes got wider. "Are . . ." He brought his hands up and then let them fall. "Are you . . . y-y-you're *glowing!* Why in Allah's name are you glowing?! I thought the photo they were showing of you was just bad."

I backed toward the door.

"No, wait!" he said, holding up his hands. "See?! See my hands! No portable, no nothing."

I looked past him. Certainly there were others in the kitchen. I wanted to kick myself for coming in here. It hadn't been a rational thing. It was the smell. The smell was so familiar.

"I just need a moment," I said. "To rest. Then I'll leave."

The houseplants near the restaurant's window began to stretch and thrust out fresh leaves. He looked at this and then slowly back at me.

"Where would you go?"

"Why would I tell *you?* Who are you?"

He laughed. "I am sorry. I am rude."

I only frowned.

"My name is Berihun. I am an immigrant from Ethiopia and the owner of this restaurant. My wife Makeda is in the back. Only her."

Then I understood what had attracted me to this place. The smell. The food. In Tower 7, the majority of the cuisine we ate was African, whether you were African or non-African. I remember the lion lady was fond of couscous and boiled yams with peppered palm oil. Nobody ever complained about the food in Tower 7. My favorite was the Ethiopian dish of chicken in red pepper paste. How I loved doro wat. Just the thought of it made my empty stomach growl. I had not eaten a thing since my rebirth. I decided to leave it all up to what Saeed called The Author of All Things, for Saeed had stopped believing in Allah long ago, and I had never believed in any gods of religions.

"Please, Berihun, I would like some doro wat," I said. "It is my favorite dish and I have not eaten in, well, a long time."

Berihun blinked and then he grinned wide. "You know our food!"

I smiled back and nodded.

"Sit," he said, motioning to the table beside the counter. "I will be right back! Makeda will be so excited. What is your name?"

I paused. Names are powerful. They have a way of becoming destiny.

They should not be shared with just anyone. But this man had given me his name without hesitation. "My name is Phoenix," I said, sitting at the table for six.

He grinned and turned to go to the kitchen. He turned back. "They say that Tower 7 was the research facility where Leroy Jackson and his group of scientists discovered the cure for AIDS, but no one ever saw him or any of his famous research team ever go in that place. My wife is sure that what they really did in there was evil and cruel. She is smart and observant. I usually believe every word she says on subjects like this. She is correct?"

I nodded. "Leroy and his team worked out of New Orleans, Louisiana, in Tower 3."

"You are not a terrorist."

"No, I am not."

He nodded and started walking away when he stopped again and came back.

"Do you have scoliosis?"

I knew what this was. The woman with the head of an owl in Tower 7 had it. Curious about her condition, I'd read about it in one of the medical books they gave me. The curvature of the spine. It was a genetic deformity that sometimes resulted from growing too quickly. "No," I said.

"My wife has scoliosis and your back kind of looks like you may have it, too."

He came closer.

"Well, really I-I don't know," I said. "Does hers hurt?"

"No," he said. "Not at all."

"Can you look at my back?" I said. "I can't really see it."

He hesitated and then stepped around me. "Well," he said, gently pulling the collar of my dress back a bit. "Oh my!" he said. "Your skin is very warm. Are you running a fever?"

"No, not in the usual way. I glow and I heat up."

That was when I noticed the counter behind him. There were several items for sale there. My eye fell on the large tub full of a yellow thick substance. Shea butter.

"Can use some of that? I'm sorry I don't have any money but . . ."

"Use what?" He looked toward the counter. "Oh. Which one?"

"The shea butter."

"Sure," he said, picking it up.

"Thank you," I said. "So aside from the heat, did you notice anything else about my back? I don't normally have any sort of hump or swelling there."

He pressed his lips together as he handed me the shea butter. I pulled the lid off and the nutty smell assured me this was the pure unrefined kind. Perfect.

"What have they done to you?" he suddenly asked.

I paused, touching the smooth hard surface of the shea butter. It softened at my warm touch. I sighed, looked him in the eye and said, "I think it is more that it is what I am, Berihun."

"Maybe," he said.

"So what did you see?" I asked, rubbing the shea butter on my arms. It felt like cool water. It felt so so good, though not as divine as the shea butter they gave me in Tower 7.

"The skin," he said. "It's . . . it's kind of puckered and swollen. Is that muscle?"

I frowned but said nothing, rubbing shea butter on my legs.

He shrugged, trying not to look worried, and quickly went to the back.

Two minutes later, a plump tall woman with many long black braids came out of the kitchen. *Why didn't they do my hair like that?* I touched my head. "Oh," I said. I had a healthy two inch afro. I pressed at it as the woman stared at me. Then I rubbed it. Pebbles and dust flew out.

"So it is true?" she asked.

"Yes," I said.

"Africans? Like me? Like my husband?"

"Yes, most of us were Africans."

"Ethiopians?"

"Not that I knew."

"But they served our food?"

"Yes."

She came over to me and touched my cheek. Only Saeed had ever touched me with tenderness. Tears welled up in my eyes, and I wasn't quite sure why. "So warm," she said. "My sister, you're safe here."

As she went back into the kitchen, I noticed what her husband spoke of. Her back was slightly crooked and she had a bit of a hump, like mine. But I didn't think her back was hot to the touch.

His wife brought the food out minutes later. By then my entire back was aching so badly that I began to wonder if my light was burning me from within. But if that were the case, then my whole body should have been in pain, not just the area around my shoulder blades. Every move I made brought a deep itchy pain that made me want to tear at my skin.

"My husband and I were about to eat dinner. This is my special recipe," Makeda said, ceremoniously placing the large round metal platter on the table. "I only make this for family."

The platter was covered with injera, a spongy delicious flat bread. At Tower 7, only once in a while did they serve my doro wat with the traditional injera. On the layer of the bread in the center of the platter, were the drumsticks and boiled eggs stewed in the spicy red sauce. On the injera layer closer to me, to my left was a small mound of boiled cabbage and carrots and on the right was a mound of yellow curried lentils. The same was on the other side of the platter.

Berihun sat across from me. "You should have the pleasure of company with your meal," he said. I felt my chest swell with emotion. Good company, a small but wonderful thing. That was exactly what I craved, next to a good meal. It seemed so long ago that I'd had good company. Makeda also set a plate with four rolled up sections of injera on the table and then sat down in the chair beside me.

"I'm not hungry for food, but I am for your story," she said, looking at me with eyes of wonder. "Will you tell us?"

"Let her eat some first, my wife," Berihun said, chuckling.

Makeda nodded, but glanced toward the door. I understood her unspoken words perfectly. I didn't have much time. The Big Eye were out there. They were looking for me. How long would it be before they came running down this street, checking every building?

I picked up one of the soft rolls of flat bread, unrolled it a bit and tore off a piece. I grasped some chicken and stew with it and popped the combination in my mouth. This is the most wonderful thing about injera flat bread; it is simultaneously food, eating utensil, and plate. My eyes grew wide as my brand new taste buds sang.

"Oh! Delicious!"

Makeda beamed. Berihun was busy shoveling food into his mouth, too.

I tore off more injera. The balance of meat, egg, pepper, tomato was harmony. Tower 7 doro wat had never tasted like this! The injera was delicately sour and light as a cloud. The sauce was colorful tantalizing heat. The chicken, savory. I ate and I ate. She brought out more of everything, and I ate that, too. Neither of them commented about the fact that I was eating like two large men, and I was glad.

All that I had been through in the last hour was smoothed away by this perfect sustenance. My entire being relaxed. My mind was calm and alive as the flavors in my mouth touched my other senses.

"My name is Phoenix," I said. We'd been eating in silence for ten minutes. Berihun and Makeda both looked at me with anticipation. "My DNA was probably brought straight from Africa. That makes the most sense to me now. I was mixed and grown in Tower 7, two years ago, though I look and feel about 40 and have the knowledge of a centenarian. I am what they call an ABO, an 'accelerated biological organism'." I sighed. "Amongst other things. I think I was supposed to be one of this country's greatest weapons."

I told them everything.

"Now I am free of it," I said, after a few minutes. I sat back. My meal was done. The three of us kept stealing looks at the front window and door. The streets seemed too quiet. But what did I know about what streets normally looked like?

"No, you're not," Makeda said. She and her husband were grasping hands. As if the tale of my life and my journey would fling them into space if they did not hang on tightly. "This is who you are."

And who AM I? I thought.

Berihun was nodding vigorously. "I didn't want to tell you this while you were enjoying your meal but your face is on every network, every newsfeed, even embedded in the advertisements. This is happening *now*, Phoenix. Everyone who looks at a television, computer, e-reader, portable, everyone who walks past a building and looks up at its screens will know your face by morning. Whatever that is you have, seed, nut, whatever, take it where it demands to go."

Makeda took my hand and for a moment, I forgot all things. Her grasp was warm, strong, as was her gaze. As the food had calmed me, she and Berihun gave me strength. My eyes stung, and I felt the tears coming again. Unlike before, when I was trying to escape Tower 7, they did not sizzle to vapor. They ran down my face, and dropped from my chin to my lap.

"You can't stop now, girlie," Makeda whispered. "You have to keep running."

She pulled me close and said into my ear, "There is an exit in the back. Leave now!"

The bell on the front door jingled as a young man in a black uniform walked in.

"Assaalmu Alaykum," Berihun said, jumping up and quickly walking to the front of the restaurant. He laughed loudly, thickening his accent and breaking his English, "We are close. Open tomorrow."

I was running again. I didn't know where I was going, but I was running. Something had happened to the streets. There were no cars. There were no people. They'd been cleared. The sky sounded like it was swarming with helicopters. I could see the flash of searchlights in front of me and to my right side. I needed to get out of the city but how would I do that on foot?

I felt something give in my back, and I stumbled but didn't stop. I felt it painfully rupture and then ooze down. Blood? This was something new. I felt the upper part of my dress pull tight, and then I heard the back rip. What was happening to me? I ran into an alley and reached behind my now exposed back. I felt . . . I had no idea what I felt. Something was protruding. Wet but hard bone? I knocked on the part I could reach. Not heavy. Hollow. I ran my hand over it. Soft things, too. I flexed my shoulder blades as the itchiness grew intense again. What felt like the skin of my middle and lower back tore some more. This time I could even hear it. But the pain wasn't pain. It was relief. Itchy relief. I looked at my hand and saw that it was red and wet with blood.

"Oh God," I wept, disgusted. "What is happening?" I shuddered as I fought not to scratch.

I leaned my face against the wall. The concrete was cool against my cheek. A door opened feet away from me, spilling out warm yellow light. Perhaps the backdoor of a shop or a restaurant. A man walked out laughing. He took one look at me and gasped, stumbling over his feet.

I tried to press my back to the wall. I froze. I couldn't; whatever was sticking out of me was too big. Then whatever it was knocked over a garbage can two yards to my right. I could feel it hit the can.

The man only stared at me, slack jawed. Another man came out, carrying a pack of cigarettes. "Holy shit," he said, staring at me, dropping the cigarettes. He made the sign of the cross and fell to his knees.

CHAPTER 3

Click

WE STARED AT EACH OTHER, the wind blowing a potato chip bag and a piece of paper up the filthy alley. Me, breathing heavily, standing there in a sweaty, bloody white dress. And the two men, one African and one Asian, standing near the open door both wearing jeans. I reached behind my shoulders and felt the hardness and softness that was attached to me. I looked over my shoulder. As I did so, whatever was on my back flexed, I could hear it unfolding and stretching. It sounded like the branches of a leafy tree in the wind. It felt like such relief.

With my peripheral vision I saw brown. I turned my neck as far as I could. Feathers. Wet brown feathers. I had *wings*.

The two men still said nothing as I backed away. They didn't follow, they did not retreat. But one of them had his portable, and its top was slid open. He was glancing at it and then glancing at me.

Running was difficult with the wings. My wingspan had to be over thirty feet. I was stressed and couldn't help stretching them out, painfully smacking the alley wall. My head throbbed as I focused on my wings. I could see them extending out. Then it was like something clicked into place in the center of my forehead. It was all there. Maybe it hadn't been there before I died but now that I was alive again, it was. My wings were mine. I knew them. They made sense. My feet kept trying to leave the ground.

When I heard the sound of a helicopter and saw the searchlight coming toward me, I tried my wings, and it was easy. The feathers had dried and all I had to do was imagine that I had another set of powerful arms. Powerful arms whose every curve, fold, muscle I could control. I could flex them, retract them, move specific parts. I ran.

Then I flew for my life.

The air reached down and took me. I reached up and took to the air. The wind hugged me. My feet left the ground. My remade body was made to fly.

Eight days ago I had never left Tower 7. I had only seen the world through thick glass. I'd never smelled the breeze. My best friend and the man I loved had killed himself when he lost all hope. Seven days ago, I had died while urging the trees and plants around me to live. Just over two hours ago, I was reborn. And now I had wings, and I was flying.

I was just above the lower buildings, gazing at what I had only seen from my window. People on the sidewalks, on apartment balconies, coming out of vehicles and homes, in parking lots, all looking up and pointing at me, the screens of whatever devices they carried glowing brightly enough for me to see from so high up. They were texting, calling, messaging, flashing, the whole world would see the new me soon.

I heard it long before they saw me. But the helicopters were moving too fast for me to really escape. The searchlight soon found me again. I was flooded in white. The helicopter flew beside me, its blades hacking at the air and forcing me to work hard to keep from losing control.

"Land on top of the nearest building," the female voice said. "We will not hurt you."

That voice. The accent. I knew it. Bumi! The woman who'd cared for and instructed me since my earliest memory of life. The woman from Nigeria whom I now realized was most likely banking on the benefits of experimentation on me to earn her American citizenship. Gain from my pain. So she'd survived to pursue me another day. And yet again she was claiming that they would not hurt me. I still remembered what it felt like to have no face and to have bullets eat away at my legs, belly, arms, and chest.

I flew faster. So they did, too.

I saw Bumi order the soldiers in the helicopter to bring out their guns . . . again. I heard her shouting at them but could not make out her words. I looked straight ahead. I would die escaping, as I had before. Someone shouted and then the guns fired. I braced my body for the pain. Nothing. But there was more shooting. And now, more shouting. Then the sound of the helicopter changed. The chopping stopped. Creaking. Screaming. I dared to look.

He was raw power. His wings were albatross-like and brown, as mine were, which meant they unfolded in three different places on each wing. When stretched out, they were straight and slim. But his were twice the size and length of mine. He looked darker-skinned than when I had freed him seven days ago in Tower 7. Had he been soaking up the sun? Nonetheless, he was no less lethal. Before, he'd killed many soldiers as soon as he was free. Now he was hurling the entire helicopter into a building. He let go, stretching his hands before him. The helicopter sailed toward the street.

Just before it smashed into a building, I caught the eye of Bumi. She'd claimed she would not harm me. Again, she'd proven that she was a liar. She was screaming and reaching for me. She'd told me stories while she caused me pain; she was what lies were made of, even though her stories were truth. My right hand twitched uncontrollably as I watched her watching me. The side of her face was patched with a blue tight bandage. I couldn't grab her. I could not save her.

Then there were flames, broken glass and twisted metal, the sound of fire alarms and other chaos. I flew on. The winged man flew behind me. Not one of the helicopters followed us, after that. Nothing followed us.

CHAPTER 4

Outer Space

AFTER DESTROYING THE HELICOPTER, the winged man flew with me for miles. I was glad for the cover of night and his silent presence. It was hard to think straight. On top of this, my shoulders and back muscles ached from pumping my wings. Yet I didn't want to land. I glanced at him every so often. He flew so effortlessly, barely needing to flap his huge wings. He was slightly ahead of me, leading the way.

Nevertheless, as soon as the blackness of the ocean came into sight, he looked at me. I looked at him and then looked away, unable to withstand his piercing stare. My heart was suddenly pounding hard. He seemed human, yet how could he be? There was something so steady about him, so even. Again I wondered how Tower 7 had captured and imprisoned him and why. Moments later, I looked back. He was still watching me.

"What?" I finally asked. "What is it?"

He looked ahead. The ocean opened up into darkness only a few miles away. I could see the lights of a large ship on the water. A luxury liner? He pointed a long finger straight ahead. I wasn't sure if he meant the ship, the ocean, or even one of the buildings.

He shot away from me abruptly and did a one-hundred-eighty degree turn. Then he flew off, back toward the city. So fast. I couldn't possibly follow him. I certainly couldn't maneuver myself like that. Not yet. No goodbye, no words of wisdom. I was alone, again. I flew on.

Minutes later, I was flying above the submerged part of the city. The tops of once majestic, now wobbly skyscrapers peeked above the dark, slow-moving water like trees in a swamp. I'd read that a species of nocturnal dog-sized rats lived in the portions of the building right above the water, and they fed on fish. They were probably out now, fishing the shallows.

I'd read that these buildings were inhabited by the poor and illegal. Hardworking people who commuted to the city using boat services provided by New York's government. I landed on top of one of the taller buildings beneath a dim light post. A baby cried nearby and someone laughed. I smelled the spicy aroma of someone cooking with a lot of curry. There was a swimming pool here but it was empty and filthy now. Beside it, plastic chairs were pushed around a rusty steel table. I imagined men sitting in the chairs as they smoked cigars and played cards and cursed and laughed. Friends just being friends, even in their poverty. No Big Eye with guns and scalpels and portables.

Several pigeons standing near the table and chairs looked at me, their heads cocked to the side. Then they went about their business of eating seeds scattered on the ground. I smiled. I had never seen these birds up close. I watched them for a moment. They strutted about but stayed close to each other, almost unconsciously. I liked the way they cooed. Clearly, someone else must have liked the birds, too. Why else would anyone scatter seeds here?

It had been hours since I'd eaten the doro wat, and I'd flown miles, yet my belly felt full. I sat down on concrete ground, feeling the breeze against my exposed back and folded feathers. My back was dry. The bleeding had stopped; the blood had dried. I looked at my softly glowing hands and the wooden box I held in them. A black pigeon with grey speckled wings walked up to me and cocked its head curiously.

"I don't know what it is," I told it. The pigeon cautiously came closer, stepping a few paces to the left as it did so. I could have sworn it was looking at my wings with its beady brown eyes. I laughed. "I don't really know what *I* am, either. What do you think?" The bird just stared at me. Then in the forefront of my mind, I had a vision of a place that was full of sunshine. The pigeon hooted with fright, turned and ran off, rejoining the others.

I pressed my forehead. There was no pain. But my head felt vast.

"Worlds!" I whispered. All the screaming chaos in my mind that stressed, dwelt, worried, lamented over what had happened to me since I stepped out of my room in Tower 7— it stopped. It was still there, but for the moment, it was on pause. I quickly understood. The alien seed was *speaking* to me in a way that reminded me of Mmuo's method. However, unlike Mmuo's nanomite communication, it didn't speak in words. It spoke directly to my mind; it touched my psyche, and its touch was magnificent.

I looked over the ledge of the building, at the ocean. Past the ship. Into the darkness. I saw images of another place. A place that was warm like New York, with the same palm trees and flooding. A place plagued with New Malaria like New York, but with people who looked like me. It was not New York. It was not even the United States. It was far. How would I get there? By plane? By the ship? Me? Phoenix, the rogue winged speciMen who was believed to have brought down the Axis and probably blamed for Tower 7's collapse as well? How would I do that?

I stood very still. The pigeons behind me were quiet, too.

I decided in the same way that I decided I wanted to escape Tower 7, on impulse.

I spread my wings. I ran and then flew, catching a gust of wind that lifted me into the sky with an ease that I didn't have the first time. Several pigeons flew with me, but they turned back when I reached the water. And that was how I started flying across the ocean. Maybe a part of me was like Saeed and wanted to die. Maybe. But it was more than that.

The first few days were pain. I did not need to eat, urinate, defecate, or sleep. Hours after I started my journey, I felt the box warm in my hands and then my entire body grew brighter, and I warmed, too. My stomach gurgled and then I felt it do something very strange. It tightened up, hard like a stone.

At first I thought the alien seed had done something to my body. But as time passed, I realized it was more likely that I had done it to myself because the seed had shown me how. While flying I had unknotted my stomach using sheer will. As soon as I did, the pain was so terrible that I quickly re-knotted it.

So the pain did not come from my stomach, bowels, bladder, or a lack of sleep. It came from my shoulders and back. I needed to build up muscles, and I had to do it while crossing the ocean. To fall into the water was death by drowning or worse. I had no time to test just how waterproof my feathers were.

I flew through the pain, and for days I could think of nothing else but flying southeast and not dropping into the ocean. I put the alien seed inside my dress where it rested close to my heart. It was like a mysterious navigation device, showing me the way in my mind. The only respite I got were the times when the wind carried me. My wings were powerful. I was made to travel long long distances. Who knows, maybe I even had albatross DNA mixed with mine. And like an albatross, I quickly learned how to fly without flying. When the wind was right, I could fly for miles and miles without doing a thing.

When the pain finally stopped, I could notice the ocean. Its vastness. In the day, the blueness. In the night, the blackness. All that had happened was and seemed so far away. The world was different here.

Hours before I saw the coast of Africa, I saw just how different the world was over the ocean. I was watching a storm churn miles away, riding some of the resulting winds, when I happened to glance below. Here, the sun was out, the water was clear, and I was flying high, so I saw the thing in its fullness. Its giant red body was bulbous like the sack of a jellyfish, but the skin looked thick and tough like an elephant's. It had three massive tentacles that it used to propel itself forth and an equally massive round head with squishy yellow swiveling bug eyes. The creature was the size of thirty houses. Large houses. It was not a giant squid or any kind of cephalopod. If anything, it looked mammalian.

The creature looked up at me with those yellow eyes, staring for a long time. Its eyes were so huge, that I could clearly see its black pupils fixed on me. I had no idea if the thing could leap, so I flew higher. It watched me with interest for a while and then eventually sunk back into the deep.

I couldn't have been gladder to see the coast of Africa. The first meal I had in two weeks was given to me by a kind old Sierra Leonean woman who spoke perfect English and wasn't afraid of women with wings. It was fried fish, fresh baked cassava bread, and thick tasty okra soup. As I ate, she said, "You will need this, I think" and held up a garment made of coarse blue cloth. She called it a burka, and it fit over my head, covering me from head to toe, wings and all. I knew what it was, for I'd read about Islamic traditions.

"I respect the religion," I quietly said. "But I don't . . ."

"Take it," she insisted. "You will need to pick and choose who sees what you are. The burka is freedom." She wrapped it tightly, put it in a satchel, and I took it. I knew she was right. I slept for two days and then after meeting her entire family, I set off, again.

The tree grew wide, tall, and crooked, as if it were dancing very very slowly. It had long narrow leaves and its branches were heavy with bunches of shea fruits. I wouldn't have known what they were if I hadn't run into the young woman who could speak English. This was a farm where the nuts used for shea butter were made.

The seed had led me to a Northern town in Ghana called Wulugu. Within Wulugu, it led me to the middle of a shea tree farm not far from a small village. To this large tree. There were people in these farms working. How strange I must have looked to them, for this was not a place where there were many Muslims, and here I was in a full burka, all alone. My folded wings, which I'd pulled closely to my back, made me look like a crippled hunchback. Beneath it, I wore my heat resistant white dress, now tan and stiff with dust, sand, and sea salt.

I dropped to my knees and began to dig with my bare hands. All day, I had eaten nothing but a few bananas that I'd plucked from a tree hours ago. My belly was empty. I had no money. I did not know what I would do after this. I was still glowing, though my body remained cool. But none of that was important. This nut. This alien seed was the focus of all things for me.

The dirt was red and moist just like the dirt at the base of The Backbone. It was easy to dig here. I dug a hole three feet deep and by then, I had an audience. I decided to give them a show. I shined brightly through my burka and giggled as all the trees and plants including the one right in front of me began to stretch, their leaves unfurling, their stems expanding. Some people screamed, but most of them sighed and murmured with awe. Some brought out portables and took pictures. While they watched the plants grow, I brought out the box with the seed and gently placed it in the hole.

As soon as I did this, I felt it go out. The light within me extinguished. The plants around me stopped growing impossibly fast. Just like that. It was such a relief that I sighed and leaned forward. I could feel the seed sucking and sucking the glowing life-enhancing energy. I could have sworn that I even heard the "clop" of the box closing. I sat up, looking at my hands. They did not glow with even the hint of green yellow. I touched my back. My wings were still there. Stronger than ever. Begging for the sky as something deep in me begged for justice. Justice for what had been done to me and all the other prisoners in Tower 7, in *all* the towers. Would I still burn and come alive? I would find out.

I stood and faced the people gathered. A woman came forth laughing something I did not understand. She switched to English and said, "Welcome." Then she hugged me. Then a man joined in. They all hugged me. I hugged them back.

CHAPTER 5

Reaper

ONE MUST STOP TIME TO LISTEN TO A STORY. The storyteller starts it again.

She starts it in her own place, in her own moment, in her own point of view. As long as you listen, she is in charge of your destiny. You and the storyteller share everything, even your existence.

Listen . . .

I started picking up the local accent. I could never fit in, so that wasn't the reason. I just liked the sound of it. I missed my love Saeed, my friend Mmuo, the other Tower 7 prisoners who weren't so nice to me. Speaking like the Ghanaians reminded me of them all. Plus, after all that had happened, it felt good to be different from what I had been, yet the same. That which was me would never change. That which was me could survive death. Over and over.

I was Phoenix.

They called me *Okore*. It meant "eagle" in Twi, though I felt my wings were more like an albatross'. But there is no word for albatross in "Twi," so Okore was fine. I was picking up the language quickly. I could speak it better than most, and it had only been some months. It was part of my acceleration. This was good because otherwise, I'd have been a problem there. The language of a people is sacred. It is their identity. Though most Ghanaians spoke English, it was good to know the native tongues, also. To lack the ability to communicate on multiple levels always means trouble. So, for once, I was spared.

But then again, I came into this village in the people's favor. When I had buried the alien seed at the base of one of their oldest shea trees, just before its strange light left me, my light had fortified all the trees of their farms. My timing had been perfect because it was harvest season; the trees were heavy. So with the coming of "Okore" came great abundance in Wulugu. Even after my life-urging light was reabsorbed into that seed and I'd buried it, the trees' fruit continued to multiply and swell, steady and strong. With me, came abundance. By the end of market season, the people of Wulugu were flush with wealth.

They built me a small two-story house and even equipped it with a solar panel, so I had enough electricity for dim lights. Some women helped me cultivate a garden. The people invited me to their meetings, marriages, parties, and burials. For the first time, I was part of a community. I relaxed, putting America behind me. What a weight that place put on my shoulders; a woman with wings should never be so burdened.

It was through the people of Wulugu that I learned what a "jelli telli" was. While I was in Tower 7, no one ever showed these to us. Our rooms— no, our cells were too small, so there was no need. We always watched small screens embedded in the walls or through our e-readers. Nevertheless, jelli tellis had been around for years.

Jelli tellis were rectangular sheets of highly elastic optic-gelatin that could be stretched to cover an entire wall. You then clicked the golden button on its tiny round remote, there was a tinkling sound and the most realistic image ever seen materialized. The village had two jelli tellis and on weekends, everyone would gather at the community house to watch noisy West African 3D movies. Once in a while, they'd screen an American one, too.

No one ever asked me where I came from or what I was. I wore the clothes of a Muslim woman. There were not many in Wulugu, but there were enough. No one bothered me. People assumed that I was hunchbacked and that was fine, too. But that didn't keep the men away. Within two months, three men I saw regularly at the market or the community house proposed marriage to me because, they said, they had fallen in love with my face. My *face*, can you imagine? I was much more than my face. Only one man truly understood this. Kofi Atta Annan. His father had named him after the UN diplomat who spearheaded the riots in Nigeria and Ghana over a century ago. For Kofi, I would take my burka off if the time came. That time was today.

He lived about a mile away from me. His home was small and had running water. He was also one of the few who could afford fuel for his generator. That's more than one could say about most of the people here. Even I went to the well and carried water home every morning with the rest of the women.

It was daybreak and the roads were empty. I'd woken up knowing what I wanted to do. So I'd bathed with my last bucket of water, dressed in a backless yellow sundress, covered up with my black burka, ate some buttered bread with sardines, and went to find Kofi before he left for work. Kofi was the town doctor. The *only* town doctor. His days were always long.

I was excited. Finally Kofi would know. What would he say when he saw that my hump was actually a set of wings? The thought made my heart flutter. I didn't love Kofi as I loved Saeed. I didn't think I'd ever love a man the way I loved Saeed. But Kofi was a lovely man. To look at him, even from afar was to smile. He was tall like a tree, and had a strong clear voice. If the great winged man I freed in Tower 7 were to speak, I suspected he would sound like Kofi. And Kofi was kind. When he treated his patients, he asked how they were feeling, he asked permission to touch, he truly cared about their well-being. He was the opposite of the Big Eye who had taken care of me in my first life as one takes care of a cow they will slaughter at the end of the year.

With Saeed, we could only be together during those times when we were eating a meal or given social time. Saeed once told me that for hours he used to pretend he was talking to me while he sat in his room. I never told him this but there were many nights where I would dream about him talking to me for hours. I wish I'd told him that. We had so little time together.

With Kofi it was different. Freer. He was there that first day when I arrived. And he was the only one who actually *saw* me bury the alien seed. Everyone else was in awe of the plants and trees growing right before their eyes. But it was *I* who fascinated him. Days later, after I was settled in the house they gave me, he approached me in the market and introduced himself. Then he asked, "What was in it?"

"What?" I asked.

"The box you buried." He paused, rubbing his chin. "I don't know what I saw. It was green, glowing. I still wonder about it."

"If I tell you what it was, will you then go and dig it up?"

"No," he laughed. "Whatever it was, it's clear it belongs there."

"It does," I said. I paused, looking him in the eye for a moment. I was wearing my black burka, so only my face was exposed. My wings were aching from being tucked close to my body for too long. I needed to get home soon. "And that's all that really matters."

His smile broadened and he nodded. "Ok," he said. "Well, welcome."

"Thank you, Kofi."

I went to him first. I was bored, and I'd decided that I liked the sound of his voice. He was seeing to patients when I walked in. There were over twenty people waiting for him, and he was sweaty and looked exhausted. However, when he saw me, he smiled a big smile. That was when I fell for him. When I saw him smile, despite all of the stress and work he had to do. He smiled at me without really even seeing *me*.

"Even a doctor needs to eat," he said. "Wait for me."

I laughed and said that I would. I quickly went to the market, found the woman who sold cooked food and bought us some jollof rice, two oranges, and two malt drinks. I returned, sat down and waited for two hours as he saw to each patient's health. Each time he touched a patient, he asked for permission first.

When an old man with a heart condition insisted that he would keep making his wife cook him soup with palm oil, Kofi asked him about his grandson. The man's face lit up and then the man quickly understood Kofi's point: If he didn't stop eating foods high in saturated fat, he wouldn't have much more time with his grandson.

I watched Kofi sing to a boy as he gave the boy twelve stitches on his leg, and I watched Kofi diagnose a woman with New Malaria in less than a minute. He was kind, gentle yet firm—all that the Big Eye doctors were not. When the last patient for the morning finally left, he looked up at me and said, "Just you sitting there made it all easier."

From that day on, we ate lunch together nearly every day. We began to meet in the evenings to go on walks and stargaze together. Kofi never asked me about my "hump." And when I kissed him, he kept his hands down. He kissed me with his lips and only his lips. Saeed and I had kissed several times, but those kisses were always rushed. The Big Eye were always watching; they never let us get truly close. With Kofi, I was free and there was more. I wanted more.

I passed the bicycle shop where two young men sat beside the bikes. They both carried guns, though they kept them out of sight. Kofi, who knew them well, told me so. One was so dark-skinned, you could only see his bright eyes in the warming darkness. I raised a hand and waved and he tiredly waved back. His partner was asleep. The roads were lumpy from water damage, but nothing nearly as bad as the streets back in the United States.

I passed the mosque, a great sandstone edifice that looked more like a sand castle than a place of worship. The two-story building was over two hundred years old. However, since there were so few Muslims in Wulugu, the morning prayers brought more ghosts than people at daybreak. The imam who lived in there was said to be a descendant of the sheik who built it. He once told me that this sheik was sure that this village was built on sacred land and that was why he built the strange mosque here, despite the lack of a Muslim community.

I think the imam's ancestor somehow knew what was buried at the base of that tree. Or maybe the tree wasn't there when the alien seed fell into the ground. Regardless, I think he knew something. And I think he was honored by, rather than afraid of, that knowledge.

I passed the spot where the men sold calling and e-port cards, portables and the ugly bulky old cell phones they called "battle commanders." I passed quiet homes, and then a small stretch of farmland. In the distance you could see the greyish green cell phone/portable tower, which had several vulture nests near its top. The villagers were both thankful and annoyed by this tower. They loved their portables and cell phones but felt the tower was an eye-sore and probably zapping them with all sorts of "nonsense." They also weren't surprised that it was occupied by vultures.

Finally I could see the hospital down the street. Just past the one and only hotel. I took a deep breath. What if he screamed and ran away when I showed him my wings? What if he was disgusted? I hoped he would not drop to his knees and make the sign of the cross, like the men in the alley back in the United States. I was no angel. I pushed these thoughts away and kept walking. A bird hooted from nearby. The air was warming faster now. I loved the weather here. The breeze was always heavy, humid, and smelled like a million green leaves. The dirt was red and rich. Trees grew well here, when the floods weren't washing them away.

I froze. Everything stopped—my fearful excitement, my enjoyment of the morning, my legs. I stood there, in the middle of the empty water-damaged road. I felt like vomiting. My wings twitched beneath my burka. Sitting in the parking lot of the hotel were three trucks. Black and shiny, except for the spattering of red dirt and mud on their tires. Large fresh-looking Toyotas, one equipped with an antenna that reached high up. All carried the same large white emblem on their sides: A hand grasping spears of lightning.

I remembered. Oh I remembered all of it clearly. Not even death could take the edge off of it. In my two years of life, before my escape, they had done things to me that I now understood were evil. Before I started to heat myself, they would place me in a heated room and watch me sweat and wheeze for hours. In my second year of life, they started burning me. With hot needles, then larger broader instruments. On my face, belly, legs, arms, they burned every part of me. I knew the smell, sound and sight of my cooking flesh.

However, I kept healing. Eventually. Fast and scar-free. Never pain-free. Despite all the books I had consumed, at the time, I thought what they did to me was normal. There was no story that featured anyone like me. And I'd never been outside. I had no way of knowing any better, until I met Saeed. Or maybe my mind opened up when I began to love him.

I still wondered what they'd done to Saeed. I know they did worse things to him. Mmuo had told me a little. Electric shock, poisoning, disemboweling then reconstructing. And they would not have used numbing medicine or anesthesia on him. That would interfere with the "test results." I'd asked Saeed a few times but he refused to tell me details. "You don't deserve that," he said. "You are so young." He was right on both counts. But I still wanted to know back then. To know someone's pain is to share in it. And to share in it is to relieve some of it. But all he said was, "I survive. I always survive it." Yes, he had survived, up until he decided not to.

I took a step back, staring at the vehicles in the hotel parking lot. And then I took another step back. I backed to the other side of the road. I hid behind a dirty parked pick-up truck, whose rear cargo area was full of shea nuts. I rested a hand on its side and leaned over for a better look. The Big Eye, the organization that had engineered, tortured, and then killed me, had come to Wulugu, Ghana.

CHAPTER 6

Red Red-Eyes

I WAS STILL BEHIND THE PARKED TRUCK when a group of gregarious young white men came out of the hotel. Even from where I stood I could tell that they were American. Their body language. The way they wore their clothes. The rhythm of their loud voices stabbing at the morning's peace. Their confidence. That aura of entitlement. Kofi would later tell me that this entitlement swagger was something white men from every part of the world had when in rural Africa, but that is beside the point.

They hopped into their cars and drove off in the direction I had come from. The Big Eye were headed toward my home. Or was it toward the tree where I'd planted the alien seed? Why were they here?

My legs shook with unused adrenaline. I continued on my way to see Kofi. As I walked past the hotel, I made a decision. I would stay cloaked. For now. "It's for the best," I said to myself.

Over the next few weeks, the village changed because of their presence.

Kofi said they'd been here before. Last year. Also at harvest time. No one knew who the white men were or what their company was named. They called them "Red Red-Eyes," a name they tended to call all white people. "Red-eyes" signaled danger, demons, envy, and jealousy. In Tower 7, we called them "Big Eyes" because they were always watching and experimenting on us. Interesting, the similarity in names.

"Since I can remember, they have been coming," Kofi said. "They always buy lots of our produce. We do business with them, but those of us who are wise, keep it at that."

Not all were wise. Especially desperate families and ambitious girls with dreams bigger than their means. There were at least forty white men who came this time, no women. Over the next few weeks, I watched them swagger about the village, buying produce, purchasing the best bicycles, chatting with whomever was willing to chat with them, usually the men in the tavern. And then there were the girls.

I walked past the field in the back of the hotel once and saw it with my own eyes. A man lay in a hammock, a straw hat covering his face as a girl slowly rocked his hammock back and forth. Another girl stood beside him, gently waving a large fan. The hotel had power. The man could have plugged in a fan or gone inside to enjoy his air conditioner. Obviously this was about a different and old type of power.

Both girls looked simultaneously miserable and content. He must have been paying them well. A few feet away, another girl was hanging freshly washed clothes. As she clipped a pair of pants to the wire, a rotund white man with silver in his hair and lust in his eyes, came and grabbed her from behind. The girl didn't fight or move as the man grabbed her breast and pressed against her. The man being fanned and rocked laughed and leered. I could also see other girls inside the hotel rooms. Working, being used, paid scraps.

In Wulugu, families had little money and a lot of pride. It was frowned upon to even hold hands with a long-time betrothed boyfriend. Here these girls were being publically handled by these men like prostitutes. Everyone was aware of it. Some parents fought with their daughters over it. And girls often ran away to stay with these foreigners, at least until another fresher pretty girl came along.

A few times, the men of Wulugu held meetings in the churches to discuss this problem. I would have loved to hear what was said, but the closest I got were reports from Kofi. "It is the white men and their lust for our women, yes, but it is also the girls," he said. "Many of them run away when their parents tell them not to go."

I'd seen the result of this when a mother dragged her half-naked daughter out of the room of one of the Big Eye men. The mother threatened the man in Twi, which he probably didn't speak. Flushed red, he'd stood there narrowing his eyes at her clearly afraid, but also unwilling to be chased away like a teenage boy. The mother turned and beat her daughter right then in the middle of the street. I knew this daughter's mother well. She was the one who'd shown me the best well from which to get my water. Her name was Mansa, and her daughter Sarah was good in math and liked to wear colorful clothes.

"Do you ever want to get married?!" Mansa kept shouting in Twi. "Will you marry Red Red-Eye? Bush men from a mummified bush? What are they? What are they!?"

Her daughter Sarah had covered her head with her arms and screamed, as people gathered to watch the spectacle. Then the girl did the unthinkable. She somehow jumped up, dodged her mother and ran to the man and threw herself at his feet.

"Please! Please!" she begged. She switched to English. "Take me away!"

The man had only looked down at her with disgust, though he seemed a bit shaken too. There was sweat on his brow and he kept looking from Sarah's mother to the other townspeople who'd gathered. Maybe he felt a little guilty. Maybe he was embarrassed, too. Some of the other Big Eye men had come out of the hotel to watch. Maybe he didn't like the idea of being responsible for this girl kneeling at his dirty feet.

He gently kicked Sarah away and walked off leaving her there. He would find an easier "washer girl" to use. Still, days later, I heard that Sarah had run back to the hotel to be with another Big Eye man, and now she walked around with new shoes.

You could almost see the tension in the air of the once peaceful town. When the Big Eye walked past groups of village men, the aura of violence shined like my skin on the day I escaped Tower 7. There was great heat brewing in Wulugu. Mostly, I stayed away from the Big Eye or at least hid when they were around. Until that night.

I was out flying. It was a dark night. It was my kind of night. As I flew low over Wulugu, I'd had a feeling. A really terrible feeling. It weighed so heavily on my heart that I landed right there behind the hotel in the grass. First I heard music. It was a song that I knew. It was not a Ghanaian song.

It was an old old song that had been included on my e-reader back in Tower 7 along with thousands of other classics. The title was "Don't Fear (The Reaper)" and though I liked the song, it had always scared me. Hearing it in the middle of a field in rural Ghana was even creepier. Then I heard the cry.

It was muffled. It was not loud. It was barely a peep. But it was a cry, nonetheless. It was a restrained shriek. From a girl. Then I saw her. She was dark-skinned, spoke rapid Twi, ate kenkey and fish, a daughter of the land. The Big Eye white man was mashing her face in the grass and dirt, a small media player sitting beside them. He was trying to take from her. This was rape. He was desperate now. Urgent. I didn't have to imagine that his thoughts were muddled—focused on grass, flesh, heat. The situation was that clear. She wasn't saying stop. Right there, yards away. This had happened to her many times. It was expected. He expected. But she didn't like it. She didn't want it. I whimpered. For a moment, too disturbed to move.

Then I beat my wings and in seconds, I was there. I pulled him off her and threw him to the side. He tumbled in the grass. I was powerful. Yes. I carried enormous jugs of water from the well, and I needed no help. My neighbors may not have seen my wings, but they were used to me. They didn't ask questions in Wulugu.

Rolling to his knees, the white man stared at me with wide wide eyes. The man was clearly drunk.

My brown wings were spread wide. My arms held up, fists clenched.

"Okore! Thank you!" the girl said in Twi, as she gathered her clothes. She started crying. I don't know if it was the sight of me or what she'd been through. She was a plump girl with tightly cornrowed hair. Had she done them specifically for this night? I blinked. I knew this girl. Sarah.

"I'm sorry," the man said. "I'm sorry. I-I-I lost control. Please. Please." He laughed nervously, standing and zipping up his khaki pants. "I always seem to lose control. I'm such an idiot. Something about this place and these people."

I only glared at him.

"What are you?" he asked, wiping sweat from his face. "An angel?"

I could nearly see his mind working. Looking at my African face, my brown skin, my brown albatross-like wings. His face grew suspicious. "No, you can't be an angel. You're just some bullshit my brain is ejaculating because that bitch won't let me fuck her."

"Leave us," I said.

"I *paid* her. She goes with me."

"Paid her for what?" I asked. "Is this what you call 'washing clothes'? 'Cooking dinner'?"

"Look, I don't know what you are, and I don't care. Everything's fucked up about this place. You probably bathed in the dirt and whatever weird shit is in it did that to you. Lord knows, you're a filthy people. But I'm fucking that girl tonight. Sarah, get over here."

Sarah shook her head and stood behind me.

"You want your mother to starve?" he growled.

Sarah whimpered.

"Or better yet, I'll let her know how much of a whore you are."

"All girls who come to you people are whores," I said. "Everyone knows that. But we don't ever reject them. They're ours. They're us." I wanted to laugh at myself. I was speaking as if I belonged in Wulugu. Did I? Maybe. Kofi felt I did.

I was watching the man's hands as we talked. At first they'd just hung there, but slowly they were becoming fists. So I wasn't surprised when he stopped talking and launched himself at me. I slapped him hard upside his head and, as my hand connected, I heard a crack. He fell and did not move.

I looked down at the media player; the song was just finishing. I stamped hard on it and the night became quiet. For the first time in my existence, I felt cold. *Is he dead?* I shuddered, the sides of my eyes stinging. *No,* I thought. *I've just knocked him unconscious.* I quickly turned to Sarah, who had run a few feet away and was now just staring at the unconscious man.

"Go," I said.

And Sarah went.

BANG, BANG, BANG!

Someone was at the door. My wings shot open, knocking down the glass of water on my nightstand. It was all that I kept in my room. For this very reason. I'd gone to bed exhausted and disturbed. I normally didn't forget to put the glass on the floor.

The sound of chopping came from outside. My mind flashed to the night above the city when they'd tried to shoot me out of the sky. There was no great winged man to save me in Ghana, and that fact got me to my feet, a scream in my throat. Still wearing my night gown, I donned my black burka and ran to the door. I threw it open, ready for a hail of bullets to tear into my chest, rend my legs into rags, eat away my face. Like last time.

The tears of anticipated pain blurred my vision. When the pain didn't come, they ran down my cheeks and I was looking at Sarah. She was wearing jeans and a t-shirt. Her nose was bleeding, the side of her face scratched and swollen. For once, she wore no make-up, and she looked younger than her 16 years, even with the wounds.

"Sarah!? What . . . ?"

"I'm sorry!" she screamed and then grabbed me in a hug. Every part of me tensed. Not since the first day here, when I planted the alien seed, had I hugged anyone. To allow a hug was to allow the person to feel my hump and understand that maybe it was not a hump at all. But Sarah already knew this. She hugged me tightly, pressing my wings. So frail in my arms, she was only a child.

I looked over her shoulder. A helicopter was disappearing over the palm treetops. Its chopping sound was fading. Was it landing nearby? Moving farther away? Where was it going? Regardless, I knew it was not gone. The Big Eye never just left.

Sarah took my hand, tears falling from her eyes as she looked at me. "I couldn't help it!"

"Help what?"

"They beat me, Okore!" she said. "My mother beat me." She took a deep breath to calm herself. "They found him yesterday. He's dead. I was the last person people saw him with, so they came to my house. My mother, she was so angry that I'd been with one of those men. She beat me until I told them what happened." Horror passed over her face. "I've betrayed you! Oh my God, I have betrayed God's messenger!"

She burst out crying. And I hugged her to me again. More than a small part of me had known that this would be the last night I spent in the comfort of my home. "I'm not God's messenger," I said. I felt so tired. The Big Eye knew who I was, what I was, and I had killed another of their own. I might as well have sat down right there in the doorway and waited for them to come and kill me. I had flown across the planet, yet here I was again.

"You *are* one of God's messengers," she said, her voice muffled as she pressed her face to my chest. She pulled back and took my hand. "Please," Sarah said. "They're coming for you. Come!"

She pointed to the car she'd driven to my home. It looked over thirty years old, at least the body did. All the doors were different colors from different cars.

"Come come come!" she screeched, dragging me toward the car. "No time for anything. They are on their way right now!"

No shoes, no money, no nothing. I was in my white nightgown and burka. I could have resisted Sarah. I was certainly stronger than she. But in me, no matter how hopeless I feel, is the instinct to survive.

I squeezed into the back seat, my wings painfully pressed against the cushions. The leather had worn away, leaving a layer of foam and wires. There was a fire extinguisher mounted to the passenger seat door. To make matters worse, the floor of the vehicle was nonexistent, eaten away from rust and age. It was my first time in a car, but I didn't have time to really consider this fact.

"Lie down!" she said.

Just as I lay myself sideways on the seat, pressing my wings more tightly against my back, I heard the sound of vehicles pulling up.

"She's not home!" I heard Sarah yell to someone as we drove off. Still I heard the sound of car or truck doors opening and shutting. Then we were on the road. As I lay there, I stared down at the road through the floor. The smell of exhaust filled the car. I hated that smell. It was the smell of self-inflicted death.

"Good," Sarah said, looking in the rearview mirror. "They're not following. Not yet. My God, that was scary. What are they . . ."

GBOOM!

"Oh my God," she moaned, staring into the rearview mirror.

We were moving away from it, but the car was not very fast. And it had no windows and parts of the floor were gone. The sound was loud and clear.

We were both quiet. I didn't want to get up and see what they had done to the only home I had ever had. I had no family. I was created in a lab. I was an ABO, an 'accelerated biological organism.' My body had stopped accelerating at what looked like the age of forty, yet I was only about three years old. I had no history. That house was all I had. I whimpered, curled into a ball, and shut my eyes tightly.

"Take me to Kofi's house," I whispered.

His home was the last one in the village. We were already heading in that direction.

*   *   *

Kofi was standing outside his house when we pulled up. He'd heard the explosion, too, along with everyone in the area. Crowds of people were heading up the road, toward where my house used to be.

"Okore! Sarah!" he said running up to the car when he saw us. He spoke in Twi, which he normally didn't do. "What's going on? I was about to go . . ." He looked into my eyes. He always looked into my eyes first.

"I'll tell you when we get inside," I said, also in Twi.

"All right," he said, frowning and looking at my bare feet.

"Tell everyone to leave town for a few days," I told Sarah. "There's going to be trouble."

She nodded. I took her hand through the window. "This was not your fault," I said. "Be glad I was there last night to save you. Make better choices from now on."

"I will," she said, tears coming to her eyes again.

For a moment we all just stood there. Sarah in her car, me beside her car, Kofi behind me. We were frozen in time, in that tight instant of intense tension. There were powerful events just ahead of us and we all knew it. I squeezed her hand tighter then leaned forward and took her face, "It. Wasn't. Your. Fault," I said. "You hear me?"

She started sobbing.

"Go, Sarah," I said.

Again, she went. As she slowly drove off, I stood with Kofi.

"Let's go inside," I said. "I have something to show you."

I took him to the center of his small house. The living room. The ceilings were highest here.

"Sit down," I said.

He sat down. Outside, I could hear the chopper, again.

"Last night I killed a man," I told Kofi.

"What?"

"One of the white men, the Red Red-Eye," I quickly said. "He was *raping* Sarah. I shoved him off her." I shut my eyes. I could feel Kofi staring at me, unsure of what to say. I opened my eyes. "But then he came at me again when he saw me. I slapped him away." I met Kofi's eyes and looked away. "I am stronger than I look. And I was angry."

"What do you mean, 'When he saw you'?" he whispered.

"I was not wearing my burka," I said. Then I threw it off.

You must know something about Kofi. He'd been born and raised in Wulugu. Like everyone else, he'd used the shea butter, called nkutu, for his skin during the dry Harmattan season. And he knew there was something in the soil that the trees absorbed. He knew that that something was in him. He knew that at night sometimes certain trees glowed a soft green. He had seen plants grow faster than normal, even before I came. He had seen nature's mysteries and accepted them. And Kofi was a medical doctor. So he also understood that these mysteries were complex.

I stretched my wings out, filling the room.

"Okore," he whispered. Then he said it in English. "Eagle."

"My name is Phoenix. That is what the Big Eye named me in Tower 7," I said as he stepped forward and stared up at my wings.

"In America?"

"Yes."

"This is what you have been hiding?"

"Yes."

He blinked and then reached into his pocket and brought out his portable.

"Can I?" he asked.

A story is not a story until it is told. I've always believed that a story is best told in many ways. "Will you stream it live?"

"Do you want me to?"

"Yes."

He pressed the on button and there was a soft winding sound and the top slid open and a camera lens came out. The electronic eye looked at me. "I'm Phoenix Okore," I said to it. "And I am in Wulugu, Ghana." I didn't know the year or the date. Something in me had stopped keeping track since my rebirth.

He turned it to himself, "I am Kofi Atta Annan, M.D. We are in my home and all that you see is happening now. It is real. She is real."

Kofi stepped around me. "May I touch them?"

I hesitated.

"Phoenix, I won't . . ."

"Yes," I said. "You can touch them."

I felt him run the edge of his hand between my shoulder blades. He pressed the powerful muscles there. He kneaded them with his fingertips and slowly ran his hand over the feathers of the long bones. He was gentle. The hands of a good doctor.

"So then, how old *are* you?" he asked running his fingers through the longer feathers of my left wing. My wings were sensitive, and I was beginning to feel blood rush into their flesh. I began to sweat. He touched the tip of my left wing and I shuddered.

"Does that hurt?" he asked. But he laughed as he said it. "Should I stop?"

"No," I said.

He moved to my right wing. "They are so natural. These *belong* on you. You're a work of art."

"There is nothing natural about me."

"It doesn't matter where or how you were made. You are God's creature."

"I'm an ABO from Tower 7, an accelerated biological organism," I said. "I am only three years old. I was supposed to be a weapon. My name suits me, Kofi."

"But then you obviously escaped," he said. "You have died and risen, then?"

"Yes."

He poked a finger between my feathers to see the skin. It felt like heaven. "You are brown even beneath the wings. Is your blood . . ."

I laughed. "Yes, it is red."

"Can you have children?" he asked. "Do you have a womb? Can an immortal bear life?" He spoke the question more to his portable than to me.

"I think I am too old," I said.

He chuckled to himself. "He saw you and attacked you because you could not possibly be an angel from God. You are African." He laughed harder.

When he came to face me, he turned his portable off and put it in his pocket. There were beads of sweat on my forehead, and my heart was beating faster than a small bird's. I know what you are thinking. Yes, we needed to leave, but this moment felt more important. I had never had anyone inspect me. Not with love. He said I was God's creature. I didn't believe in God, but those words were like magic to me. They said that I, too, was an earthling. That I belonged here. I belonged.

Every part of my body was heated and my thin nightgown hid none of it. My nipples poked right through and I was glowing. Not green, however. Beneath the rich brown of my skin, I was a soft orange red like the rising sun or the inside of a sweet mango.

"*Chali*," he said. "You are lovely."

The front door burst open. Through the doorway in the living room, I could see the Big Eye had black uniforms and guns. They were looking around, spreading to all the rooms, screaming. "Anyone in the house, Get DOWN, GET ON THE FLOOR NOW!!" They hadn't seen us yet. With the door open, the sound of the chopper was clear. We'd both been hearing the sound of the chopper since I arrived. We'd both ignored it.

Kofi grabbed my hand as I grabbed his. We turned just as we heard the back door bursting open in the kitchen, too.

"Step away," I told Kofi. "They want me, not you."

"No."

He met my eyes. We ran up the stairs to his bedroom. He shut and locked the door just as someone banged on it. I looked at the window. I could carry him. We could have flown away, but there was a chopper hovering over the house. They had me, again. We pushed the bed in front of the door.

"Kofi, you don't know what these people are capable of."

"YES, I do!" he snapped. There was a bang at the door, as they tried to beat it down. He looked at me with wild eyes. "They took my family! My parents, my sister! Maybe they took them to one of the towers, maybe even your Tower 7."

Bang!

"They were like you, I think. Different. Possibilities," he said. "I wasn't, so they left me." He ran to his closet and threw it open. He brought out a rifle.

"No," I said. "They'll kill you if they see you're armed."

The bedroom window cracked, then chunks of glass fell to the floor. Big Eye soldiers started to climb in.

"Get on the floor!" one of them yelled.

I ran in front of Kofi as he brought up his rifle.

"Leave him!" I screamed. "PLEASE! Take me! Take me!"

"GET ON THE GODDAMN FLOOR!"

"No! Get out of my HOUSE!" he screamed. "You've taken enough from me! You will NEVER have her." Tears flew from his eyes, spittle from his lips. He turned to me, his eye twitching and blazing with warrior's blood and rage. "I won't let them take you, Okore."

I loved Kofi. He was the gentlest man I'd ever met. Wulugu needed him more than anything. Who else had been born and raised here, educated and trained elsewhere, yet *returned* to give back? Who else?

Kofi stepped in front of me as he raised his gun. He was as tall as me. I wondered what it was that his family members could do. Maybe I had even known them. Most of the others in Tower 7 were Africans— Egyptian, Cameroonian, Kenyan, Senegalese, Nigerian, and yes, Ghanaian. Yes, maybe I knew his family. I grabbed him and shielded us both with my wings. But not before I heard what sounded like the chirp of a small bird. Kofi's blood sprinkled my face, as my wings closed around us. All went dark.

He dropped the gun. He started choking. I opened my wings a bit to give us some light. He was bleeding from his neck, his eyes staring at me in shock. Not from the fact that the Big Eye had shot him, that I know. I didn't know what they did to his family, but Kofi did not expect it to end this way for him. Not for him. His body bucked as his life blood ran over my arms, reddening my white garments. All he'd had to do was get behind me. He'd gotten in front of me, instead.

I loved him.

And now the Big Eyes had taken him, too. Just as they'd taken Saeed. They were always taking from me. Always taking the best. Of my people. Of my world. Take take TAKE! *Sssss*. I was hot, now, glowing orange. Kofi choked and gurgled weakly. He was leaving. He was in pain.

The tears evaporated on my face as they crowded around me. I looked down at Kofi, he was still staring up at me, his mouth open as he tried to speak. I shut my wings, blocking off the Red Red-Eye.

"GET OUT!" I screamed at them. "GET OUT NOW!"

I didn't wait.

I put Kofi out of his misery.

That's why I burned. I burned hot. Hotter than I'd burned the first time. I could do that. To make it quick for him.

Everything went brilliant all around me. Hues of red, orange, and smoke. Kofi was growing lighter in my arms, so I looked up. I wanted to remember him as he was. My flesh was pain. But I held my consciousness. I held Kofi in my arms. In my head I heard that song from last night about the reaper . . .

We'll be able to fly . . .

Around me, the house blew away like castles of ash in the wind. All of Kofi's life disintegrated. As I died with it, I noticed something in the space before me. There was fiery chaos everywhere, except for this strange black slit. I raised my hand. I paused, looking at my fingers, which had burned down to the bone. Bones that weren't *bone*. They were *metal*, red from the heat.

I slipped the metal bones of my hand into the pocket of blackness before me and that part of me disappeared. I brought it out, and it was there again.

Curious, I thought.

Then I was gone.

CHAPTER 8

No Fight, No Flight

I'M ALIVE, AGAIN.

I am the villain in the story. Haven't you figured it out yet? Nothing good can come from unnatural bonding and creation. Only violence. I am a harbinger of violence. Watch what happens wherever I go.

The Big Eye have no idea. Below, they travel on a tanker heavy with crude oil. It's on its way to the United States; I ride the angry winds just behind it. How arrogant they are to believe that I am compliant. How naïve. I thought scientists learned from experience.

This second time I returned to life, I woke to the smell and sight of rich red earth. Then the stench of burned dirt. *First my Saeed*, I thought, staring blankly at the moist soil. *Now my Kofi.* I moaned as the grief of both their deaths washed over me. I kept coming back, but I could not bring them back. Not even once. They were dead. Before their times. I didn't believe in God. How could I believe in God? So this meant that they were gone. Both of them, forever.

Heat. I heard the ground below me hiss and then crackle as it smoldered. Heat. Within my body; outside of it. I grabbed handfuls of dirt and squeezed, curling my body in on itself. Heat. Nothing eased the pain.

I was in Ghana. It was a hot sunny day and I was me. I was brown, but as I stared at my skin, just beneath, I saw the hint of glow, now that glow was red. I didn't need to inspect myself this time. I knew. And I remembered everything. Saeed. Then Kofi. I tried to curl tighter and couldn't.

Click click.

These people again.

"Don't move," the woman's voice firmly said. Her accent was not American. Bumi. The Yoruba woman from Tower 7. How was she alive? She pushed the barrel of her gun against the back of my head and waited for me to comply. As if I were afraid of dying. Why did they always think I feared death?

"Get up," she said in her flat voice. I turned to face her as I sat up. She now had a network of sharp light brown scars on her cheek, and her short straightened hair was streaked with grey. She wore the black uniform and there was a fist grasping lightning bolts on her left breast pocket. The symbol for the Big Eye was always stitched over their soldiers' hearts like a blindfold. She certainly couldn't see me. Not really. Even if she'd known me from when I was a baby.

I looked up. All around me was red dirt. Then the blue sky and the yellow sun. I was in a pit the size of Kofi's house. This was where his house used to be. Where on the second floor, his body had died. There were about thirty Big Eye standing around me, some more on the rim. All pointing their guns.

Slowly I stood up. Tall, naked, bathed in bright sunshine. The ones closest to me, moved steps away. I stretched my back and then my wings. In the corner of my eye, I saw shiny red gold. My feathers had changed color. I stretched my wings again and again, giving them big flaps that sent half the Big Eye running for cover. I laughed, folding them behind my back. The ones who hadn't moved away probably wanted to shoot me. But they didn't.

"There is no need for all this," I said. But in my head I thought, *It is the calm and silent water that drowns a man.* An old Ashanti woman once said this to me as we'd angrily watched one of the Big Eye men lead a young local girl to his hotel room.

I gave myself over to them. No fight. No flight. They gave me a heat resistant white dress. The back was cut to accommodate my great wings. I dressed there in the pit that used to be Kofi's house.

Seven days and nights had passed. And for all seven days and nights,

Big Eye soldiers were stationed in the ditch watching for me. I do not know what they saw when I came back to life. Did I simply rise from the ashes at the bottom of the pit? Did I appear cell by cell? Or did I just appear? I don't know. I never asked. I didn't care.

There had nearly been a riot when they escorted me into the Big Eye truck. In many of the American movies I watched in Tower 7, whenever terrible things happened in African towns, the Africans would flee like a pack of primitive unthinking beasts. Hooting and scrambling, their black skin powdered with dust, mindlessly stepping on jutting rocks and sharp branches with their rough bare feet.

For the first year of my life, in Tower 7, I'd wondered if I was made from inferior DNA. Then I started mixing books written by Africans about Africans into the ones I was reading. These stories were different. My time in Ghana taught me even more. So when they escorted me out of the pit and walked me at gunpoint past what used to be the hospital and was now mostly rubble, past the empty market, the mosque which still stood, and the burned bicycle shop, toward the waiting truck, I only smiled when I saw the armed crowd.

For days, the Big Eye had been watching for me and they didn't realize that there were people watching them, too. I was loved by the people of Wulugu. And I loved them. We all loved Kofi. I'd told Sarah to tell everyone to flee. But they didn't. Even Sarah stayed. They had given me another name when I arrived in Wulugu, Ghana. They named me Okore, which meant eagle. But they also knew the name I was given at birth. And they knew its meaning. So they knew to wait. The people of Wulugu had probably started gathering at the armored truck as soon as the lookouts saw me come out of the pit. Everyone was probably flashed or sent text messages.

As I came up the road, the crowd started shouting, and the Big Eye pointed their guns. "Okore! They took Dr. Kofi Annan, we will not let them take you, too!" Sarah shouted in Twi. Yes, in all the noise, I heard her.

"Phoenix Okore lives!" several men shouted.

Some women started singing a jubilant song praising Jesus.

"Leave her!" a young man shouted, a cudgel in hand. He was one of the men who sold bicycles. He wore a tattered t-shirt, old shorts and flip flops, but he looked ready to take down a dragon.

"Let her go!" roared a muscular dark-skinned man in old jeans and a dashiki, shaking a machete in the air. He was a shea nut farmer who owned several of the healthiest trees in Wulugu, including the one where I'd buried the alien seed. Several enraged men stood menacingly behind him, equally armed with machetes, knives, and probably a few guns.

All of their protests were in Twi. How did they expect the Big Eye to understand them? Or maybe they didn't care or want understanding.

Someone threw a stone at one of the soldiers. The soldier ducked. He looked at the largest group of men, bared his teeth and started raising his gun. In that instant, I had a flashback of what happened to me in Tower 7. If the Big Eye started shooting, I knew they would not stop. I met Bumi's eye. She smiled a smile that said, "Just give me a reason."

"Please!" I shouted in English, spreading my wings wide. The deep golden red shine of them had the desired effect. Everyone quieted and stared, Big Eye and Wulugu townsfolk, alike. A soft breeze blew through the lush trees behind the old houses, beside the road. *Shhhhh.* I quickly spoke to the people. I spoke in Twi. "I don't want any more of you to die! Wulugu must survive all this!!"

I hoped that they understood *exactly* what I meant. It was too risky to say *exactly* what I wanted to say, even in Twi. The Big Eye were in Wulugu because of the alien seed, directly or indirectly. That had always been clear to me. They might have known it was here and were searching for it. Or maybe they were scouting out unique people (like Kofi's family) affected by the seed; people they'd then take to one of the American towers to "enhance." Or maybe they merely sensed something exceptional about the shea products here—the nuts, the fruits, the unprocessed butter. That "special-ness" was because of the alien seed. The people of Wulugu may not have all known I'd replanted the seed, but they knew I'd done something there. They had to survive to *guard* it.

"You will give them a good challenge but they will wipe you all out in the end," I said in Twi. "Save it for a better day. I will be fine."

There was a moment where they angrily surged forward, but thankfully the Big Eye held their fire. Then the people of Wulugu who'd come ready and willing to risk their lives to defend me—mostly men, a few women, and no children—reluctantly pulled back. They let the Big Eye shove me into the truck, my wings painfully bending in the restricted space. Bumi got in and sat beside me. "Nice wings," she said.

I looked out the window at the people who were the only family I had. The truck drove off before they could say goodbye.

So I agreed to return to the United States with the Big Eye. Across the ocean. However, they couldn't bring me by airplane. It was too dangerous for them, and my wings would not fit. Thus, they made a quiet deal with an oil tanker set to leave from the coast of Lagos, Nigeria, two days later. The cramped drive from Wulugu to Lagos took twenty-eight hours. Even when we stopped for breaks, I was only allowed out of the truck to relieve myself. My wings throbbed, the muscles twitching and constricting. The Big Eye didn't want people to see me and start talking. Africans like to tell stories, and stories travel and germinate. And sometimes, stories evolve into trouble.

Bumi dismissed my suggestion of wearing a burka while outside. "I've chased you to the other side of the world, all the way to my native land, how stupid do you think I am?" she asked, looking at me with cool eyes. "I know you. Stay in that truck, you will be fine." Before, she'd have had three or four Big Eye point guns at me, but allowed me to stand in the fresh air for a few minutes. Bumi was still the short pretty Yoruba woman I'd known in Tower 7. However, now she had deep scars on her cheek, a slight limp and a state-of-the-art cybernetic arm she'd been given after the helicopter crash. She could snap my leg bones in two with that arm and wouldn't hesitate to do so if I gave her the slightest reason. She was hardened. We'd both changed so much since our days in Tower 7. I wondered if she'd been given her American citizenship yet. I didn't ask.

Nevertheless, there was one time where they allowed me out for more than relieving myself. It was in a city not far from Lagos called Ikare. We'd stopped at a mosque built by the brother of one of the local Yoruba kings. We parked in the back, and Bumi got out to talk to the lean but strong old man in the white flowing sokoto and buba. The man ignored her, came up to the vehicle, and looked in at me.

First he spoke to me in a language that I could not understand. As he spoke softly, he motioned for me to come out. I looked at Bumi for guidance.

"Go out," she said. "He wants to see you."

"Who is he?" I asked.

"My father."

I frowned but slowly got out. I glanced at the mosque. It was open, and I could see the room inside. It was empty, so was the compound.

"Allah is great," he whispered, looking over my wings.

"Allah has nothing to do with it," Bumi muttered.

"She is Allah's will," he said. "Come, my wives have prepared a meal for all of you. *All* of you."

His wives would not come near me. They would not serve me, though they served the four Big Eye soldiers like servants. Bumi seemed to find this hilarious. "Mommy," she said to one of them, laughing and placing a bowl of soup and fufu in front of me. "She won't bite."

Her mother only shook her head and quickly left the room as the other wives did. I ate fast and then asked if I could stand outside near the car. Bumi went with me, while the others finished up and made small talk with Bumi's father.

"We can cure you," Bumi said, as we walked to the SUV.

I chuckled. I had died, lived, crossed the ocean to Africa, fallen in love and watched that love die. I was no longer so naïve. "Cure me of what?" I asked.

She considered me, then her face hardened. "Just don't give us any trouble along the way."

"You have my word," I said.

She leaned against the truck and took a sip of her water. "Your word is shit to me," she said. "When I get you to Tower 6, we will finish what we started."

"And what exactly was it that you started?" I asked.

"Never you mind," Bumi said.

And I didn't mind. It was warm outside and the yard was wide open. I was not flying, but I felt free, for the moment. I inhaled the dry air with my eyes closed, and I opened my wings wide. The muezzin called the afternoon prayer, so there was at least one other person on the compound. I let it wash over me with the breeze. And in that moment, I felt at peace, regardless of Bumi's ugly presence. I felt in my soul that in due time, all would be well. Life was so easy.

Then Bumi said it was time to go, and I had to climb back into the truck, folding my wings close to my body.

"Pray to Allah to keep you safe and sound," Bumi's father said, opening the door, taking my hand and patting it.

"Or maybe you can pray for me. I never had time to learn."

"I will," he said. "You are a fallen angel, but you can still fly. All is not lost."

Then Bumi shut my door and we were off.

When we got to Lagos, the Exxon representative who handled the deal took one look at me and decided he didn't want me on the tanker, despite the deal that had been made by phone. This made what I had to say much easier.

"I will fly," I flatly proclaimed. "No ship. I will never get on any ship." I was not resisting the Big Eye, but I'd never intended to get on that ship. I'd planned to fly my own way.

It would sail to Miami, Florida, the location of Tower 6. Bumi didn't trust me to follow, so after consulting with her superiors via portable, Bumi, herself, injected tracking nanobots into my bloodstream. These slipped into my blood cells and multiplied within the cells whenever mitosis occurred. These tiny tracking devices essentially became part of me. The Big Eye would know where I was, what my temperature was, what I had eaten. Obviously, this was an upgrade that they'd made just for me. Unlike the nanobots Mmuo had used to communicate with me in Tower 7, these nanobots wouldn't melt unless I became hotter than 6000 degrees Celsius, the approximate temperature of the center of the Earth. I was back on the grid; it was Tower 7 all over again.

As soon as they stuck that needle into my flesh and pressed down on the syringe, I felt naked. But at least I could fly.

CHAPTER 9

Villain

ALL STORIES MUST BE TOLD.

I've been telling you this one as I cross the Atlantic again. Below me, its waters ripple and roil. There is great wind here. An angry type of wind. But it's moving in the right direction, which means that all I have to do is keep my wings open. The wind is taking me to my false home in America. To pass the time, I tell you *The Book of Phoenix*. My turbulent accurate memory. My oral unfinished tale. Unfinished because it will finish when I finish.

If I stray too far from the ship below, I have no doubt that they will come after me in their helicopters, with their weapons and their fearful self-entitled intent. However, they have nothing to worry about. For now, I comply.

How long have I been telling you this tale? How long have I been flying? For days. I've shut down my system again. No straining muscles, this time. Flying is natural, and I am stronger than I was when I left the United States. My titanium alloy bones are not light, but my body is made to fly. The Big Eye built me well. I'd have been a good weapon if I were not human, if I did not have a brain that could remember after death after death after death.

And there is more. Last night, he came to me. I was flying low, listening to the calm of the water and fantasizing about dropping into it. If my wings got wet, I wouldn't be able to fly. The water would pull me into its great belly, as it had so many other Africans on unwanted journeys. *Will the Big Eye be able to come after me?* I was wondering. I almost wanted to find out. *Do they have deep diving gear ready? Will they be able to reach me? I can fly, but I am not light. I will sink fast.*

The smell of the ocean out here, away from everything, a mile from the ship whose lights I follow, is of fine salt and the flesh of bodies large and small, plant and animal. I felt good. I inhaled the fresh air, feeling my brain and spirit vibrate because I clearly understood that I was so much more than I was before. Tower 7 would never have held me for long. I wished Saeed could see me now. "Saeed," I whispered. "So much has been lost, but all is never lost."

It was too dark for me to see anything but the sliver of moon above, the lights of the ship, and the soft glow of my red gold wings. The wind was gusting, so I couldn't hear him. The ocean's musk was in my nose, so I could not smell him, either. But I sensed him with the tips of my longest feathers.

There he was, flying below me, slightly to my right. His enormous wings spanned past my left. He rode the air inches above the water. Something told me that he didn't risk a watery death if his wings got wet. It was hard to believe that *I* had freed *him* from Tower 7. Already I was putting next to no effort into flying; his presence made flying even MORE effortless. He was carrying me, for the moment. I stared down at him. His skin was so dark that I only clearly saw his brown wings. I heard his voice as if there was no roar of ocean wind, and he was right beside me. He spoke to me in Twi.

"Phoenix the Okore returns to the United States of America, her birth place, the prodigal daughter." His voice was rich, and it sounded like he was smiling.

I frowned and spoke aloud, despite the noise of the wind. "I've had one other 'birthplace' so far. And there will probably be more."

"Yes, but Tower 7 was the place of your *creation*," he said. "There is nothing to love or hate about it. It is fact."

"Tower 7 no longer exists."

"Phoenix of the Okore," he said again, this time laughing, deep and throaty. "Reckless impulsive child."

"How did you get here?" I asked. "Who are you?"

His voice grew deeper. "*I* am your father."

I paused. Then I burst out laughing, glad that he was carrying me. I'd had the time, equipment, and access in Tower 7 to stream and watch thousands of movies, old and new. But how had he managed to see the fifth movie in the Star Wars series while trapped in his glass dome?

"Not all questions have answers," he said, chuckling.

"I know."

"I know what you are planning," he said. "You've no intention of letting them take you to Tower 6. You want to go to New York. But, Phoenix, you can't just go to The Backbone."

I paused. How did he know? "I'll do my best," I finally said, pressing my lips together and frowning. I didn't want to think about *the how* yet.

"Your 'best' will get you captured quickly," he said. "Your blood is tainted."

I laughed. "My blood has never been pure."

"They can track you wherever you go."

He was right. But they might let me at least flee as far as the city. I just had to reach The Backbone.

"I'm here to show you how I got here," he said. "Because you can do it, too. And you might like to have some fun with it."

"Do what?"

"You are not what I am," he said. "I'm immortal. I cannot die. You are super-mortal. You can live and die to live and die again. You are speciMen, beacon, and reaper, life and death, hope and redemption."

Villain, too, I thought. *And I have plans.* But I hoped he couldn't read my mind. No one needed to know that. Not even him.

He chuckled, again. "That is to be decided by your actions, Phoenix. Not by your thoughts. I want you to remember the ends and the beginnings, of birth and death. Remember."

"I can't remember when I was first born."

"No. But what of the other times?"

The first time I inhaled my first breath in the ruins of Tower 7, it warmed my warming body. I remember noticing the breeze first, how it smelled of flowers and then exhaust. The second time was in the pit that used to be Kofi's home. A hot shiver from my toes to the top of my head. I'd thought of Saeed, but then Kofi. I remembered both times that I died, when there was also heat. I frowned, remembering something else.

"There was something." I squeezed my eyes shut for a moment, pushing the memory forward, and then I opened them. "When I died in Kofi's house."

"Good." He said. "You've found it."

But I hadn't. Not yet. It was right on the tip of my mind but I couldn't grasp it. *There was something when I died. With Kofi burning up in my arms. As I burned.* For a whole minute we flew, not speaking. I still couldn't remember it.

"I live outside of life and death," he said. "So I can slip through time and space. You live *inside* life and death. So you can do the same."

I looked up at the moon. It was a tiny sliver. Like an opening, a cut into another place. That was when I remembered. A sliver. The moon. Like the slice of otherness I'd seen when I was burning up, when I was trying not to look at Kofi's disintegrating body. My heart ached for a moment, as I remembered Kofi's face blowing away, becoming ash, showing bone, then bone becoming ash.

With effort, I focused on the opening into nothingness I'd seen. "There was something into something else," I whispered. It was black. A black slit. No not black, it was nothing. I'd stared at the "bones" of my hand, realizing that my bones were some kind of metal. Then I'd slipped my hand into the slit and my hand disappeared. I brought it out just before I died. My bones were still intact, made red hot by the flames.

"Will it hurt?" I asked. I'd only slipped the skeleton of my hand into it.

"No."

"I can control what it does?"

"Oh yes."

I felt my heart begin to pound as I realized what this meant, what I could do. I smiled in the dark, above the ocean. I looked at the oil tanker that carried the Big Eye, and the tanker's crew, and wished that sea monster I'd seen last time would emerge and swallow them all up.

The Big Eye had no idea what was coming to their coveted country, their beloved city. I am reminded of the chant that the African market women over a hundred years ago shouted when they battled against the white colonialist foreigners. One woman would cry, "What's that smell?!" and the other women would shout in response, "Death is that smell!"

Something scarier than that sea monster is coming.

That was yesterday. It is today. It is afternoon. Up ahead is the American coast and the Big Eye are signaling me to come and land on the ship. I'd told them I would never set foot on that damn ship, *any* damn ship. That should have been their first clue. I would never arrive in this country on a boat. Never.

I take one last look at the coast of Miami. Then I do as the winged man taught me last night over the ocean. I look deep within myself, as I hear the Big Eye's helicopters approaching me. I count to five as I focus inward. I am heating up. My wings are probably glowing. Then I fly forward, and I am gone. "Slipping," that's what I will call it. And it isn't hard to do because I am "slippery." And it doesn't hurt. I am made for this, too.

And I know exactly where and when I am going.

Tower 1 is a large building in the middle of a Chicago northern suburb called Naperville. It is surrounded by bushy unkempt palm trees, but it is easy to find. I can practically smell what they are doing in there. Once you've smelled captivity, greed, and abomination, you know the grey nose-stinging scent anywhere. I don't need to go in through the entrance. They have high security to make sure only cleared personnel enter and none of their creations get out. This place is no Tower 7 where guards and security relied too much on technology. Here they have true Big Eyes. Especially after what I had done to Tower 7. Also, security is tighter here because Tower 1 is where it all began. Tower 1 is the nexus.

I read about Tower 1 in my days at Tower 7. It is where the Big Eye created their first abomination. They "adopted" a ten-year-old girl from Ethiopia. They believed that she was a traceable direct descendant of "Mitochondrial Eve" and thus carried the complete genetic blueprint of the entire human race. On top of this, the girl was afflicted with hyperthymesia, an extremely rare condition that made her able to remember every moment of her entire life. They gave her the code name, "Lucy." The portion of the records that gave her real name was deleted.

To the Big Eye, this girl was the complete Great Book of Humanity. They did two things with her. 1. They made a perfect clone of her (when you have one Great Book, you make a back-up copy). 2. They tried to make Lucy immortal by reprogramming her DNA to not age. For eleven years, Lucy remained in the body of a ten year old. When she was twenty-one, she escaped and threw herself from the roof of Tower 1. She left no suicide letter. Nevertheless, her case was still deemed a great success. And they still had Lucy #2.

From that point on, the programs in Tower 1 were heavily funded. They built Tower 2 in Boston, where they focused primarily on creating methods of dealing with climate change and buoy technology for floating towns and cities. Soon after that, they built Tower 3 in New Orleans, where Leroy Jackson became famous for curing AIDS and several of his students began studying the New Malaria. And so on. Behind the good intentions and amazing science, however, was abomination. Weapons, the quest for immortality, how far could we go . . . The foundation of all the towers was always always always corrupt, driven by a lusty greed.

To kill a snake, cut off the head.

No one has any idea what is about to happen right here in the dead of night. It doesn't matter who is patrolling the hallways or the streets and parking lots outside. It doesn't matter who is perched in the trees, guns ready. None of it matters.

Somewhere a tracking device receiver is beeping. At first, it claims that the nanobot's host is in a department store. Then it claims that it's outside of Tower 1. Then inside. But that does not matter either. They will dismiss this information as a malfunction because no one has injected me with the tracking nanobots yet. Not to their knowledge. That won't be done for another two days. I've stepped into a different space and time. Naperville, Illinois, United States, Tower 1, Floor 4 out of 9. The most extreme research is usually done on the middle floors.

The walls are white and low. The floors are grey, shiny, and cool beneath my bare feet. There is steel railing running along the walls of both sides of the hallway. We didn't have that in Tower 7. The hallway is narrow, so I fold my wings tightly against my back. It's painful but I have no choice. I've wrapped a black sheet over myself so that only my face shows. I pinned it below my head, so that it doesn't fall off. I have used make-up to shade my dark brown face a light peach color. I grabbed all these things from the department store. If I am seen by their cameras, they cannot know it is me.

I walk down the hall, the soft slap of my feet the only sound I hear.

"Like a hospital," I whisper. But I know it is not. This is not a place of healing. Pathologies are created here. It smells strongly of rubbing alcohol. I turn a corner and step into a hallway with walls full of glass doors. I tug my black sheet over my forehead to hide the upper part of my face and peek into the first door. I want to scream, but I hold it in. It's not his fault. And as I look at him, my eyes understand what I am seeing. He is no different from me.

He is a man with rich brown skin and a wide puffy crown of black hair. He could be Kofi's brother, for all I know. A jelli telli is stretched to cover the wall in front of him. He is watching an ancient Western that I recognize immediately because the theme song had scared me so deeply when I watched it over two years ago: *The Good, the Bad and the Ugly*. As if something is mocking me, the awful theme song plays, and I shudder. It still sounds like a chorus of starving coyotes.

Both of the man's arms and the lower parts of his legs are complicated masses of red, black, and green wires meshed over jointed metal rods. His hands remind me of the metal bones of my own hands. Computer parts are strewn about his room, and he is standing at a table heavy with more parts. His thin metal fingers are highly dexterous as he weaves wires into what looks like a green circuit board. There's a spark. He laughs to himself and nods his head. I can't tell what he is building.

He looks up, and his eyes grow wide with surprise. I hold a hand up and wave. He waves back. He looks up to the side and all emotion drops from his face. His room is under surveillance. I quickly look at the ceiling in the hallway. As soon as my eyes notice the camera, a siren goes off.

The man's mouth opens with surprise, and he frantically points at me.

"Hey!" he shouts.

No, not at me.

"Behind you!" he says.

I turn just in time to see the guard about to grab me. There is a gun on his hip. I inhale. Then I am instinct and I'm fast. I pull my wings even closer to my body, whirl around and shove him backwards against the wall with one arm. I grab his face with the other. He is a big man but no taller than my six feet. And I am stronger. When did I become so strong? Was it the flight across the ocean? Or maybe it is the dying and coming back to life.

The guard has blue eyes, a sparkling earring on his left ear and a bushy black beard that is scratchy beneath my pressing hand.

My body floods with the rage that has wanted to burst from me since I left Ghana. I let it wash over the guard; I let it drown him. I slam his head to the wall, and there is a soft crunch. He goes limp. He sinks to the floor. There is blood now. I've crushed his head. His gun is still in its holster. He had no intention of killing me. But I have killed him. I shudder and frown, my nostrils flared. My belly flutters. What am I becoming?

I stare down at the man. My mind feels cloudy. *I am villain*, I think.

Bang, bang, bang! The man in the room is kicking his door as hard as he can. "*Forget* him, o," the man says. His thick accent sounds Ghanaian or Nigerian. "He is rubbish. And he don' *peme*, anyway. Go down 'de hall! Look for 'de square. Smash it."

I blink. "Square?"

"Yes! You will see it! Go! Move, now!"

I can barely hear his words over the siren. I look at the glass door holding him in. There is no knob. I push at it. The door doesn't budge.

The man looks like he is going to go mad. "You cannot release me, o!!" There are tears in his eyes. "*Biko*, do something! They kill us every day. They kill you soon!" He is pressing his face to the door and looking down the hall. "Run!"

I nod. I don't run. I am gone. I slip.

The third time is easier. It is natural to me. I was made to do this, whether the Big Eye meant to make this so or not. I am like a horse who has just discovered what it is to run.

I have slipped to the same place just an hour earlier, just further down the hall, out of the camera's view. I have not killed the guard yet; I hang on to that fact and think nothing else of it. I run in the opposite direction, this time staying in the blind spots of the cameras. When I cannot, I slip and reappear where I need to be. What do I see behind all the glass doors? More cybernetic humans, more sophisticated than I have ever seen. That must now be Tower 1's specialization. Most have mechanical limbs, some more than others. One woman has a mechanical lower body, but with human legs. I see three people in the same room with skin that glows a soft green. At first I think they are what I used to be, but when I look more closely, I see that their skin is embedded with millions of miniscule screens.

"How can I get you out?" I ask them.

"Get to the glass box," one of them shouts. "Break it!"

I'm relieved to hear the same suggestion.

"Keep going down the hall!" a young man with only one cybernetic arm says. He seems to expect me to run by.

I am fully convinced that they are all able to communicate electronically when I pass the next door several feet down the hall. The old woman inside is the first Caucasian captive I see. She is entirely robotic except for her head and left arm. "Don't let them see you!" she says.

"I won't," I say. My heart is pounding like crazy. Heat pours from me, and I hope that my black sheet doesn't catch fire. For the second time in my existence, I feel that if there is a God then I am doing God's will. I do not think of the guard I will brutally kill in an hour. All who see me understand what I am. All creatures of the world want to be free, even when they've never tasted freedom. So all of these caged people are glad to see me.

A minute later, I stand before the large room staring at the wooly mammoth sleeping on an equally massive bed of hay. I am wondering why the enormous creature does not free itself. Then I see the square. It's the size and width of a sideways refrigerator and it's made of glass. There is something foggy and vaguely red inside. There are screens and other equipment along the far wall, but I am focused on two things. The sleeping beast and the glass square.

I think of the glass dome back in Tower 7; I'd made the plants crush it. I smile. Here I am again, unsure of the consequences but sure that I needed to break the glass. But what of the beast?

My desire overcomes my fear.

I slip.

Blackness.

I step out.

I look up. Its head is nearly as big as my entire room in Tower 7. It breathes. Deep. Calm. At peace in its unnatural life. It smells like freshly broken plants with a hint of manure. This human-made beast is my kin, too. It's resting its head on its thick folded hairy legs. Its eyes are closed, its thick brown eyelashes over an inch in length. Its sharp yellow tusks reach and curl many feet beyond me. Without thinking, I reach out and touch its huge furry forehead. The long brown-red hair is rougher than it looks. The mammoth's breathing doesn't change. Deep and full.

I move toward the glass case. Upon closer inspection, the thing inside looks like a ball of forming and disintegrating red dust. A soft hum vibrates from it, and I can feel it in the tips of my wings and in the back of my head. It's a pleasant feeling, however. Calming. Is this what is making the mammoth sleep? Is this why the mammoth doesn't free itself? Beside the case is a smaller glass cube about the size of a shoebox. It was also full of something red, but more solid.

Another louder siren sounds off over the still blaring one. There must be cameras in the large room. I make the decision and put my fist through the glass case. As the glass shatters, the thing inside sends out a vibration so strong that the rest of the case crumbles. *Puff!* For a moment, there is red dust everywhere. Then the dust particles pull into a solid ball of red sand on the shards of broken glass.

I am stamping on the smaller glass case with the heel of my foot when I hear a grunt from behind me. I whirl around to see the wooly mammoth rising slowly to its feet. It shakes its head and lets out a horrible trumpet-like roar. Meanwhile there is something tall and red standing behind me. I turn to it as the mammoth runs toward the glass. The red creature is tall and praying mantis-like, its body made of something like thick glass and full of red smoke. Even as I look at it, the glass-like shell of its face billowed out to form a second eye. The stuff in the smaller glass case was its exoskeleton.

"I need to free the others," I tell it in Twi. Why not English? I have no idea. When you are terrified, you do what you do, logical or not.

The mammoth is ramming its body against the solid wall outside in the hallway now. The arm I punched the glass with is bleeding, cut by the glass. People are shouting. And shooting. When did more Big Eye get here? I focus on the thing in front of me. Did they create this? WHAT is it?

The air around me vibrates, and I stumble back. The creature looks up at the high ceiling and then, like a giant grasshopper, it leaps. It disappears into the vent. The mammoth throws its body against the wall again and there is a loud crash as the enormous thick slab of concrete falls out, revealing the night sky. There are Big Eye huddled in the blocked hallway shooting at the mammoth. But it's clear that its skin is too thick to be harmed. They cloned the creature too well. Or maybe they cloned it and then enhanced it. Stupid.

They seem to have forgotten about me. I slip.

It is still night. I stand outside of Tower 1 in the parking lot covered by a black sheet. I have slipped fifteen minutes into the future. The mammoth has left a path of destruction behind it. There is the enormous opening in the side of Tower 1. The five crushed vehicles below it, embedded with rubble and the imprint of the mammoth body when it fell out. The torn gates. The car accidents down the road from when it ran into the street. In the distance I can hear its wild roar.

And as I stand there, men and women run past me. As they run, some swing cybernetic arms, some run on cybernetic limbs. The woman with a torso of machinery slowly struts past me. "*Daalu*," she says. Then she smiles and says, "That means 'thank you' where I'm from."

"You're welcome," I say.

As I wonder what happened to all the Big Eye, I see the young man with cybernetic arms and limbs who first told me to find the glass box. He stands in the parking lot and turns toward the building. He holds up both of his hands and splashes of orange-yellow liquid fire shoot from them. The skunky smell of propane hits my nose. When the side of the building is burning, he brings his arms down and slowly walks up the parking lot. He will move round the building and set the other side on fire. And then another side, and another. Tower 1 does not have nearly as many stories as Tower 7. However, what it lacks in height, it makes up with width. Still, I am sure this half man half machine, this speciMen, this abomination—my kin—will find a way to single-handedly bring down Tower 1. Oh yes, Tower 1 will burn just as I had intended.

Before I slip, I see a backward shooting star. The orange-red light leaps from the top of Tower 1 into the dark night sky. I doubt this "shooting star" will burn out, though. I doubt it's a shooting star at all. I think it travels far into the night and then crosses the Kármán line and keeps right on going. Returning to wherever it came from before the people of Tower 1 captured it.

The Backbone is as tall as I remember. I look up at its spiked trunk and softly glowing leaves in the warming sky, all the way up until I can't see any further. It has grown so much since I last saw it. I clench my jaw, pushing all this aside.

It is the early morning before I disappear from the eyes of the Big Eye over the coast of Miami. Just before sunrise. The air is warm and humid, and I can hear the rush hour traffic; I can smell the exhaust. I am crying and the tears become steam before they can even roll down my cheeks. My black sheet burns up, the white make-up on my face turns to ash. My white heat resistant dress begins to crackle. I increase my heat, keeping my gaze on The Backbone. I am villain. I will break The Backbone's back. I will burn the entire city starting from this arboreal heart.

The tree shivers and some of its leaves fall. A groan comes from its roots; they are writhing deep below my feet. And the noise echoes across the city. I hear people exclaim from nearby, but I don't turn to look. They'll soon be dead, anyway. Good. These people are the same people who went about their lives, walking past Tower 7 every day, when it still stood. It made no difference to any of them what they were doing to us only a few floors above.

And even if I care to see these indifferent people, I can't see them. The mile wide area where Tower 7 used to stand is now gnarled wild jungle in the middle of the city. They have tried to contain the plants and trees by surrounding it with a high concrete fence. I smile with disgust. These people haven't learned from their many mistakes. You cannot contain The Backbone. But I can burn it and the rest of this remorseless city to ash. They made me here. I will be exactly what they wanted. Since no one else seeks revenge for all that the Big Eye have done, I will. Let me be the villain for the sake of justice.

"Is this what they've made you?"

I pull my wings in. He is naked, but I know it must be terribly hot for him. Immediately I pull in my heat. I am so glad to see him.

"Mmuo!" I whisper. I fall to my knees on the soil, suddenly very very tired. I look up at him. Now the tears fall down my cheeks, through the white ashes of make-up on my brown face. Wet. Water. They feel so cool. He reaches out a hand and helps me up. Mmuo, the Nigerian man who can walk through walls. Mmuo, who helped me escape Tower 7. Mmuo, one of the only two who survived its fall. Mmuo, who knew that I would rise from the ashes and had left me a dress to clothe my nakedness.

"He said you'd be here at 6:55 am, a minute before dawn. And here you are." Sweat pours down his face. He blinks as a drop falls into his eye.

"Who?"

From above, comes the loud flutter of wings and a burst of air that blows the trees, cooling the air further. The winged man lands on one of The Backbone's lowest branches. Then he flies down and lands before me. He stands tall, peering down his nose at me. His eyes are still soft, still kind.

"Will you kill everyone in this city, Phoenix?" he asks. He speaks with his mouth now. His voice is fatherly, and I feel like sitting back down and listening to him tell stories as the children did with elders on moonless nights in Wulugu.

"Isn't that what they want?" I whisper.

Behind me, I hear Mmuo laugh.

"You're not a villain," the winged man says.

"I *am* a weapon," I insist. "I'm a bomb. Isn't that a villain? I'll be doing what I was made for."

"Who made you?" The winged man asks, his beautiful face serious and intense.

"That's a tricky question," Mmuo added. "Phoenix, it is not so simple."

But I still want to do it. Not only do I want to do it, I want to burn so hot that I would not come back. Saeed is dead. Kofi is dead. My only home has been blown up. The alien seed is safe. Mmuo is my friend, and he can sink into the ground to safety. The winged man is my guardian, and he can fly away. Let them leave me. I want to do evil. I want to do great great evil. More tears fall from my eyes as the thought squeezes my heart.

"You both should leave," I say flatly.

"Should I leave, too?"

The voice came from beside me. Slowly, I turn my head. Slowly. The sky is warming. My eyes focus on him. He is dressed in a simple white dashiki and pants. He wears leather sandals. *Saeed*. I press my hands to my heart, curling my wings around myself.

He slowly comes to me. A stunned smile on his face. "Phoenix," he says. "I thought you were dead!" He opens his mouth wide and inhales a deep breath.

I cannot speak. I cannot think. I cannot process.

He takes my hands. He sighs, his mouth quivering. "You are real," he breathes.

I can't keep my tears from coming. My world is falling apart.

"I-I'm sorry," he says. "Phoenix, when I saw what they were doing, I couldn't . . ."

"You ate the apple," I say. "You died."

"No, that's not what happened," Saeed says, shaking his head. "And they only *thought* I was dead. They flew my body to Tower 4 on the U.S. Virgin Islands." He pauses, a dark look crosses his face as if he were remembering something ugly. "I woke in a morgue. I don't know exactly what they planned to do with my body. But no one was watching me. So I escaped."

"You survived," I say flatly. That's what he always used to say.

He nods. "Yes. But I had no money, I had no way of contacting you. It took me weeks to get back here, but I *came* for you. But by then . . ." He motions to the jungle and the majestic Backbone. "There was nothing in the news but talk of poor architecture and toxic waste." He looks at the winged man. "I was in the Library of Congress searching fruitlessly for information about Tower 7. Over the months, I managed to take a reading class but still can't; it's hard. I was trying to read a general history book about the city when this man appeared and nearly got us both arrested." He points at Mmuo.

I can't help the smile on my face as I imagine Mmuo appearing stark naked in the middle of a library; a tall glistening dark dark African man rising through the floor or stepping out of a wall.

"*He* found us soon after," Saeed says motioning to the winged man. He pauses, looking at my red gold wings. I have unconsciously uncurled them as I listened to him speak.

He pulls me to him, and I rest my head on his shoulder.

"I'm glad you're alive," I say.

"Phoenix," he says, kissing my ear.

"*I* was the one who did it," I say. "Tower 7 went down because of . . ."

"I know," he says.

"I have a lot to tell you."

"I do, too."

We stand that way for several moments. Then he holds me back, his eyes on my wings.

"May I touch them?" he asks.

I laugh, glancing at Mmuo and the winged man. "Maybe later."

Mmuo steps up. "That was you, too, wasn't it, Phoenix? You did that to Tower 1?"

I press my lips together. Then I stand up straight. "Yes."

I catch the winged man's eye and then look away. I know that he will come to me over the ocean as I am following the oil tanker tomorrow and teach me how to move through time.

"See?" Mmuo tells Saeed.

Saeed is looking at me with wide intense eyes. "We want to do that to all the towers," he says. "We want to set every speciMen *free*."

Like an egg, a plan starts to hatch in my mind. There are several we can recruit who will want to help. If we can find them. I'd watched them escape Tower 1. My mind focuses especially on the one who'd set the building on fire. He will join us. That, I am sure of. But there is one problem. The tracking nanobots inside me. Even if I burn to ash, they will survive and immediately re-infect me as soon as I begin to reform.

"The Big Eye will find me wherever I go," I say, after explaining this to the three of them.

"You have to die," the winged man says. "And you must burn hot. You have to destroy all the tracking nanobots in your body." He looks into my eyes, leaving the worst of what he meant unsaid.

I didn't just have to burn hot. I had to burn 6000 degrees Celsius. The temperature of the center of the earth. Can I do this? Might this burn away that which is *me*? Phoenix or not, I am still a creature of this earth. But do I want to have to run from the Big Eye forever? Or even worse, get recaptured?

"I won't let them hurt you," Saeed says.

I wince. Kofi had said the same thing. I take Saeed's hand, and I look at the winged man, "I will have to find a desert or go to the moon."

"I will contain you," the winged man says. "Come."

Saeed is frowning. "Phoenix, you . . ."

"Saeed," I calmly say. "There is no other way. You know it." I pause. "If I don't come back, make sure you destroy them all. Every single goddamn tower. Every brick, piece of concrete, shard of glass. Make those buildings your greatest feast!"

This makes him actually smile, and I know I am making the right decision.

I look at Mmuo, who has taken my other hand.

"There are others like us out there," I say. "I helped them escape Tower 1. Find them. What they are doing in the towers will be the end of humanity if it is not stopped. We are living in darkness and, I swear to you, one day the Author of All Things will pull a star to this planet to burn all the evil away, taking all the good with it. I don't believe in God, but I feel this so deeply. In my bones. But if we bring down the towers, maybe this will not happen."

Saeed hugs me. He whispers into my ear, "My special bird. Don't fly away."

Mmuo squeezes my hand. "Don't forget, we have work to do."

"Like what you did in Nigeria to your government?" I ask.

But he only frowns. Still, even now, Mmuo refuses to tell me what happened in Nigeria that ended with his imprisonment in The United States, in Tower 7.

"You will tell me someday," I say.

"No. It's not a story with a happy ending," he says.

"No story ever really ends anyway," I say. "Especially not the good ones."

The winged man curls his wings tightly around me, and I shut my eyes. I rest my head against his bare chest. It feels so cool. I hear no heart beat. I do hear the rush of the wind over the trees, the movement of the ocean, the shift of desert sands. *Who are you?* I wonder. I don't believe in angels.

I heat. With all my strength. I heat. I am so strong. I am so powerful. They made me a villain. But these people whom I love, they help me to make myself more. I have purpose. I go beyond that which I was made for. I heat. I burn. All around me are a thousand spinning suns. Oooh, I heat.

Then I hear the wind in the leaves of The Backbone, and I understand the deeper meaning of my name.

Chapter 10

Wazobia

I KNEW SO LITTLE ABOUT THE WORLD AND SO MUCH. As you listen to me, you should take that into consideration. I would, if I were you. I was two when I decided to escape Tower 7. How long was I in Ghana? A year? And once I crossed the Atlantic after leaving Africa, time stopped meaning anything to me. I had died three times, and I had learned to slip outside, between, through time into other times. And I had lost two men that I loved and gained one of them back.

It was quiet where I was, but inside I was burning with fury. I carried it with me into the darkness of death, and when I brought it out into the light of life, it had evolved, matured, intensified, grown wings. I would free the others. I would crush those who had the nerve to make me. They had no respect.

The winged man had kept me from killing myself. Thus, he'd kept me from doing the worst: killing my soul by killing a million other souls with my heat. As I became ash for the third time, I wondered yet again, *Who is he?* I didn't wonder *what* he was.

I never had any control of when I returned. This time, it took me a month. Mmuo and Saeed were happy to tell me how it all happened. "When you were nothing but ash, there was a final flash that nearly blinded us," Mmuo told me the night after my full return. We sat in the living room of the apartment Mmuo rented in Soho. "He took most of your heat in his wings but we could feel it, too. It felt like a burst of hot wind."

Saeed had turned back first and fallen to his knees before the winged man. On the ground were grey ashes. In death, I looked like any of earth's flesh when burned. The winged man stepped back as Saeed gathered my ashes into a pile, tears falling down his cheeks. He hadn't been there when I burned the first or second time. Such a thing is always worse when you actually experience it.

"She will be back," Mmuo had told Saeed. But he wasn't sure.

The winged man flew off without a word. Mmuo and Saeed just sat there in the jungle of Tower 7. Mmuo said they spoke words over my ashes. They'd mourned me. Seeing me as ashes made it nearly impossible to not assume the worst. Nothing natural becomes ash and then returns to life. Ashes to ashes, dust to dust. Neither Saeed nor Mmuo would tell me what words they spoke over my ashes.

"A few minutes later there were lights in the sky," Mmuo said. "And I swear to you, they made a weird whooshy almost musical sort of sound. Saeed denies hearing it, but I *know* he did. The whole city did, even above all the city noise."

He didn't know what they were but I did. I'd read about them while imprisoned in Tower 7, and I used to wonder what they'd look like. They were called Northern Lights. Aurora Borealis. As I died, I'd flared like the sun and the atmosphere over the city was reacting to *me*. Later that evening, though there had been no previous recent activity spotted on the sun, the meteorologists and geoscientists speculated that the strange auroras and the blackout right after that killed service to computers, jelli tellis, skyscraper screens, and all portable devices for two days were caused by a solar flare. And the newsfeeds mentioned the noise, too. I guess they needed some sort of explanation after the resulting twelve hours of rioting and stockpiling.

Mmuo and Saeed guarded my ashes for the entire month. At all times, at least one of them was there. I do not remember a thing, not until that last three days when I started to . . . reappear. That's how Saeed described it.

"It was the dead of night and I was in my tent," he said. "It was raining."

They had left my ashes. It had rained many times, the wind had blown, my ashes washed away, scattered far and wide. But Mmuo and Saeed stayed there, using a camouflaged tent, though the cover of the wildly growing and twisting trees was enough to hide them from the Big Eye when their surveillance cameras flew by. Saeed and Mmuo waited, in the very place I had burned while enfolded in the winged man's wings. They patiently waited.

Then one dark rainy night, Saeed heard a loud sigh. He heard it even over the noise of the rain. He crawled to the tent entrance and looked outside. Creeping over the spot where I had died was a soft mist. The wind kept blowing it away, but then it would return to the same spot. "The mist was warm and smelled like concrete cooking in the heat," Saeed told me. "That's how I knew it was you."

Soon, Mmuo returned to give him a chance to go to the apartment to bathe and eat a hot meal. But Saeed didn't want to leave me. I was now more than mist. I was a softly glowing, slowly shifting shape. Like a nebula. Red orange yellow. Always warm.

"Go and wash, at least," Mmuo told Saeed. I remember him saying this because it was at this moment that I came back to myself. I could hear, see, and smell. Saeed did indeed need to bathe. "Is that how you want her to see you after all these weeks?" Mmuo added.

I listened, reveling in their voices, the scent of the jungle around me, the after-scent of exhaust, the warm night air, the wetness from the rain, and the sight of the magnificent Backbone. *I'm sorry*, I thought as I looked at it. *I'm sorry I ever sought to destroy you, magnificent creature.* It looked wider and taller than ever. I could see three hundred and sixty degrees around me, from the dirt below my non-body, to the stars in the sky, to the jungle around me, and the skyscrapers beyond.

It was when Saeed had finally agreed to go bathe and sleep, when it stopped raining, that Mmuo started to tell me the story I had twice asked him to tell me: the story of what he did in Nigeria that landed him in Tower 7. The first time I'd asked was just before my escape from Tower 7. I'd asked again before I burned, cradled in the winged man's wings. Both times Mmuo refused. Maybe now he hoped the story would bring me back faster. I could not move. I could not feel. I could only listen. I so wanted to hear his story. Finally. What did Mmuo know about going up against a government? I remember every word. Mmuo is an interesting man . . .

Phoenix, you must be very bored there, unable to move and cause trouble. You look like a sleeping bolt of lightning. Power at peace.

I remember you well in Tower 7. Whenever I came to the 28th floor to meet with Saeed, you were the only other person that I always made sure I saw. Sometimes I let you know I was there, other times, I just quietly peeked in to make sure you were ok. I was often nearby during mealtimes. I used to steal whole roasted chickens, like a fox in a hen house. I saw you when they took you to the lab. Once I made their equipment cart fall over. Do you remember that? Phoenix. You are special. Come back to us. Wake up.

I know you like stories, so I will tell you mine. There is not much time. Your Saeed will be returning soon, so I will try to keep my story moving. I may tell Saeed these things in due time, but for now, I will only tell you. Because you asked me twice. I am Mmuo, and the man I will tell you about is long gone, but I will tell you of him. I was my father's fourth child and third son. He named me Ikenga Emezie Nnachukwu. My mother was a schoolteacher and she loved books.

She met my father when she was about twenty. He too loved to read, but he liked books that were worlds away from the literary canon. He read things by legendary agitating African writers from long ago, like Ngugi wa Thiong'o and Wole Soyinka. And he listened to old old tunes from Fela Kuti, and he loved the American golden era rap music. He'd learned the meaning of colonialism and about the "colonized mind" from the deep Internet when he was twelve years old.

Ah, Phoenix, mentioning these musicians and writers seems to have gotten your attention. Of course you read them. What *haven't* you read?

You glow more strongly now, and you have added a hint of blue to your orange, red and yellow light. Yes, you would have liked my father and he would have liked you, my mother, too.

You know what he told my mother when he first met her? "I never *had* to DE-colonize. I've never been colonized." You were the opposite of him when you were in Tower 7. How you have changed.

My father instantly liked my mother, and my mother liked him. And soon they were both angry militant young people intent on taking back the "motherland." My father went on to become an engineer and a local politician. But though he put faith in science, he put his greatest faith in what he called the Old Ways. These included things he'd learned from his own father, the masquerade secret society he belonged to and the Old Ways of other ethnic groups like the Yorubas, Efiks, Ogonis. He took what he could use. And he knew it all very well.

I had two older brothers and one older sister. Whenever we travelled anywhere during election season, my father would take us behind the house to the shrine he kept there. He'd cover us with a special shea butter he mixed himself.

Phoenix, what is this lightning that you just tried to kill me with? You zapped me with a thread of electricity when I mentioned shea butter. My hands are shaking and the air smells a bit acrid, but I am still here. I will make sure that your Saeed brings you some when you return. Would you like me to keep telling you my story? Ok.

My father said his special shea butter would stop bullets. He'd learned how to make it from a close friend of his who was Yoruba. This friend had covered himself with the shea butter and then made my father shoot him. My father said that after he shot him there was nothing but powder on his friend's chest and that the bullet had fallen to the ground, hot and spent. We all believed my father.

And we were right to, because one night during the time when my father was running for Imo State Governor, we were driving to one of his speaking events. My mother was already at the place where my father would speak, waiting for us. We were in my father's black Jaguar and my siblings and I were in the back. My father was in the front seat. I remember this well. The driver, whose name was Endurance, was driving.

I was laughing at my sister, who sang along to the song Endurance played in the car radio when she suddenly stopped singing and gasped, looking past me out the window. After that, I only remember screaming, noise, and the sound of the tires screeching as Endurance mashed the brakes and swerved off the road. Some people had opened fire on our car. Several of the windows were open when they began to shoot. There were holes in the car doors, the windows that were closed were shattered, but not one of us was hit.

We'd all been covered with the shea butter, even our driver Endurance. Earlier, my sister had complained about how shiny it made her skin and how she could never apply the proper make-up. But she knew to put it on anyway.

My father won that election, easy.

By the time I made it to university, I had learned everything my father knew. I was his favorite because I was the one who took a vested interest in the two things my father loved— juju and politics. I learned how to make the shea butter that stopped bullets; my father initiated me into his masquerade secret society; I knew how to make a man hurt, forget his name, and stop chasing women; and I could speak to the goddess Ani, that's the goddess of the land.

You are an American, Phoenix. So though you know Africa well, you will believe in the power of science over all that we know. But you are an African, too, so you know it in your flesh, your strange flesh, that the spirit world rules the physical world. Where is it that you are returning from as I tell you my story? Is it from a test tube? Or from somewhere else? They made you, yes. But something made them make you, Phoenix.

Anyway, by the time I went to university there was something else that I had learned to do. My father taught me about the mystical, but I came by this knowledge on my own. I was not at the top of my class, but I was one of the smarter students. I loved and understood the spiritual, yes, but I also loved the sciences. I loved nature's structure, rules, logic, its playfulness and the sheer scope of its creativity. Science has always been aligned with Ani. It was clear that my path of study would be engineering.

One night, I was pondering the laws of physics and the will of Ani as I stared at my bedroom door. I'd been lying on my bed for an hour, think-

ing and thinking. Maybe at some point I'd fallen into a trance or medita-
tive state. Something came together in my mind as I stared at the door and
considered the flesh of it, the tree it had once been a part of, its power, its
weakness, its dead cells, molecules, and atoms. The space between them.
The spirit of the tree that clung to this piece of tree flesh.

I got up, walked up to the door, and I walked right through it. I
emerged outside of my bedroom, and there stood my father staring at me,
shocked. He'd been on his way to the kitchen. He smiled and I smiled too.
After that, I did it over and over again, walking through wooden doors.
Now you see how it started for me.

In university, I became like a miniature version of my father. I didn't
do it on purpose; it was just a natural progression of things. I was my father's son. Like him, I was drawn to mysticism. As he did, I believed that
Nigeria could be better if it just changed. I loved Fela, as he did. I wanted
to walk around half-naked like a real African and spit in the face of the
West. I joined the student government, and by the end of my second year
was its president. By the end of my third year, I was one of the top engineering students but I was most known for being a part of WaZoBia.

"WaZoBia" means "come, come, come" in the three most widely spoken Nigerian languages. Yoruba, Hausa, and Ibo. *Wa* in Yoruba means
"come," *Zo* in Hausa means "come," and *Bia* in Igbo means "come." The
word "come" is an invitation of togetherness, and represents unity and
diversity in community. Phoenix, WaZoBia was a radical student group
bent on challenging the ever-present and meddling oil companies and corrupt military Nigerian government. No campus cults for me. I wanted to
join a group that was about more than *wahala,* petty trouble. I really *did*
want to change Nigeria.

At some point, WaZoBia decided to overthrow the government.
Maybe it was after the fuel riots. How can you be one of the world's last
leading producers of crude oil, and yet still have a shortage of kerosene and
vehicle fuel? In Nigeria, we use solar generators but solar powered cars are
rare, and it's next to impossible to find a place to recharge an electric car,
especially outside of Lagos and Abuja. Hybrid vehicles are still quite pop-
ular, some even still use fuel-powered cars. So fuel is still in demand there.

But no, no, I remember now, it wasn't the riots that convinced us that it was time to overthrow the government. It was the introduction of the Anansi Droids 419. The Anansi Droids were, how do I explain them? They were digital android killer soldiers! They were the size of dogs and looked like shiny silver spiders. They were robot spiders. The Nigerian government's engineers created the prototype. Can you imagine? We came up with these things ourselves FOR ourselves. We're so colonized that we build our own shackles. Some young engineer by the name of Obinna Ukamaka came up with the idea after reading a science fiction story about robot spiders guarding the pipelines of the Niger Delta. Life imitated art, except this particular story was actually *critiquing* the government not giving them a blueprint. The author must be rolling in her grave.

Chevron, Shell and a few other oil companies helped fund the project. The purpose of these machines was to prevent pipeline bunkering by guarding them . . . by any means necessary. Though the machines were supposedly artificially intelligent, they killed senselessly. If you so much as touched a pipeline, they came running and tore you apart. These pipelines ran right through the backyards of villages. They ran alongside roads, past schools. Within the first month, hundreds of people were killed.

None of us in WaZoBia could live under a government that would sell out its people so thoroughly, so brutally. We were strongly united in this understanding. We'd grown up with technology. And everyone knows that after the prototype is put to use successfully, they upgrade and then they upgrade that next generation and so on. The Anansi Droids were a slippery slope, especially with Nigeria possessing a still sought after resource.

The daughter of Nigeria's Vice President was a member of WaZoBia. Three of us could build bombs. Four of us had fathers high up in the military, five of us had been area boys before entering the university and had only recently shrugged off bad habits, one of us was a mistress of the Nigerian president himself, and one of us could walk through wooden doors.

Our plan was perfect. We had guns. We could get in. And none of us was afraid to kill or die. We were idealists. We'd all seen our parents, families, ourselves, suffer. And we knew we were capable. But there must have been an informer. That is the only way to explain what happened the night before we were to put our plan into action.

We'd gathered at Rose de Red's house. She was the leader. She could shoot a gun like her soldier father, and she could shout like her Minister of Communications mother. She had a small apartment in the capital of Abuja close to Aso Villa, the office and residence of the president. We'd all travelled there, some by air, others by car or bus. None of our parents knew where we were. They all thought we were at the University of Lagos preparing for exams.

We sat in that room on the 4th floor with white walls and expensive leather furniture. Rose de Red came from an oil rich family. She knew so much. We were all accounted for. Everyone in WaZoBia. We were smiling, young, excited. Right outside the window you could see the Aso Villa. It was a warm night. Our weapons were ready. WaZoBia's most charismatic member, Success T, was getting everyone excited before Rose de Red spoke by shouting, "Victoria, Victoria, Victoria acerta to the great of the great Nigerian students, both home and abroad . . ."

And that's when the door banged open and masked men in black suits burst in with AK-47s. Without hesitation, they opened fire. I was sitting in a chair near the balcony window right in front of Success T. The lights stayed on so I saw it all.

Success T's chest exploded. Rose de Red's left eye popped as a bullet smashed through it. WaZoBia members tried to run, but there were too many men in black with guns. The room that moments ago had been immaculate and full of optimism now smelled tangy with gunpowder, blood, urine, and was full of death. The window behind me shattered. And through it all I just stood there. Right before the meeting, in my hotel room, I'd taken a shower and the soap dried my skin. It was itchy, and I realized that I'd forgotten to bring lotion. So I'd used some of my special shea butter. I'd brought it for the next day, when we planned to storm the capital.

But I don't think I'd have been shot even if I *hadn't* put the shea butter on. They didn't want to kill me. How else can I explain the people who grabbed me, put a sack over my head, and dragged me out of there? How can I explain being cuffed, blindfolded and shoved onto a plane by men and women with badges on their chests of a hand grasping lightning? How else can I explain why they took me across the Atlantic Ocean to the United States without a passport and drove me straight to Tower 7? Was that an accident?

The Big Eye agreed to serve as the strong arm of the United States and Nigerian governments and the invested oil companies who wanted to prevent a coup d'état for their own various greedy reasons. And the Big Eye got to grab the engineering student they'd heard could walk through wood. They killed two birds with one stone.

Who are the Big Eye? Are they a secret part of the American government or a powerful private corporation? Is there a difference? To me, it doesn't matter. It's the same ends. So while they did what they did to me over the years in Tower 7, fusing and altering my body and forcing me to show them how to use my father's juju, Nigeria remains under the latest crippling military rule as oil companies suck the last of its black blood.

I knew I could escape them once they succeeded in enhancing my ability to the point where I could walk through all matter. I only learned that they'd coated all the outer walls with their "just in case Mmuo escapes" substance when I ran face first into the wall and lost consciousness. The only way I escaped was because I came to in time to sink to the room below. I was trapped in Tower 7 until *you* got me out, Phoenix. I've never been able to properly thank you for this, dear.

Come back to us. We need you.

CHAPTER 11

Return

I CAME BACK.

Mind.

Wings.

And other flesh.

Under the blue sky. In the city.

This time it is different. I will be different. I am different. I was different. You must know that by now. You've watched me, heard me. I speak my life into existence with each expressed breath I take. I tell you a story within which are more stories. Universes within universes. We are all spinning like small suns. I am like my own sun.

I could feel my lips. "Praise Ani," I breathed, for Mmuo's story was on the tip of my mind when I finally found I could speak. Mmuo laughed loudly. I blinked as I looked at him. It was the first time I'd ever seen him wearing clothes. He wore white pants, leather sandals, and a beaded necklace. This was a lot for a man who never wore clothes at all. He looked different.

"What is Ani?" Saeed asked, frowning, as he grasped my hand. He must have wondered if I'd lost my mind.

"She's the goddess of the land," Mmuo said. "I spoke of her to Phoenix while she was recovering. I guess Phoenix heard me." He looked at me knowingly. "Good."

"She's the sister of the Author of All Things," I said to Saeed. Then I smiled. I was weak but I felt so good. The air was fresh and I inhaled it deeply.

Saeed helped me up. My muscles worked and my skin prickled, absorbing the sunshine. Mmuo averted his eyes from my nakedness. Saeed didn't. His eyes swept from my body to my wings. "When they made you," he whispered. "Something good was touching their minds."

I smiled, basking in his gaze.

"When they made you, planets must have aligned," he said. "When they made you, they made one of a kind."

Saeed, always the artist. Maybe he'd draw me next. I looked up, through the trees, at the sun. I shut my eyes and was happy. Absolutely, completely happy.

Saeed gave me a small jar of yellow raw shea butter. "Thank you," I whispered. I coated my skin with it, the nutty smell reminding me simultaneously of my happier days in Tower 7 and my happiest days in Wulugu, Ghana. The dress Saeed gave me was yellow and the back was open for my wings. It wasn't heat resistant. It fit perfectly. Then he handed me the black burka. I looked at it, perturbed, as I stood tall in my dress. Then I looked back at the sun, and then back at it. Thick, black, rough. I put it on. I was the veiled hunchback, again. This time on a different continent. But I had plans. *We* had plans. The first was to get out of there before the Big Eye spotted us.

Mmuo reluctantly shrugged a t-shirt over his lean muscular chest. "We leave these walls and enter barbarism," he said.

It was broad daylight and I could see the tall tall buildings clearly. We had to walk several blocks to get to Mmuo's car and as we walked, I held Saeed's hand and gazed up. The palm, iroko, and ebony trees that grew between the buildings reminded me of Ghana. In Ghana, men would climb the palm trees to tap palm wine. Here, they pruned the palm trees until only the top had the bushy leaves. I could never see this from the top of Tower 7, and when I was running I didn't care. Now, I had to smile. The trees looked naked.

Beyond the trees loomed the tallest human-made structures I'd ever seen, aside from The Backbone. At first, I clung to Saeed and listened hard for the sound of walls crumbling and buckling. I'd seen Tower 7 and the Axis fall. It was more than easy for me to imagine these ones doing the same. When I realized the appearance of the buildings falling was just an illusion created by the sheer height of them, I began to relax and enjoy their enormity.

The buildings flashed and chattered even in the daylight with commercials, TV shows, the latest news. One building was covered with a giant screen that only showed a little girl smiling and smiling. As we passed it, the girl puckered her lips. People around us exclaimed and started moving quicker. Some laughed, two women yelped and started running, covering their heads with their briefcases. I found out why moments later when a spray of mist burst from the mouth, dampening everyone. We were right in the middle of it all.

Mmuo loudly sucked his teeth. "These people dey craze," he muttered. "Waste of solar power."

The mist felt wonderful in the heat. It blew beneath my burka and dress, cooling my entire body. I giggled, delighted. It was all so silly. It was nice to see a lighter side of the city for once.

The sidewalks were packed with people coming and going, Asians, Africans, blended, Hispanics, Muslims, Hassidic Jews, Hindus, suited businessmen, a blind woman carrying a very loud navigation companion. Americans and visitors. All kinds of people who unknowingly accepted the existence of the towers. Who reaped the fruits of the tower's callous labor. Few of them looked twice at me.

They talked on their portables. They drove in solar and hybrid vehicles. They sat in office buildings draped with eco-clean vines. I wondered how many of these people were "mild speciMen," speciMen who turned out too normal to work with; these people were released and begrudgingly accepted and integrated into American society. And who in amongst these people was a "quiet clone", always hiding his or her belly-button-less waist? Who had a cybernetic limb that had replaced one damaged by an accident or by a birth defect?

"It's going to be a tight fit," Saeed said when we got to Mmuo's car.

I turned to the side, squeezing in. My second time in a car was an even tighter fit than my first time, when I'd gotten into Sarah's car in Ghana and fled my soon to explode home. My wings were bent in such an excruciatingly awkward position that I hissed with pain. The seats were not made for a Phoenix. But it was the only way to get away from the area without the Big Eye seeing me. I decided this would be the last time I got in a car. It didn't turn out to be true, but the sentiment certainly was.

CHAPTER 12

Seed

MMUO'S BALCONY WAS WIDE, facing downtown. The Backbone was in clear view. I wondered if Mmuo had gotten this apartment with me in mind. He'd put a lawn chair out here but I pushed it aside, preferring to sit on the floor. I pulled my knees close to my chest and shut my eyes as the breeze cooled my face. Mmuo's apartment was on the twenty-first floor, and though the air smelled like exhaust and the mosquitoes still hung around, at least I was high up. These days, I was most comfortable when I was high up. I sighed and relaxed my shoulders and wings as I let it all crash down on me. I was here. With friends. I was alive. I was free.

"Phoenix."

I wiped the tears from my face as I looked up at Saeed. Then I looked away. He sat down beside me and for a moment we were quiet, looking at the world before us. The apartment was in the city but far enough away from the busiest part to have more trees than tall buildings. A tall palm tree grew so close to the apartment building that I could reach out and touch its top leaves.

"What are you thinking about?" he finally asked.

I looked him square in the eye. "I was thinking about apples," I said, feeling a sudden flash of anger. My temples ached, and I shut my eyes again. "I was thinking about how they taste."

Saeed muttered something in Arabic.

"I will learn Arabic one day," I said. "Just so you can't do that anymore."

"I said that you don't know me," he said, looking annoyed. "You're too young to understand a man like me. You're only three years on this earth."

"I've died," I said. "Three times. Have you?" I twitched my wings in annoyance.

He looked away and sighed. "Phoenix, you really don't understand."

I felt the heat in the middle of my forehead first. Then, in an instant, it had reached the tips of my toes, fingers and wings. Saeed frowned at me but he didn't move away. *Good*, I thought. *Stay. I hope it burns.* A tear fell from my left eye, and I could feel the warm mist brush my eyebrows as the tear slowly evaporated. *What if I burn and take this entire building with me?* I mused. *Saeed, Mmuo, New York.* I fought back tears, shocked by the power and violence of my rage. "Why did you try to leave me?" I finally asked. "You saw the bad thing they were doing and then you just decided to subtract yourself as if you were Allah or Zeus? Who are you? What makes you . . ."

"Wake up Phoenix!" he snapped. "Think. What does your mind tell you about what happened? You can read all those books yet you still can't unravel the *truth*." He muttered something in Arabic.

I wanted to shout. I wanted to scream. But those things have never come naturally to me. I was quiet. But my body felt hot. And in the darkness of the evening, there was a glow around my eyesight.

"Calm yourself," he said, finally moving away. "People will see you."

I took a deep breath and closed my eyes. Behind my lids I saw a blazing sun slowly set. Then it was just the dark again; I was calm. I heard him move back to me. He took my hand and squeezed it. Then he brought it to his lips and kissed it. His lips were so cool and they felt good.

In my calmness, I realized something. I opened my eyes and looked into his. My heart was beating like crazy. Saeed's beard was bushy and a rich black. His eyes were clear and dark. He had a strong nose. His face reminded me of the imam in Ghana who'd built the mosque that looked like a sand castle, but Saeed was much younger, and there was nothing Muslim about Saeed.

"Tell me what they did," I said.

"Ah, so you *do* have critical thinking skills," he said quietly.

"Tell me."

He pulled at his beard and rubbed his face. He nodded. "Ok," he said. "Ok. Phoenix. Well, remember the lines? The lines on the floor?"

I nodded. Every speciMen deemed tame and trustworthy "walked the line," a computerized line that would appear on the floor and lead you where you were supposed to go when there was no doctor or guard to lead the way. "Mine was yellow. Yours was red."

"I hated that line," he said. "I would have nightmares about it. I had nightmares about a lot of things there." He pressed his lips tightly together.

"One day, I stepped off the line that was leading me to the lab," he said. "They were so slow to respond. They were so used to us behaving. Only Mmuo had escaped them and even then, they saw that none of us followed his example. I was halfway across the floor, when they caught up with me. But by then, I'd seen their device, whatever it was. I still had the apple in my hand. I'd planned to paint it. But by then, I was squeezing it as I tried to cope with what I was seeing.

"Before that night, Mmuo and I had been conspiring. We had a plan of escape that was actually quite similar to yours. I cannot read but I've listened to many audio books. There is a verse in a poem that has always stuck with me. I didn't have to even try to memorize it. The poem was so powerful that it stuck to my brain the first time I heard it: 'Things fall apart, the center cannot hold,' by a man named Yeats.

"The towers have changed *life*. Not just in the States but all over the world, I suspect. You know this more than me, but I sense it. All the cures, inventions and enhancements have changed so much. But the core of the tower's philosophy has always been rotten. And in due time, it will collapse on itself and everything will go down. Mmuo knew this, and I knew this. We were planning escape because we didn't want to be there when it happened, and we wanted to *make* it happen, if that makes sense.

"I was dying inside, Phoenix. They brought me here after living on the streets of Cairo. I had no family, just survival, primal powerful survival. Yet after only a few years in Tower 7, I was dying inside. They did things to me, they changed me, and I watched them do worse things to others. I'd come into that dining hall and see the changes with my own eyes. Then I met you, and I watched them do things to you.

"You came to me that first day. I had never seen anything like you. You do not know what you look like to others, Phoenix. No words can describe it. Yet, I knew you were doomed. There were female Big Eye who wanted me as their plaything but saw how much I felt for you, and they would tell me things, raw painful facts. They wanted to draw me away from you. The Big Eye women are cruel in ways you would not want to know. But the fact is, I knew what you were, Phoenix. Destined to burn. A weapon.

"Then I met Mmuo and once we got to know each other, he saw in me a partner in crime. I saw in him someone who had escaped. We fed off each other. He visited me often, but not too often. The Big Eye knew it but did not worry. Our time was close but not yet."

My eyes stung. *How come he had never spoken of all this with me?*

"Never," he continued. "I would never have left you. I was waiting for the right *time*. Ask Mmuo." He paused. "But seeing that device, all that death, death from I don't know when, I forgot all that. Phoenix, it showed a time and place where mounds and mounds of Africans were dead! What were they doing? When was . . . ?"

"I didn't see Africans," I said, frowning. "I saw Caucasians."

He stared at me for a long moment, then shrugged. "Genocide is genocide. Maybe you saw them looking through a different time and place."

I nodded, wanting him to continue.

"When I saw that machine, I went mad," he said. "I don't remember much other than red. Red lines, many of them, clouding my vision. I still had the apple in my hand that I'd taken from you. That was red, too." A blank look crossed Saeed's face. "I burst into that room and threw it at the

Big Eye. I threw a scanner and anything else I could get my hands on to destroy that black machine. I don't remember if I caused any momentary break in transmission. I was just picking things up and throwing them. It took ten Big Eye to restrain me. They dragged me back to my room and beat the hell out of me. All through, I kept thinking about you. You didn't know anything and there was always so much hope in your eyes. I kept thinking about what would happen to that hope if I told you about what I'd seen or if I never returned to you." He paused, frowning at me. "But now I see something new in your eyes. Now, when I look into them it's like looking into a mirror. Your innocence is gone."

"Death will do that," I wanted to say. But I did not.

"They left me for a few hours," he continued. "I floated in and out of consciousness. Then they must have decided that I was damaged goods because later that night, they burst into my room and injected me with something that was supposed to kill me but didn't. That's how I woke up in the morgue in the US Virgin Islands in Tower 4. There was a tag on my finger that said 'Dismember. Organs will self-preserve. Use for transplant'. I was more valuable to them dead than alive."

I waited for him to go on and tell me exactly what happened then but he said nothing. I was glad. I'd gone digging for answers and pulled up something naked, ugly, and upsetting. However, by the next day, I was still simmering.

"There is no 'long time ago' for me," I snapped. Saeed and I were sitting in Mmuo's car while Mmuo was inside, buying groceries. Saeed had been telling me about his other life, when he was "a homeless kid in Egypt," and I just didn't want to hear any more.

I had no real reason to be irritated, but I was. I didn't want to hear his tale of torture, survival, and misery. I didn't want to hear about how his father had indentured him at the age of six to a successful but physically and verbally abusive pharmacist who wanted a child slave, not an apprentice. I didn't want to hear how his mother never spoke a word of protest as she watched the pharmacist drive away with him. I didn't want to hear about how Saeed ran away at the age of seven from the pharmacist the night the man beat him unconscious because his paranoid over-medicated wife didn't like the "conniving" way Saeed had looked at her. I didn't want to hear about how he lived for three years on a digital dumpsite making money by burning old computer parts and selling the exposed copper wiring.

Saeed stopped talking. He smiled. "People like you have always been."

I frowned. I didn't understand what he meant. I didn't want to understand anything. Or anyone. I just wanted to be free of all the weight, free of my constant anger, free of being a fugitive, of Saeed's awful recent and distant past, of all our murky futures. At least for a little while.

However, I had to stay in the car. It was the closest to being in public that Mmuo felt I should be. After seeing the in-depth news stories that marked me as a dangerous, murderous speciMen that authorities were "close to securing," I agreed with him. They gave me no name, but the lesser viewed stories showed images of my face from when I'd "brought down The Axis" building, and none of them referred to me with a pronoun other than "it." Saeed insisted that the Big Eye were making sure every journalist "coordinated" in the image presented of me. A woman was not dangerous, so no need to panic. An African was a threat, so do not hesitate to kill her. A winged human being was an abomination, not angelic; so when it's over, forget her death quickly.

Still, my days in Ghana had taught me that I was no longer a creature who could be comfortable being indoors for long periods of time. I never knew whether this was because I was a winged creature now or because of some sort of fallout from my days in Tower 7. I banged my fist against the car door. A beeping sound came from the front seat and my door opened. The car thought I wanted to get out. It really was a "smart car."

Saeed reached over the seat, leaned across me and shut the door. He looked into my eyes. I instinctively leaned back.

"They're looking for you, Phoenix."

I scoffed. "They are looking for a non-human nonentity."

"No, they are looking for *you*," he said.

"They won't find me," I said, looking away.

"Maybe, but you'll have to run," he said. "Wherever you expose yourself, you'll have to flee from there." He paused. "And we can't follow you, either."

Everything in me clenched and the pain of it surprised me. My wings pushed my burka away and slapped the car ceiling. I gasped, regaining control. Saeed looked around as he quickly pulled my burka back over my wings. Tears squeezed from my eyes as I took a calming breath.

"Relax, Phoenix," Saeed whispered. "Relax."

I grimaced and sniveled, rubbing my temples. The pain.

He climbed over the seat and sat beside me cradling me with his arms. I leaned against him, shutting my eyes. I never saw darkness. Just red. Especially in the sunshine. I lifted a hand and slowly ran the back of it over Saeed's short beard. The roughness felt good against my skin. I turned my hand and stroked it with my fingertips.

"I've mourned you," I said. "I wept, beat myself up, cursed, bled for you. Then I *healed*. I buried you here." I put my hand over my heart. "And now . . ."

"I'm sorry," he said. "I couldn't . . ."

"I loved a man named Kofi Annan," I said, shutting my eyes again. I could see Kofi clearly. I remembered him over two lifetimes. He was dark-skinned like me and beautiful like the few African men allowed to star in 3D movies. But he was also humble and unaware of his beauty because he had so many more important things to focus on. He had a head full of rough black hair, and he stood an inch shorter than me. "The Big Eye took his family away years ago. And then they killed him years later because he tried to protect me. He died because of me."

"Mmuo told me, Phoenix," he said, looking at his hands. "I know everything. You don't have to tell me, again."

"I lost you. I lost him," my voice shook, and I wished I hadn't started talking. It was like scratching at a fresh scab. "I . . . I can't lose . . ."

"We have nothing to lose," he said, taking my face into his warm hands.

He kissed me.

I saw Tower 7. The dining hall. We sat close to each other and he'd kissed me. It was fast. His lips were cool, and we'd looked at each other afterwards, first with surprise, then delight, then we'd veiled our faces with secrecy. SpeciMen were not allowed to pair unless the Big Eye deemed it good research.

Now, this kiss was not like the ones we shared in Tower 7. There was heat and humidity. I was able to wrap my arms around him and him around me. I was able to feel him. Saeed may have been lean, but he was strong. And unlike in Tower 7, this kiss lasted. Saeed could not eat fruit yet his mouth tasted like mangos. He pulled back from me, a surprised look on his face. Then his face broke out in a smile, hunger in his eyes. "Warm," he breathed. "You're always so *warm*."

I felt heated but it was not the type of heat I had come to know too well. This was something new and exquisite. My entire body felt like it was humming. My wings wanted to stretch and fly. I needed to get outside. I wanted Saeed to take me outside.

A knock on the window made us both jump. We scrambled away from each other. The doors unlocked and Mmuo opened the door on the passenger side. He peeked in and chuckled, shaking his head. Then he placed two grocery bags on the seat. He walked to the trunk and opened it and started loading in the rest of the groceries. Saeed opened his door and leaned out. "You need any help with those?" he asked.

Mmuo held up a hand, still laughing. "I think it best if you don't get up."

Saeed glanced at his lap and then looked at me. I turned and looked out the window, embarrassed. It wasn't because Mmuo had caught Saeed and I being intimate. Mmuo was my family; he did not wish me ill. He would protect me, and I would protect him. What issue would he have with my closeness with Saeed? It was certainly nothing surprising or new. He'd known about us in Tower 7.

No. What I was embarrassed about was something more basic. Saeed was twenty-one years old and had lived a rough life both in Egypt and then in Tower 7. He'd told me that he'd been intimate with several of the Big Eye female guards over the years. This was why when I came along, they had hated me and told him ugly details about me and what I was.

But despite the fact that I looked and felt 40 years old, I was only three. I was still processing the intense feeling that had swept through my body. I'd felt whispers of it minutes before Kofi died, when I'd shown him myself and he'd touched my wings. I shivered. There was a sweet aching between my legs and at the tips of my wings. As Mmuo started the car, Saeed took my hand, wove his fingers between mine and grasped.

I looked at my hands grasping Saeed's and realized something else. I wanted to laugh out loud with relief. Instead I sat back and looked out the window. We passed office buildings and one had a large urban garden, full of sunflowers, tomato plants and possibly dasheen bushes.

I wasn't glowing. Praise Ani, I wasn't glowing. I was warm, not hot, and I wasn't glowing. This was good for Saeed and good for me. It was good for everyone.

CHAPTER 13

Terrorists

I LOVE BOOKS. I adore everything about them. I love the feel of the pages on my fingertips. They are light enough to carry, yet so heavy with worlds and ideas. I love the sound of the pages flicking against my fingers. Print against fingerprints. Books make people quiet, yet they are so loud. I love the smell of the pages, even of the newest physical books, which were so rarely made. These new books had stiff grey pages made from doubly recycled paper and were printed with vegetable ink that was 100 percent biodegradable and smelled strongly of spoiled broccoli. I loved them as I loved the 300-year-old books that threatened to crumble in my hands.

I loved the immediate page shift of digitals. The crispness of high-definition photo and print. Manipulating and flying' through information and story was my first real lesson in the art of flight. Before my own wings grew in.

And then there is the information itself—the stories, the voices, the worlds within worlds. When I was in Tower 7, I felt like I was everyone and everything. I was ignorant in my knowledge. Ignorance was my bliss. Even when they did their painful tests, the burning . . . I knew I could always return to my books. Not escape, return. I knew so much, but so little. You can have knowledge, but you are nothing without wisdom.

But this was what the Big Eye relied upon. They gave me whatever I wanted to read. They gave me top secret books and documents because I requested them; I didn't even know that these were classified materials. To them, I wasn't human enough to be a threat. I was their tool. I was nothing to worry about or fear. They saw me as they saw the Africans made slaves during the Trans-Atlantic Slave Trade hundreds of years ago. They saw me as many Arabs saw African slaves over millennium and how some still see Africans today. The Big Eye didn't think they needed to put a leash on me because my leash was in my DNA. They were the definition of arrogance and entitlement.

For several months I not only read about the towers, but I read about the history and proliferation of information, both oral and written. I was obsessed with it. And this led me to read about the biggest library in the world, America's de facto think tank: the Library of Congress. While in Tower 7, I'd never dreamed of going there. Escape never crossed my mind, not until Saeed "died." But a part of me certainly wished to enter its walls.

Many hard copies of the downloads I read were stored in the Library of Congress. Especially when it came to information about the towers. The Library of Congress had the world's only Tower Records, they were located in its Special Collections and Archives. From what I'd read, these records even had their own room. What was most unique was that every record was kept as a hard copy. There were no digital files. And only one copy. The towers were places of intense stealth research; archiving and documentation were integral to their very existence, but so was keeping information close and within.

Now that I was awake and aware, I understood several things about the Tower Records. If the United States housed the only information there was about the towers, they could monitor control one hundred percent of who got to read these files. The second was that they clearly had something to hide. Why lock down information in this way if they did not? Thirdly, they didn't want people to know they had something to hide, thus placing the information in "public." People knew where to find it, even if access was highly restricted. Fourthly, whatever they were hiding in these files was something they wanted to eventually destroy. One copy of a file on paper. Paper did not last forever. All it would take was a fire, or for the cooling and moisture system in the building to malfunction for a week, or a flood, or a thief. They were making these files easy to get rid of. I wondered about this, but had no answers.

It was shady. But this was what I now expected of my first and third country of birth.

It was my suggestion to go to the Library of Congress's Special Collections and Archives section before we formulated our plan of attack. I'd read plenty but not everything. I'd never thought to research myself. I'd never asked the Tower 7 Big Eye to show me the "File of the Phoenix." I'd never asked to see the files on any of the speciMen. I wanted to see those now.

We'd discussed it over dinner at Mmuo's small apartment. Saeed was eating a plate full of crushed concrete, rust flakes, and rubble he'd harvested from a soon to be demolished building. Mmuo and I were eating egusi soup and pounded yam and fried plantain Mmuo had prepared. He'd learned how to cook from his older sister. I just wished he'd agree to wear clothes when he cooked. My belly still ached from quietly laughing as I watched him squirm and curse whenever droplets of hot oil from the pan hit his skin. Mmuo hated clothes so much.

"You don't have to be a member of Congress to get in there," Saeed said, finishing his concrete. He had a pad of paper on the table and was doodling on it with a red pen. He was drawing circles and loops. He always did this when he was thinking. "The user cards that Mmuo and I have are for everyone."

"But those weren't easy for either of us to get," Mmuo added. "You have to have a license, passport or ID card, *and* submit to a background check."

"So how . . . ?"

"Black market," Saeed said.

After he'd returned from the Virgin Islands looking for Phoenix, Saeed had gotten a job teaching Arabic at a local Madrasah in New York. They hadn't been so impressed with his command of Arabic as much as they were with the stories he had to tell about Egypt. Parents brought their children to come hear him talk about the streets and how he'd survived. The imams at the Madrasah loved and embraced Saeed and gave him a room to live in along with his pay. It was here that he learned a bit of how to read in both Arabic and English. They asked no questions about his background but

Saeed suspected that they knew he was some sort of speciMen. Saeed said he'd used all that he'd saved up over the months to buy illegal access to the Library of Congress before Mmuo ran into him that day. Saeed could barely read, but he felt the answers he needed were in this building. He hadn't known about the Tower collection.

Mmuo refused to tell me where he got his money. All I knew was that he had a lot of it.

"If I can meet with a contact, I have an idea," Mmuo said.

When Mmuo had escaped from Tower 7, the nation's one and only black congressman managed to find him. Mmuo said the man was the most two-faced person he'd ever met. But he was one of those who used his bad for good. This congressman hated the tower projects and had promised Mmuo a favor.

Mmuo's rented solar-powered "smart" car had manual drive, a beat-up exterior, and nearly bald tires. "The rental car rep was a racist," Mmuo said with a shrug. "The man even asked me if I knew how to drive. I saw plenty of fine vehicles in the lot but this one was all he said he had available. The idiot could have rented me a much nicer vehicle and made more money."

It was a five hour drive to the Library of Congress in Washington D.C.

"I look colonized," Saeed muttered as he gazed at himself in the mirror. I agreed. I didn't like European suits, and I certainly didn't like them on Saeed. The colors were a dull navy blue, the tie looked like a noose and he looked so stiff. Saeed didn't look like the African Arab he was.

"I feel like a robot," Mmuo growled.

I stifled a laugh when I glanced at him. His suit was custom-made, covering his expansive long legs and arms. And it was grey. He did look like a robot.

It was 80 degrees outside, balmy December weather. I still couldn't understand why men in this day and age had to wear this outdated attire to look professional and respectable. These clothes were from cold times, before the climate had changed. Why couldn't the United States incorporate the world's fashions as the English language incorporated so many of the world's words? It was plain meshugana.

Our hotel room was small, but we had no intention of staying the night, so this was fine. After the long drive, I took a nap. Mmuo went for a walk. And Saeed quietly sketched fruits on his pad. We all had our ways of calming our nerves.

It was early afternoon. The Library of Congress was a few minutes' drive away. Saeed would take a quick cab there. We hadn't dared go to the building earlier to scope things out. The area was always under high surveillance, and we were fugitives.

I straightened out Saeed's collar and said, "It's for a purpose."

"Doesn't make it right," he only mumbled. Mmuo also muttered something, in Igbo. At least *they* didn't have to wear a burka.

Although Saeed was an Arab and thus would be profiled, he was the most safe-looking of the three of us. He was an attractive young man who could easily pass as the son of a wealthy businessman from Saudi Arabia. And that was what Mmuo was going to make him. Mmuo could not only walk through walls but he was also an intuitive hacker. If electronics were involved, he could manipulate them. This was how he'd gotten me to the 9th floor in the elevator in Tower 7, and it was how he "found" money now, outside of Tower 7. It was also how he was going to get us into the Tower Records. Not only could I read very very fast and remember all that I read, I knew how information was catalogued—from the old ways to the newest methods. I was our best bet in quickly finding what we needed.

However, I couldn't just slip and reappear in the Tower Records room. I'd read the Congress Library map many times and viewed the 3D image online. But the small room in the Special Collections library wasn't on the map. I could slip but I wouldn't know exactly where to come in and I couldn't risk being seen as I had been in Tower 1.

Saeed needed to escort me in to the Tower Records section. I was to be the meek hunchbacked Muslim woman with her curious, wealthy, politically influential husband. They would watch us, but they would let us in as they did so. Then Mmuo would cause the cameras to malfunction for ten minutes. I'd have to read fast.

A half hour later, Mmuo and I walked toward the White House. A storm was brewing and the air felt charged and smelled soily. It was probably raining somewhere nearby. The streets were busy as was the sidewalk. I could see the White House up ahead and a part of me wanted to stare at it. But that part was small. Most of me was focused and very aware of my black burka and hidden wings. There were men in business suits and women in high stylish heels, tourists with cameras and a few joggers. Almost everyone on the sidewalk was Caucasian. My wings itched. I missed Ghana. Kofi. I pushed the painful thoughts out of my mind. Saeed. Was he in yet?

Mmuo brought out his portable and looked at its round screen. "Almost," he muttered to me.

"Ok," I said. But how close was Saeed?

We were nearly at the White House.

"Nice weather, isn't it?" Mmuo said.

I met the eye of a man with sunglasses. He was jogging across the street, as we passed. I heard him jump onto the sidewalk not far behind us. I pressed my wings closer to my body.

"Yes," I said, trying to keep my voice from shaking. "I think we are overdue for some rain."

"Long overdue," Mmuo said.

His portable buzzed again, and we slowed down as he read. "He's going up the steps," he whispered to me. "I hope that Congressman was telling the truth about his signature."

"I thought you trusted this guy," I hissed.

"I don't trust any black man savvy enough to become a member of Congress," he snapped.

I sighed. "Sometimes all you can have is trust."

There was now another man walking behind us. The man in front of us was walking too slowly.

Mmuo checked his portable again. He smiled and said, "Okay."

I smiled too. Saeed was in.

We walked several more paces. The portable in Mmuo's pocket buzzed, and we stopped. We were at the White House gates. My heart was slamming in my chest as I looked at the elegant white building. This was not how I'd imagined seeing it for the first time. But then again, I'd never imagined I'd see it in real life. I glared at the symbol of all that had imprisoned me. I imagined it burned black, charred by my Phoenix-fueled flames.

There were seven men and one woman surrounding us. Just standing there. Four in black suits, one in jogging attire, the rest in street wear. Would they grab us? Shoot us? Not in this crowd. They knew who we were. Or maybe they were just profiling the tall African man and the tall crippled African Muslim woman in the burka. We perfectly fit the ridiculous profile I'd read so much about. In the capital and in other focal points of American society like Hollywood and certain parts of New York City, government officials were known for arresting minorities for no other reason than being a minority in an important place. Nevertheless, this time their profiling was dead on. We *were* terrorists.

"Sir, ma'am, please come with us," the suited African man beside Mmuo finally said. He was almost as tall as Mmuo but much more strongly built.

"We won't hurt you," the stocky white woman in jeans and a t-shirt said. Why did these people always think I was afraid of them "harming" me? But these people weren't the Big Eye. There was no hand grasping electricity patched to their chests. These were Secret Service. If I were a terrorist, shouldn't they have assumed I wouldn't "fear harm"? Shouldn't they have assumed I'd "give my life for my cause"? These people thought so little of minorities and terrorists. Deep down, they saw us all as cowards, no better than misguided sheep.

"Why?" Mmuo asked. I hesitated. This wasn't the plan.

"We just want to ask you a few questions," the man behind us said. They all looked tense, as we awkwardly stood at the intersection. The signal flashed white and an automated female voice told us to walk. None of us moved. People started to impatiently maneuver around us.

"Do you think we don't have places to go?" Mmuo asked.

"Sir, if you would . . ."

"Why do you people think you should control everything?" he snapped.

"We're not trying to do that, sir," another man said. They pressed closer, and I began to feel anxious.

"Not yet," Mmuo said to me.

"We're authorized to use force, if we must," the man in the jogging suit said. "All of us here deem your responses as suspicious activity."

Mmuo's portable vibrated in his hand and made the sound of a rooster crowing. In that strange moment, I was reminded of Ghana, again, where the roosters crowed at all times of the day. The seven police surrounding us jumped into motion, pulling out guns and shouting.

"Put your hands in the air!" The woman was screaming in my ear.

Mmuo handed the portable to me and it instantly started emitting an acrid stench of burning circuits and computer chips. I dropped it. Mmuo met my eyes, and I didn't wait for him to sink quickly through the concrete into the sewer system directly below us.

I slipped.

I arrived in the corner of the Great Hall on the first floor. This was a public area, so the 3D map I'd studied gave me the knowledge that I needed to arrive in the exact spot, not an inch off mark. Once I could imagine it, I could arrive there. I cannot tell you how I did what I did. It is not something words are equipped to describe. However, I could guide it. When I was so close, merely miles away, I could arrive on a specific spot. When I stepped into time, I carried my essence with me. So when I stepped out, I remembered they were malleable, both time and space. The closer, the softer.

I heard a gasp as the cool air hit my face. Then someone grabbed my hand and squeezed.

"Act natural," Saeed said. "Adjust. You're my wife. Meek, poor English. I am just curious about the towers. Walk with me, Phoenix."

Saeed and I started walking. My sandals softly tapping the shiny floor. When we reached the center of the elaborate hall, I stopped. "Wait," I whispered. "Mmuo needs time to get here, anyway. So give me a moment."

The hall was spectacular with Renaissance art carved into embroidered white columns and staircases. There were colorful panels in the archways and the ceiling reached high above the second floor. I was overwhelmed by the shift from being outside in the balmy air surrounded by Secret Service men and women outside the White House to being in the Library of Congress. I looked down at the floor to stabilize and orient myself. Marble, like Tower 7's but not white. Brown and yellow with brass inlays. I looked across the floor. The design that we stood on looked like a blooming sun.

"We were surrounded," I whispered, staring at it.

"Secret Service?"

"Yes."

"That fast?" he asked. "They must really hate our kind."

I chuckled despite myself.

"I think the library is on alert," Saeed said. We started walking again. "About a minute ago, I saw some guards jog past. They looked like they were heading to the front of the building, and they looked worried. But they haven't asked anyone to leave, so I think we're ok. They're likely focusing on the White House and the area around it."

If so, our plan had worked. This was why Mmuo and I had been at the White House in the first place. A diversion.

"Did Mmuo make it?"

"I don't know," I said. He had to catch a cab and this thought did not set me at ease.

We looked at each other and then looked away. I nervously surveyed the room. We were the only people of color in the Great Hall. I was an oddly shaped woman in a black burka, and I didn't have a library card. I felt ill. What would they do to Mmuo? And what would we do without him here?

My eyes fell on a tapestry on the wall. It was of a tall regal woman holding a scroll. This was the Minerva mosaic that I'd read about when studying the building's layout. Minerva was the protector of the United States. But I focused on the smaller statuesque woman standing on some sort of globe just below the regal woman's scroll. She had wings. This was Nike, the Greek goddess of victory. I stared at her realizing that I'd admired this image on the screen at Mmuo's apartment yet, for some reason, I hadn't connected her to myself. But now I did.

"They told me it's that way," Saeed said.

I nodded. He led the way.

"If Mmuo isn't able to alter the file, will they arrest us down here, do you think?"

"Me, but *not* you," Saeed said. "If anything happens, leave."

Minutes later, we were in an underground tunnel that led us to Special Collections and Archives. The man at the help desk had looked at us with such scrutiny when we'd asked about the Tower Records that I thought it was over right then and there. Then he'd said, "Right this way." We followed him through the stacks to a glass door. He typed in a code, pushed the door open, scrutinized us again, and then held up a portable. He touched the screen and the face of another guard appeared, "You've got two, today," the help desk man said.

"Ok," the guard on his screen said. "Send them in."

The pathway was long, the walls white. I shivered. It reminded me of the hallway in Tower 1. All it needed was the grey railing on the sides.

Only two people were allowed in at a time and clearance was tight. As we waited for the guide to check us out, I held my breath and looked through the second set of sealed glass doors into the sterile white room. The glass was most likely bullet-proof. There was nothing on the walls, nothing on the ceiling. The guard only had his silver chair to sit in. I wondered how he withstood spending hours in this place.

He frowned at us. Then took Saeed's library card and touched it to the flattest portable I'd ever seen. It looked like a hand-sized sheet of glass. It lit up a soft periwinkle then it turned green and said, "Prince Osama bin Abdullah of Jeddah, Saudi Arabia and wife are allowed into Tower Records. One hour. No photos, please."

I forgot about Saeed guarding the door. I didn't think about whatever it was that Mmuo had to do to get me into the full system. I ignored the silver buttons that were security cameras stationed in every ceiling corner. I didn't think about what would happen if anyone checked on us. I thought only about information. Answers. I thought back to my time in Tower 7 when I had their e-reader in hand. Before I began to heat.

These small stacks were arranged in an ancient format called Dewey Decimal. I'd studied it, so there was no need to ask the guard for help. I went to the card catalog in the middle of the room. I paused. "LifeGen Technologies," I whispered. I knew the name, but this was the first time I brought it to my consciousness, the first time I'd spoken it aloud. I'd always called them the Big Eye, as had the other speciMen I knew. But this was the official name of the company behind the towers, the hand that grasped the lightning bolt.

I looked up Tower 7 and found much of what I'd already read in digital format. Histories, the mystery of The Backbone, architecture. I also found what we were looking for. A single volume containing the "speciMen files" of Tower 7.

I can read fast and retain just about every detail, so I didn't need the pad and paper that Saeed gave me. As I read, I felt sweat between the feathers of my wings. Even though the room was kept at a cool temperature and low moisture level, I was burning up. My body felt as if it were on fire, but this time it was because I was burning so much as I processed what I read.

"What are you doing?!" Saeed hissed as I threw off my burka.

"Mmuo got us in, right? So, he had to also have done something to the security cameras," I said. "I remember when I was escaping Tower 7. He's thorough." I took a deep breath and let it out. "I need air. It's too hot."

"Phoenix, what if . . ."

"We take the chance," I snapped. "I need to breathe. This is a lot."

Saeed bit his lip, glanced at the cameras on the ceiling and then quickly nodded. He picked up my burka and got it ready to throw back over me. "Ok."

My eyes were watering from the stress of what I'd just read about Mmuo. Had they really peeled away all of his already special skin, injected it with some sort of sentient molecular shifting compound and then grafted it back on? I wiped my forehead as I read the most shocking part of his file. I glanced at Saeed.

"What?" he asked.

I shook my head and continued reading. He wouldn't believe it. I couldn't believe it. But I could. I'd seen the red creature in the glass box in Tower 1. It had looked like a light dust until I broke the glass and it came out. Then it had shifted and solidified into a tall praying mantis-like creature. The more I read, the gladder I was that I'd freed it.

According to the information in Mmuo's file the creature was an intelligent alien from Mars, befriended and then captured and brought to earth by a young man from the Mars colony. This young man had forced the creature to divulge its technological knowledge about molecular control and reorganization. This information was passed to Tower 7 scientists and then used to create Mmuo's skin.

Mmuo had endured the peeling and grafting without any anesthesia.

This was why he could slip through more than wood. He hated clothes because his skin wanted to see everything. I shuddered. Mmuo's file marked him as "fugitive."

The idiok baboons who could speak in sign language were having their brains tested and extracted. They'd been caught in the Congo and even then were able to fully communicate with their captors in perfect sign language. The Big Eye believed the baboons had quickly taught themselves the language in order to communicate with their captors. What got Tower 7 interested in them was the fact that they could tell the future. One of them, the only female, kept telling Tower 7 to stop doing what they were doing, that if they didn't, they'd bring the end of the world. But no one listened to her. All the idiok were marked as "deceased," most of them dying in Tower 7's collapse.

Saeed was a weapon, as I was. In his file they called him, "The Seed." (The play on his name was surely not a coincidence. The Big Eye scientists were known to have a sick sense of humor. Even The Backbone was created as a joke.) He was the prototype of the soldiers created to seed disaster zones after dropping nuclear bombs on enemies. "The Seed" were human killing machines who would go in and kill off survivors to make sure the enemies were fully defeated. Saeed didn't know it but he was resistant to radiation, too. Or maybe he did know. Maybe this was one of the many ugly secrets he kept from me. Saeed could never die of cancer. His file marked him as "deceased."

There was no file on the winged man. I hadn't expected there to be. The winged man was someone that Tower 7 probably kept secret from even *itself*.

My file had its own LifeGen Technologies mini-booklet. My belly dropped. Why did I have so many pages? Why was I a company-wide speciMen, as opposed to just Tower 7? There was nothing more extraordinary about me than Mmuo or Saeed. Saeed was classified as a weapon, just like I was.

As I read, my legs grew weak, and my mind tried to grow cloudy. The information I learned was poison. How could I have no father? How could I be nothing but a cataclysm spurred by weapon engineers and scientists? I was nothing but the result of a slurry of African DNA and cells. They constructed the sperm and the egg with materials of over ten Africans, all from the West African nations of Nigeria, Ghana, Senegal, and Benin. Then they combined all that with DNA from Lucy the Mitochondrial Eve, the ten-year-old Ethiopian girl who carried the complete genetic blueprint of the human race. The girl who could remember every part of her life; the girl whom they tried to make immortal.

My eyes watered, but I read on. Something was coming. But I didn't stop reading. An African American woman carried me to term, and when I was born, she wanted to keep me. They wouldn't even let her kiss me goodbye. The woman had eventually gone mad and had to be committed to a psychiatric ward in New York, not far from Tower 7. The doctors could not figure out why she had grown so attached to me. They had told her nothing about the type of child I was, and they'd paid her and her family several millions of dollars; she'd rejected her portion after my birth. They gave the address of the psychiatric ward. I would remember it.

I kept reading. There it was. My surrogate had given birth the day after a sizable solar flare. There was a black out, and I'd been delivered in the darkness. When I was born, I was the brightest light in the room. They didn't know what happened or how it happened. They speculated that maybe there was a chemical reaction because of all their mixing and the solar flare. What they quickly understood was that I was special. And they could cultivate my specialness.

I died when I was 1 month old. I looked about two years old. I'd run a fever, begun to glow brightly, then simply burned up. Minutes later I came back, good as new, a naked two-year-old-looking brown child with a head full of black puffy hair. I don't remember any of it. The Big Eye were so excited about me, and this excitement was expressed in the way my doctors and the scientists documented my case. They used words like "epochal," "monumental," and "revolutionary." I could burn and then live again. A reoccurring small nuclear bomb. They raised me like an android, not a human. I hadn't burned again until last year.

There was nothing about me sprouting wings. Not a word. I wiped my face and sniffed. "They didn't predict that," I whispered. I stretched my wings until they grazed the ceiling, loving them more than ever. "They hadn't really predicted anything. They just let themselves think they did." It was easy to see how they lost control of me.

I slammed my file shut. Then I opened it again and flipped to the very end. I was marked as "Fugitive and lethal. Acquire and manage before end of Solar Cycle." Then there at the bottom of that page there was one small note. "Information to be used in tandem with HeLa, Tower 4, US Virgin Islands".

"HeLa?" I whispered. "Interesting."

Lastly, just before we ran out of time, I had a chance to skim the financial status of the towers. Billions and billions of dollars, euros, and yuan were poured into the towers each year. But here was the twist: even more money was earned through patents, research results, and other things that were called names like "Project X" and "Experiment 626" or simply coded numbers. I had very little time to read and process the information in the financial book but one thing did catch my eye. Eighty percent of the billions earned came from Tower 4 in the Virgin Islands, where Saeed had been sent when they thought he was dead. Tower 4 was the hub of the towers' income. The money was accredited to the sale of 2839, 2840, 2842, 2843 and 2844. There was also a large portion accredited to "harvests."

My mind was so full that I barely noticed when Saeed threw the burka over me. I wasn't paying attention to the guard swiping Saeed's card again. I didn't hear him wish us a nice day. I barely felt Saeed's bone grinding grip of my hand as we quickly, but not too quickly, exited the library. The taxi ride to the Pakistani restaurant twenty minutes away was a blur. Only when I spotted Mmuo at the table did I leave the ocean of Tower Records information that now lived in my head. I joined my two friends in a victory dinner.

Mmuo and I ate beef seekh kebabs and chicken biryani, and Saeed had only water. And at that corner table surrounded by gregarious immigrant men taking breaks from driving their taxies, I told them everything. We spoke of violence, revenge, revolution, and more violence. Mmuo stabbed at his kebabs with a fork and then ate the mangled pieces. Saeed had to hide his angry tears.

When it was all said, discussed, and done, we realized that our plan was the same. Tower 4 in the US Virgin Islands was going down next.

CHAPTER 14

Flight

THE WIND TOOK ME. It was warm like the breath of a kind yet wild beast. And it was fragrant from the city's open night flowers and maybe The Backbone's blooms, too. When I closed my eyes and inhaled the heady air, I saw the red of roses and the light soft purple of lilacs and hyacinth. In the sunny sky where no skyscrapers reached, I spread my wings and climbed higher.

I laughed deep in my chest and I wept. This was the first time I'd relaxed enough to do nothing but enjoy the sheer groundlessness of flight. Nothing was beneath me, and I was alive and reveling in it. The rush of air caressed my sensitive wings. I felt my blood reach every part of my body. The buoyancy of the warm air was like the hand of something that loved me.

I pumped my wings hard and flew higher. My cheeks ached from grinning so hard. Nothing was chasing me. Nothing was trying to imprison me. Below, Saeed and Mmuo waited on my return, talking about whatever it was they talked about when I was not there. Plans. Not for revenge, but for justice. For the first time in my existence, I felt balanced.

Was this what the birds felt every day? This joy? I hit a thermal, and I felt like I'd slipped outside of time; everything stopped and grew peaceful. The rush of air in my ears was gone, the gentle press of the wind ceased; I no longer had to flap my wings. The warm coil of air held me, gently. If there was a God, it was up here.

Slowly, I spiraled, up and up. Every part of me was alive, awake, in tune. Humming. And it was to the beat of the earth below and the stars above. We'd driven far enough from the city to escape the worst light pollution. So on top of all this, I could clearly see the stars. For the moment, I made complete harmonious sense. No matter the genetic selection, the forced fertilization, the careful cultivation, the skeletal molting. I made sense. I was natural. A child of The Author of All Things. I giggled in the silence. "Thank you," I whispered.

In the distance I could see the city's downtown skyscrapers, The Backbone standing tall and audacious, as if it belonged there more than the solid buildings around it. *What must you have seen in Tower 7,* I wondered for the first time. Of all the prisoners of Tower 7, only The Backbone had witnessed everything, because it grew through floor after floor. When I shined my light on it, the energy of its rage was the greatest, and it was no wonder. The Backbone knew all the secrets of Tower 7. It had borne witness. It had witnessed them make me. *I want to know, too,* I thought. *How did they make me?*

Mmuo once told me that his father was fond of this phrase, "When a student is ready, a teacher appears." Mmuo's father was an extraordinary man.

"Phoenix," he said.

I screeched but I managed to hold my wings steady. Where had he come from? The winged man flew like an owl. His feathers and light clothing made not a sound as he flew above me.

After regaining my composure, I looked over at him for a long time. I wanted to frown at his invasion of my privacy, but that is the thing about the winged man, each and every time I saw him, instead of feeling fear, I felt relief. I pondered this for a moment. Was this what having a "father" felt like? The presence of relief? The presence of safety? I spoke the first question to pop into my mind.

"What do I call you?" I asked.

I could hear him chuckle, deep and amused. His voice was in my ear.

"Always, people must categorize those things that defy their understanding," he said. "They must name. Without a name, how can one command or control?"

"That is not what I meant," I said.

"We should fly lower," he said. "We are not astronauts."

He was right. I hadn't noticed how high we were. The air here was thinning, and it was harder to breathe. I followed his lead, and we flew out of the thermal column, swooped close to the ground and caught another thermal.

"It is good to fly," he said after several moments. "There is freedom in it. I'm a firm believer in freedom, Phoenix."

"And justice," I added. "You love justice."

"I do."

Saeed had collected several newsfeed articles written up about "the winged human speciMen on the loose" who stalked the skies and repeatedly came to the rescue of people in need—from people in car accidents, to mugging victims, to attempted suicides. They were calling him "Seven" because everyone knew he was one of the experiments who'd escaped from Tower 7. His escape had been caught on camera.

Mild speciMen, especially clones who'd emerged from the experiments too normal to be of use, were a tiny accepted part of the American population. This was common knowledge. However, rogue extreme speciMen like myself, Mmuo, Saeed, and the winged man were fugitives. Why the winged man had decided to become the city's vigilante was beyond me. True justice was in freeing those in the remaining towers.

"Call me what the newspapers call me. Seven," he said. "That is not my name but it will help you with your problem."

"Ok," I said.

"I wanted to speak to you alone," he said. "Before you three leave for the island."

"Aren't you coming with?"

"No."

"Why?! We need you!"

"There is something I must do here," was all he said.

I frowned, fighting back tears of frustration. We'd all assumed the winged man, Seven, would know of our plan (the way he always knew how and when to find us) and come with. If he didn't go with, then maybe it wasn't a good idea. Maybe.

"Phoenix, you all must go," he said. "You will find something there. I need to find something here, too."

"Is it in The Backbone?"

"No," he said. "But you are right to think in that direction. It is not done here with Tower 7. But above all things, above what I find here and what you three find there and what the others find—"

"Others?"

"You need to find that which is in you," he finished, ignoring my question.

"What? I don't understand."

"You didn't understand how to slip, either," he said. "But you could do it." He paused. "Why do you want to destroy the rest of the towers?"

"To free the others."

"But you don't know what lives in them."

"I don't care," I said. "I know enough. I know the specialties of all the towers. I have read about them. I had access to the information. The Big Eye were so stupid, they thought I would remain content, so they never really worried about what I read." I considered how right they'd been for the two years of my life. Until Saeed and the apple. "Freedom. We *all* should have it."

"All things are a part of The Whole," he said. "All things can heal. All things have a spirit. Everything is powerful, Phoenix Okore. But the towers are violating all that is natural, they are endangering life on earth in its totality—animal, plant, soil, sand, iron, stone, and sky. You three are correct, something must be done; the others need to be freed. You know this instinctively. Even when you freed me in Tower 7, so unsure of what you were or your destiny."

"What's my destiny?"

He laughed.

"What's yours then?" I asked. "Why were you in that glass prison?"

"You don't ask the right questions," he said, growing serious.

I gasped, suddenly understanding. "You let them capture you," I said. I tried to think of a better question but nothing came. My mind was too full of wind.

"Fly," he said, looking at me. He looked toward the downtown of the city. "I must go."

Before I could say more, he was gone. I wanted to ask him who he *was*, *where* he came from, *what* he was. I wanted to ask him why he'd allowed them to catch and "crucify" him. How long had he been there? And how much did he know about *me*. What was he and what was I? He'd said I had to understand myself but . . . when I thought about it, well, what was I, really? How'd they *make* me? There were only three ways I could get these answers—from Seven, the Big Eye, or The Backbone. None of them would give me any answers. In the meantime, I wanted justice.

I rode three more powerful thermal columns. In the third one, I was joined by a large brown and white sea hawk. We flew together in silence for five minutes. It gave a few sharp whistles when it finally flew off. The gesture was so sweet that my heart ached. I had friends. I decided to return to my friends on the ground.

Saeed and Mmuo were leaning against the hood of Mmuo's car rental. Saeed was eating from a bag of rust flakes and crushed glass, and Mmuo was peeling and eating a mango.

"What did you talk about?" Saeed asked me, shielding his eyes from the sun as he looked at me.

So Seven had been to meet them either before or after me. "He said I should call him Seven."

Saeed and Mmuo laughed. "It doesn't matter what you call him," Saeed said. "No name will ever suit him."

We had a plan. A good one. The first step was to get on the ship.

CHAPTER 15

Cruise Ship

THEY WERE CALLING MY NAME.

We'd been too busy doing what terrorists do to realize it was all over the newsfeeds. How did they even *know* my name? "The Phoenix Okore burned our chains!" they shouted, waving what I recognized as the Ghanaian flag, their fists in the air. Some of those fists were flesh, some were metal and some were claws. I stared out the tiny window at the ocean, trying to ignore the broadcast Mmuo and Saeed were watching on the jelli telli stretched across the entire back wall of the small room. But how could I ignore revolution?

The speciMen who were calling themselves the "Ledussee" ("let us see") must have hacked into the system of the Big Eye. Or . . . the footage Kofi recorded of me just before the Big Eye came to his house for us, it must have automatically uploaded to a page online. Yes. How else would they know to call me "okore"? Why else would they wave the Ghanaian flag? "I'm Phoenix Okore, and I am in Wulugu, Ghana," I had said, looking into the eye of Kofi's portable.

"This isn't a bad thing," Mmuo assured me. He grinned. "Phoenix, this is a *movement*. You started a movement."

"No," I said. "*We* did. You opened that elevator for me, didn't you? Saeed, you tried to destroy that evil machine." I narrowed my eyes, feeling my anger with him flare. A part of me was still upset at him, though I knew it wasn't his fault. "You threw the 'apple of knowledge' at the devil's machine."

"Someone had to," Saeed said, looking me in the eye. My fury didn't bother him. "But they are not shouting *our* names, are they? Just yours."

"What?!" Mmuo exclaimed. I turned around. He was staring at the jelli telli with his mouth agape. "But that can't be!"

Now there was a well-dressed African anchorwoman on the screen speaking directly to us as she sat behind a desk. " . . . just breaking, but the standoff between Nigerian soldiers and the Anansi Droids 419 has been going on for days. Sources say that these spider-like artificially intelligent robots, whose job is to protect the nation's oil pipelines, are malfunctioning and the only person preventing a bloodbath is a woman named Eme. She is a local from the Niger Delta and she seems to have managed to befriend one of the droids. The local people here call the droids 'zombies' after the song 'Zombie' by afro-beat legend Fela Kuti, a song about corrupt government officials who do not think and only kill.

"All of Nigeria's pipelines have been shut down by the droids and no human being is allowed near them. This standoff will affect the world. Expect fuel prices to increase. American President Chan will speak tonight on how the United States plans to help Nigeria with this crisis."

Mmuo laughed ruefully. "When the roots of a tree decay, it spreads death to the branches. Trust me, this is happening elsewhere."

Saeed called up the jelli telli's virtual controls, when he shifted to search mode and they turned blue. "Most likely the speciMen have made it to Mexico or even managed to get on planes," Saeed said. "The United States isn't the only country producing us."

"Anansi Droids will cross the ocean, ready to hate whatever human beings they find," Mmuo added. He shook his head.

I turned from the jelli telli and smoothed out my dress. I looked at the open door into the night.

"You don't have to do this," Saeed said.

"Stop saying that. I know," I snapped.

"You'll really be all right?" Saeed asked.

"Of course. I'll be *flying*." I paused, anxious to get going. " I can't believe I've even set foot on this ship. It's only for you two that I do. If you two were black Americans, you'd understand better."

"But you could lose the ship," he said. "What if there's a storm and you get blown away?"

I laughed, turning back to him. He looked embarrassed, but still expected an answer. "I've crossed the ocean twice," I said. "The second time, I followed the Big Eye's ship. It was easy."

"But this time, during the day, you can't let them see you," he said.

"I know. I'll just fly very high." I kissed him on the lips and forehead. "I'm going."

Saeed only frowned.

"And food?" Mmuo asked, as I stepped toward the door that led outside to a service walkway on the side of the ship. "I know we've been over this, but you're really ok without food?"

"I can go the whole three days without food," I said. "My body will take care of it. But I'll stop in every night, to see Saeed and eat." The sun had gone down and the ship was setting off. I stepped out onto the narrow walkway on the side of the ship.

Can you hear me? Mmuo asked just as I took off.

"I hear you," I said, flying into the night.

"Good," he called after me from the walkway. I glanced back and saw that Saeed stood behind him. But it was too dark to see his face.

I flew with the stars and the early full moon, alone and away from everything and everyone, the ship a twinkling mass of lights below as it waded out to sea.

We'd driven hours from New York down to Port Carnival, a Florida cruise ship, cargo and naval port not far from Orlando. Mmuo's congressman connection had come through for him a second time by procuring a ticket and false papers for Saeed on a Disney Cruise Ship leaving from Port Canaveral. Saeed effortlessly got through customs and onto the cruise ship with his suitcase carrying all of our things. Once onboard, a man wearing a white uniform with copper-colored skin and the jet-black hair of a TV star had stepped forward and immediately escorted him to room 31 in the servant quarters. This man was named Andres.

Mmuo had to use other means to get to room 31, a room right next to a door that led outside to a narrow walkway linking to another part of the ship. First Mmuo dove and swam to this side of the ship and entered from its bottom. Once inside, he had to find room 31. He was naked; Mmuo could not pass through walls with clothes. All he had were the room number the congressman had given him, of the dining room, and his memory of the detailed 3D image of the ship. The plan went smoothly until he was onboard. He'd passed his hand through both Saeed and me giving us his nanomites; in this way we could hear him as he searched for us. He ran about, passing through wall after wall before he found our room.

My job was less complex. I waited until night and then flew around the ship until I saw the narrow walkway on the starboard side of the ship where Saeed stood waiting for me. The ship was over a thousand feet long, 125 feet wide and could carry 4000 passengers. My job wasn't nearly as difficult as Mmuo's, but finding a small walkway on such an enormous vehicle wasn't easy, either. I flew back and forth several times, and there were people on deck and on the busier main walkways, as well. I had to stay out of sight.

The cruise ship would take three days to get to the Virgin Islands. I could have slipped or flown, but neither of those ways allowed me to travel with Mmuo and Saeed. It was too risky for anyone of us to take an airplane. There was a rebellion of speciMen cyborgs happening and they were calling my name. Saeed was considered dead. And both Mmuo and I were also all over the news for being spotted near the White House.

The whole country was on high alert for the "two escaped and dangerous African speciMen" and the Big Eye were scouring the nation for us. As far as we could tell, they had not figured out that we'd been in the library. Not yet. If I separated from Mmuo and Saeed now, we'd never find each other. So this was the best option, Saeed and Mmuo on the ship, me in the air. I finally had to set foot on an actual ship. Our plan was to destroy Tower 4; good enough reason.

CHAPTER 16

Limbo

THE WINGED MAN WOULD HAVE understood how I felt. Seven was out there protecting and saving people like some New Mythology super-hero. Where the new myths had villains like Penguin Men, Goblins, and Human Magnets, Seven had the Big Eye. To both of us, the taste of justice was sweet, metallic, and warm. However, up here, in the sky, above and away from everything, with no one but the sun and the spiraling columns of warm air during the day and the moon and whipping cool winds at night, it was easy to be that which was separate from anything alive. It was easy to be that which knew death, intimately. During the hours where I had to fly high above the ship to stay out of sight, I often had to work to keep the ship in sight—not because it was difficult to do, but because I'd become Other up there.

It was not silent. The air rushed past, below, above, into, and behind me constantly. It was noisy, harsh, and smelled like the ocean even up here. I spread my bright red wings wide, feeling with every one of my cells but at the same time blending with the air. Then the sun would set, and I would hear Mmuo in my head, "Phoenix, come back." Familiar words to me that always managed to bring me back to myself, no matter where I was. And it was when I set foot on that ship, smelled the food cooking and chlorine from the ship's many swimming pools, got a whiff of sewage from the ship's plumbing, when I smelled the general smell that human beings give off when in a community, that I remembered the burning, rolling, vibrating ball of heat inside me.

I saw Saeed and Mmuo for about two hours in the evening. "We stay out of sight and help some of the workers when we can," Saeed said. He shook his head. "They work these people too hard."

Because he was good with machines, Mmuo worked with two men from Colombia in the engine room. Both of these men had been engineers in Colombia and couldn't find work. Neither spoke English, but they knew exactly who Mmuo was and were delighted. "They are constantly grinning at me and shaking my hand," Mmuo said. "One even brought a piece of paper and a pen for my autograph."

Saeed said there was also a Yoruba worker on the ship named Omo who had taken a liking to Mmuo. So much so that Mmuo kept disappearing with her. "She's not an engineer," was all Saeed said. I never saw her, but I was glad for Mmuo. From what Saeed said and what Mmuo refused to discuss with me, Mmuo hadn't been with a woman since he was imprisoned in Tower 7. That was seven years. I didn't know much about men and knew even less about sex, but if I had to guess, this was a long time for a man.

Saeed volunteered to help wait tables at one of the restaurants near the swimming pool. He said several women made passes at him, even going so far as giving him their room keys.

"The women here behave worse than whores," he muttered that second night as we ate in the small room. Today's meal was roasted chicken, asparagus, some kind of salty rice, and a dessert of canned peaches. I found the meal disgusting and only nibbled at the rice. Mmuo turned on the jelli telli, and the next thing I saw was my face and the words "Phoenix Rising" in charred letters and "Ledussee the Future" just below it on the CNN channel. No anchorperson explaining, warning, or discussing. No ads scrolling by on the top, sides or bottom of the screen. Just my face and those words. A full minute passed, and my face and those words were still there.

"They've hacked CNN," Mmuo said, grinning. He sat down on his bed, staring at the screen.

Saeed giggled and then glanced nervously at me.

I got up, my legs shaky. I glanced at the image one more time. The image of me looked intense and unsmiling; like I was staring right at the camera, at you. My bald head was shiny with sweat, and I was glowing. The image was from Tower 7, maybe right after I realized I could wipe my hair away. When had that image been captured? The Big Eye and their big eyes.

I sighed and ran my hand over my short hair, enjoying the feel of its roughness on my palm. "I will see you tomorrow night," I muttered. Then I quickly threw open the door to our room, then to the outside, and I flew off. I had one more full night to fly alone before we'd arrive at the Virgin Islands. One more night in limbo.

The ship arrived at the Ann E. Abramson Pier that morning. And when the time came, Mmuo disrobed, sunk through the ship's lower deck into the water and swam to a nearby quiet beach whose location we'd each intensively studied on the 3D map. He hid in a small cluster of palm trees and waited for Saeed to arrive with some clothes. I slipped and met him there a half-hour after he arrived. Saeed packed on the ship then got through customs using his passport. Once on land, he took a cab to the hotel near the beach and this is how he rejoined Mmuo and me.

But there is one more thing that I will speak of now, that I did not tell Saeed and certainly not Mmuo. I'd seen them just after the sun rose and only because the waters were so calm and the sky was so clear. The sunshine glinted off their shiny metal domes as they moved along. They had to be Anansi droids. They were about a mile from the cruise ship, moving in the opposite direction. I'd flown down for a closer look. There were at least fifteen of them, and they really did look like robot spiders! They were about the size of a small child. As I watched, several of them extended their long legs and spun over the surface of the water. Dare I say their movements were . . . playful? Some of them would drop beneath the water and come back up and spin some more. There were four that swam slowly a foot or two below the surface of the calm clear water, one on each side of the group, making a diamond formation.

I watched them for a while, wondering if they saw me, a bit afraid that they had developed the ability to fly, wondering where they were going, and wondering how much hatred they harbored for human beings. Then I flew back to the ship.

Human beings make terrible gods.

CHAPTER 17

Sandcastle on the Beach

IN THE US VIRGIN ISLANDS, they drove on the left hand side of the road though with American cars where the driver's seat was on the left. I never knew something so minor would make such a big difference. I felt so off balance.

The air was wonderfully humid. I wanted to tear my burka to pieces and let the breeze caress my wings. Instead, I walked meekly behind Saeed as we left the hotel to catch another taxi. There was a taxi station down the road just as the congressman said there would be and the man in the white van named Lurrenz was waiting in the driver's seat. Lurrenz turned out to be a Rasta with long bushy dreadlocks, an even bushier beard and green yellow and red wristbands on each wrist. He was chewing on a piece of coconut.

Lurrenz looked us over with wide almost scared eyes. "Good marnin'" he finally said, as he chewed. He pointed at Mmuo. "Are you Mmuo?"

"Yes," he said, firmly shaking his hand. "Lurrenz?"

"Correct. Welcome," he said. I'd expected his Caribbean accent to be stronger. He sounded as if he'd spent some time in the States. "Wow, cannot believe this." He looked at us with what I can only call admiration. "Get in," he said, looking around.

He scrambled out when he saw me slowly stepping up. "Let me help you," he said, firmly taking my arm. It was a tight fit for me, though not as tight as with a car. When I sat down, with my closely pressed wings facing the window in the first row of seats, I nodded my head so he could see my thankfulness. "Thank you," I said.

"You can take that off, if you like. The windows are tinted." He slammed the door shut, and I cringed as the door pressed my wings more tightly to me.

I looked at Saeed and Mmuo, who both nodded. Then I threw the burka off, shifted to face the door, and stretched my wings as much as I could in the cramped car. They pushed at the ceiling and seat uncomfortably curling over, some pressing into the side of Saeed's face. "Ahhhh," I sighed, even half-stretching my wings was relief. Lurrenz was watching me in the rearview mirror.

"Praise to the most high," he said. He started the car, and we set forth into the island of St. Croix.

The drive made me want to vomit. He drove carefully enough but the terrain was slightly hilly, and it was very windy. I held on as the car threw me from side to side. Saeed was quiet as he looked out the window beside me. Mmuo sat in the front seat.

"How de trip?" Lurrenz asked Mmuo.

Mmuo smiled and then laughed. "Uneventful."

It was a half hour drive to our destination. About halfway through, I realized I was feeling hot in a way that I could not control or understand. I wasn't glowing, and this heat wasn't intense, but I didn't feel right. Saeed pressed his hand to my cheek. "You don't feel hot, like . . . not like your kind of heat."

I nodded, trying to stay calm. "And I feel waves of hot and then . . . cold." I shivered, feeling a cool wave. Never in my life had I felt cool within my body. I'd have enjoyed the sensation if it weren't so wrong.

"Maybe, it's just fever," Mmuo said.

"I was goin' to say that," Lurrenz said, laughing. "I know what to do."

Five minutes later, he pulled to the side of the road. The stand was owned by some of his Rastafarian friends and they too had long dreadlocks. There was even a young boy smoking something that looked like a cigar. One of the men used a machete to slice off the top of a large coconut. He handed it to me, eyeing my wings. He offered me a brilliant smile and a wink.

"Do I need a straw?" I asked.

"No," he said. "Take and suck." He brought his hands together as if he were holding the coconut and pretended to bring it to his mouth.

I pressed my lips to the opening and took in the coconut water. It was refreshing and delicious, the temperature of the warm air. I drank the whole thing. By the time we arrived at the resort, my fever was gone.

We pulled up to a small white stone building whose top was tipped with pink. It looked old and comfortable, as if it had withstood many hurricanes. The road beside it was narrow and quiet, nothing but thin bush across the street and no buildings to the left or right of this one. Mmuo and Saeed got out of the car, but I hesitated.

"It's ok, darlin'," the driver said. "Just get into the building. You'll be fine. No guests here until day after tomorrow. Your man bought it out." He smiled. "Go and stretch your wings."

I don't know why, but his words made me want to cry. I saw no cybernetic limbs, mutations, alterations, additions, or subtractions on Lurrenz. He was just a man. He was like the people I met on my way to Ghana. He accepted what I was as if it were normal. He gazed at me but didn't stare. His world was big and there was room for me.

Saeed took my hand as I slowly got out and came around to the driver's window. "Thank you," I said to Lurrenz.

He took my free hand. "Jah will protect you." Then he kissed my hand and let us go. I felt like I'd been blessed. Coconut water sloshed in my belly as I walked with Saeed across the street to join Mmuo. We went inside. There were only three people in the hotel. The owner, his wife and his wife's brother. They stared at us as if we were, well, speciMen. However, they were kind, too.

They showed us to our rooms, promised to bring an early dinner in an hour, and quickly left us alone. The Sandcastle Hotel was right on the ocean. Our rooms opened to the most spectacular view I'd ever seen. White sands, light blue clear water. What struck me most was the noise the water made as it rushed up the beach and tumbled back. I'd never had a chance to actually *hear* the ocean. I'd never had a chance to just sit and listen to it like this. I was always flying over it. When I left Tower 7 the first time, I'd barely glanced at it as I flew clutching the alien seed. When I saw Africa's coast, I was so relieved to see land, that I didn't glance at the place where it met water. When I let the Big Eye capture me, I was too angry to care about seeing the beach. And when I arrived back in the United States, well, I skipped over the beach entirely and went for Tower 1.

Saeed and I had one room. Most of the furniture was wicker and had a beach theme. There was a jelli telli stretched across the wall of the main room and a kitchen stocked with fresh fruit, bottles of water and snacks. There were also bowls of rust flakes, crushed glass, and chips of concrete.

"They didn't have to do any of this," Saeed said, though he looked pleased. "I am fine making a meal of sand." He popped a flake of rust into his mouth and chewed. I shivered. His type of sustenance was not something I'd ever get used to.

The best thing about all the rooms was that the ceilings were high. I could move about freely. The shower was the grandest thing. Made of smooth marble, it was so wide that you had to step down into it. Using it was like stepping into a room with shower heads on the walls.

Mmuo disappeared into his room, shedding his clothes right at the door and walking through it. When I stepped out, his clothes were still there. Right outside my door was a table, shaded with an umbrella. Our early dinner was laid out on one of the tables. There was a plate of rust and a large glass of water for Saeed and for Mmuo and I, whole lobster tails, spiced rice, and slices of fresh mango.

"Very nice," Saeed said, sitting down.

I knocked on Mmuo's door. He didn't answer.

"He's probably asleep," Saeed said, his mouth full of rust. "Mmm, crumbles right in my mouth."

I sat down, and Saeed pushed my plate in front of me. I'd never had lobster. It looked like the nether region of a giant insect that had been broken open. I poked at it with my fork. It was soft, but tough. I speared it and when my fork barely penetrated it, I put it down and used my hands.

Saeed only laughed and shrugged. There was no one around, and we were speciMen. Who needed manners?

"Peel it from the shell," he said. "Dip it in that right there. It's melted butter."

It tasted like rubber dipped in butter. But I was hungry, so I ate it anyway.

Mmuo came out wearing nothing but white pants. He sat beside me and gazed at the food. He smelled as if he'd taken a shower. "This looks good," he said. He poked at his lobster tail with a fork and then dug into his rice. "When did they bring it?"

"I don't know," I said. "It was here when we came out."

He chuckled. "I think we are alone in this hotel."

"Good," I said.

"No, we're not," Saeed said, quickly getting up. He was looking behind Mmuo. I gasped and got up, too. The man had come around a corner right beside our room. He skulked and then lunged, less than a yard away. I saw him raising his hand, and I saw what was in his hand.

I slipped.

I was standing right beside him a second before he raised his gun; I grabbed it from his hand. Mmuo moved forward just as Saeed reached into the pocket of his pants. The man held up his empty hand, still unaware that there was no gun in it. He even tried to squeeze the trigger that was not there. Mmuo grabbed him by the neck and flung him against the door, sinking into the door and pulling the man against the wood. As the man choked, Saeed ran at him with his switchblade and held it to the man's neck.

I stood there, wide eyed, grasping the gun. The man wore a black military uniform and shiny combat boots. His hair was shaven close to his round head, his dark skin made his black uniform seem to fit even better. On his chest, at his heart was a white circle with a black hand grasping lightning bolts. He was a Big Eye. And Big Eye were like ants, where there was one, there were always more.

"Why are you here?" Saeed asked, pressing the blade to the man's neck.

When did he start carrying that? I wondered. He held it easily. Naturally. Maybe he'd always carried it.

The man squirmed. He was tall and strong. But Mmuo was taller and stronger and pulling his neck against the door from inside it. The man coughed. He might have been in his early twenties. "Please!" he managed to gasp. But Mmuo pulled harder.

"Call off the others!" Mmuo shouted from behind the door.

"I . . ." He hacked, gasping for breath.

Saeed pressed the blade closer. "Mmuo, let up! Let him talk!"

He gasped when Mmuo released his throat. "I came to ask for your help," he pleaded. He coughed. "Please! There's no one else!"

"Then what's the gun for?" I shouted.

"I'm not stupid," he said. "I work with your kind. I'd never come near any speciMen without bearing arms. Y'all crazy."

"How did you find us?"

"I work in Tower 4," he said. "Some . . . there're speciMen there who know of y'all. Especially you." He pointed at Saeed. "They said you'd come back, and you'd be staying at the Sandcastle Hotel. I been coming by here, checking."

Saeed looked as if he'd seen a ghost, the switchblade nearly dropping from his hand. Mmuo was silent behind the door. He lessened his grip on the man some more. I had his gun. Saeed stepped back. We waited.

"Don't kill me. Please," he said, raising both of his hands. "I'm on your side. For this. I'm asking for your help."

Saeed kicked one of the chairs to him as Mmuo shoved him forward and stepped through the door. The man slowly sat down. Mmuo stood before the man watching him, his arms crossed over his broad chest, stark naked. His pants had slipped off when he stepped through the door. The man stared back at him, but said nothing. Smart man.

"It was stupid to come with a gun," Mmuo muttered, moving to his plate of food. He picked up a lobster tail, peeled back the shell and bit into it.

"Maybe," he said. He was staring at me now.

"Talk," Saeed said.

"I guard the fifth layer," he said.

Saeed's hand twitched, grasping his switchblade. For a moment, I was sure he would shove it into the man's chest.

"Don't look at me like that, man," he said. "I never hurt any of those children. I . . ."

"Were you in the lower level?" Saeed snapped.

"Yeah. Sometimes," the man said quietly.

"And you did nothing to stop it?"

"What was I gonna do?" he said, looking away. "I know guys who tried, and they weren't just fired. They disappeared in the night, never to be seen again!"

"What is in the lower level?" I asked.

"That's where I woke," Saeed said.

"Shit," Mmuo said, looking hard at Saeed.

"Yeah," Saeed said.

"*What?*" I asked, annoyed.

Saeed shook his head. "Not now, Phoenix," was all he said. He turned to the man. "What is it that you want?"

"I didn't do the harvesting. I swear! I—"

"You just watched it happen!" Saeed shouted.

"Let him speak," I said. "Who are you? Why are you here?"

"My name is Dartise Lenard," he said, focusing on me. He was right to do so. I was the only one who wasn't looking at him with murder in my eyes. "I'm from Atlanta, Georgia and I started with LifeGen Technologies right out of college three years ago. Joining erased my ten years of academic indenture.

"I was stationed in Tower 4 a year ago and . . ." he looked at Saeed who was glaring at him.

"Go on," I urged.

He looked back at me and smiled sadly. "It was a dream come true. The Virgin Islands, like getting a job in paradise. They had me guarding the speciMen in the innermost layers because, well, they said I had a kind face, and I was black. The speciMen in this area preferred guards who were black and looked nice. I found out later that this is because these speciMen, though they long-lived, some over 70 years, stayed children. Children like faces that are soothing, friendly, smile easy. And children like faces that look like theirs. All these children were black—African, to be specific. Most of them were from Ethiopia, some were from Sudan. They were all real dark-skinned." He took a breath, glancing at Saeed. "So, these children . . ."

"Yes, tell us," Saeed said, though gritted teeth. "What about them?"

"They were special," he said. "I don't know the details. I just know we weren't supposed to ever touch them or let them touch us. They stayed in their rooms most of the time, so this wasn't a problem. But once in a while, we had to move them to places, to be . . . harvested."

I shivered. Saeed had been sent there when they thought he was dead. His body was still of use to the Big Eye, though I did not know what for. I didn't like that word, 'harvest.'

"The children were long-lived," he said again, looking away from me now. "And if you took a piece of them, it grew back. I don't know why or what LifeGen did to them."

I frowned at Mmuo, disgusted, then at Saeed, realizing why they'd taken his so-called body there. They'd wanted to harvest his body parts, too. Maybe even in death, his body survived. However, they'd been too right. Saeed wasn't dead at all.

"They didn't age," Dartise continued. "And a few of them could *see*, like, see the future!" He leaned forward. "The first day, one of them grabbed my arm when I was taking her to a lab. Contact was brief and none of the cameras caught it, I guess. There're lots of cameras there." He paused. "She said I was in the right place to make a difference. Didn't know what she meant, and I didn't care. Six months later, I had to escort a speciMen in the innermost layer. I was about to go home for the night when I was told that I had to walk number 782 to lab 12. I had to put on a radiation suit and mask. They told me not to speak to 'it' and to have 'it' walk in front of me at all times and to keep my gun pointed but never ever shoot or I would be fired. They hinted that worse would happen, too.

"I was tired and scared. Its name was HeLa and 'it' was a woman." He looked up at me. "She reminds me of you. But without the wings. That first time I met her two things happened. I took her to a lab where they harvested something more important than body parts from her and I fell in love."

I wanted to laugh. Mmuo actually did laugh. Saeed made a sound that sounded like hacking. This man wanted us to save a woman he'd fallen in love with. A Big Eye had fallen in love with a speciMen.

Saeed and Mmuo grilled Dartise for information and he seemed eager to give it once he calmed down. We listened to his stories of discovery, rupture, and blood in Tower 4. More of the wildest, darkest, rabid scientific sorcery. I kept quiet, but inside I felt my heat, my furious flames roiling.

At some point, the three of them started strategizing and a plan came together. Thanks to the desperate Dartise, the plan was solid. Once he left, we used the jelli telli to bring up the digital image of the earth. We zoomed in on Tower 4. It's amazing just how much detail the public world map will show of the towers. They certainly won't show you everything, but they show enough and give you a limited guided tour. To me, it's just more hiding out in the open. They pretend the work they do is innocent and non-secretive to keep people from asking more questions.

None of us spoke the obvious, that there was no turning back from here. Nor did we check the news. Whatever was happening in the rest of the world was not our business, at the moment. We were focused on Tower 4. We assumed there would be heightened security, and if there was not, better for us. We would free and destroy. There were only three of us, but as the world knew, even just one rogue speciMen could do a lot of damage.

Mmuo left, saying that he was going for a long walk. That left Saeed and me. The sun was setting.

Outside I could hear the ocean lapping at the beach; the sound soothed me. I leaned against the door and watched the sun slowly set. There wasn't a human soul on that beach, but I imagined there were plenty of other types. I imagined the Nigerian spider robots. What if they showed up on this beach? But I had a feeling they were more interested in bigger busier places that liked to consume energy.

Saeed rested his chin on my shoulder as he leaned against my wings. "Do you want to know the last time I was in a place like this?" he asked.

"When?"

"Never."

We both laughed.

"I saw the Nile River every day," he said. "It ran through Cairo, sluggish and muddy. This water is like liquid glass." He kissed my neck. "It's beautiful."

He breathed against my ear and everything shivered. The tips of my wings felt as if they were touching the world. "My goodness," I whispered. I wasn't sure what was happening to me. I touched my forehead as Saeed came around me, took my hand, and we went outside. The sun had set, but this didn't matter. There was no one else on the beach. I looked over my shoulder as we stepped onto the sand. Mmuo's door was closed.

The sand was soft on my bare feet and the water was warm. We walked out up to our knees.

"Have you ever tried swimming?" he asked as we stood looking out at the dark ocean. I was glowing slightly, and I could see hand-sized white fish swimming around my ankles and legs with curiosity.

"Never," I said. I bent down and touched the water. I was wearing one of my white dresses, and its hem was already wet. I touched my hand to my lips and tasted the salty water. "Maybe I'll die."

"You won't die," he said.

"I'm not you."

"Well, dying isn't exactly your worst enemy."

Laughing, I splashed him. He looked at me utterly shocked. Then he splashed me. I tried to run away and fell into the water instead, soaking my wings.

"Phoenix!" he said, running to me.

The water was so warm on my wings. For a moment, I just lay there, looking up at Saeed's extended hand. "Come," he said, hauling me up. I stood there, my wings soaked and heavy. He looked at me, breathing hard, nervous in the dim moonlight and the light from my glow. I was glowing brighter now, but I was not warm. "Are you all right?"

"My wings feel . . . oh, I love how they feel," I said. I waded out further and lay back in the water and floated on my back, my dress billowing around me. It was amazing; I intuitively knew how to swim. I didn't sink, the water carried me. The ocean was my father. The sky was my mother.

"Water is life," Saeed said, as he floated with me. For minutes, we were like that. Right on the edge of the ocean, on the precipice of something so much grander and long-lived than us. We could both feel it. Tomorrow was going to be something big, but for the moment, we were in a safe place. The water carried and cared for us. As I looked up at the moon, the ocean all around me, Saeed my love beside me, my brother not far away, in that beautiful place, the joyful salt water of my eyes mingled with the salt water of life.

It was the happiest moment in my life. There was sunshine pouring through me. Sunshine of the morning, not sunset. Life, not death. Tomorrow would be different.

I can't tell you how it happened. It's a blur in my mind. As if I became one with the ocean. Saeed and I. We shed our clothes at some point. We swam further. He'd learned to swim in the Nile and, like flying, swimming was built into my DNA. Neither of us feared the ocean though I knew there were things inhabiting it that not even human beings had glimpsed.

His skin was cool and his mouth tasted like sweet fruit and salt and his hands felt like the ocean's rough waves. I didn't know my body could do what it did. I had no idea it could feel what it felt. He kissed my lips, my chin, my neck, my breasts, and every part of me sang. I glowed, lighting up the fish below us. My wings stretched out in the water. I lay back as he lay on me. I carried us both.

Saeed pulled my hips to his, holding me down as my wings stretched. He wouldn't let me fly off even if I tried. I wasn't just on fire, the whole world around me was aflame.

There was pain and then there was heat. I opened my mouth and inhaled the ocean air.

"Are you all right?" he asked.

"Yes," I whispered. How could he understand what I was seeing? How could I explain it?

I was still seeing the night on fire.

When he finished there was blood, and we moved out of the water. I wasn't sure what he'd done to me, though it felt right. Was this sex? I'd read about it in several of the books I'd consumed in Tower 7. I hadn't screamed. I didn't feel dirty or sad or guilty. I didn't feel I'd lost anything. I wanted to ask Saeed what it was we'd just done, but I didn't. I felt refreshed with salt water. I felt clean. Even my wings seemed to glow a deeper gold red. Why lose that feeling by talking about it? My wings felt like a thousand pounds when I got out of the water. I shook them and they felt a little better.

"Will they dry quickly?" he asked, worried.

"I'm not worried," I said, smiling. As we walked to our room, I heated my wings and steam rose from them in a soft mist. By the time we got to the door, they were dry. I shook the salt from them and stretched them out wide.

"Look!" Saeed said, running his hands over the feathers. "The color!"

I held them out and looked at the tips. I was not glowing but the golden red was so brilliant that it made my eyes ache. Even in the darkness, it was like seeing blood. I gasped. It was not only the color. My wings felt light and loose and powerful. I shook them out, again, and folded them behind my back. Pulling them close was easier than ever. A few old feathers fell to the sand and Saeed picked up the biggest one.

"Mine," he said.

I laughed. "If you want it."

He put it into his pocket after he put his shorts back on.

We went inside. The shower was wide and open and I had no problem fitting in here with him. He bathed me from head to toe. Avoiding my already clean wings, he lathered my skin and then he rinsed me. Three times. Almost like a ritual.

Then he did the same for himself. After, he washed his hands, then arms, then his feet, then his face three times. "It's the only thing I remember my father teaching me," he whispered to me when he finished.

He dried me with one of his towels. Then he dried himself. "I feel stronger when I touch you," he said, as he rubbed shea butter into my skin. "You're always so warm."

"And you are always so cool," I sighed. His flesh didn't warm when it touched mine and the cool sensation of his hands moving along my body was heavenly. We lay in bed and fell asleep before I remembered to tell him that I loved him.

CHAPTER 18

Deus ex Machina

I WENT FLYING BEFORE THE SUN CAME UP, an hour before we would leave.

I'd woken up beside Saeed, my body sweetly aching. I couldn't enjoy it, however. My eyes were open wide. I was seeing something terrible, again. I was seeing what I'd seen while with Saeed in the ocean. The world was on fire. Even the air. I couldn't breathe because the air was being sucked from my lungs.

I gasped, my mouth wide and Saeed's hand came across my waist and held me tighter while he slept. It didn't help.

I quickly but quietly slipped out of bed, threw on my dress and stepped outside. The night was warm. It felt close, pressing against my body. Behind me, the first and third man I'd ever loved slept. I fought the urge to go back and join him for a last two hours of rest. But I was seeing something terrible and to return to him would only prolong the vision. I needed the sky.

I cocked my head and listened to the ocean crashing against the earth for a moment. Then I opened my wings and took off. The air was light, and I immediately found a nice strong thermal. I flew faster, as if my wings were on fire and I was trying to put them out. My entire body burned and that image was still in my mind.

As I flew in the warm air, I cooled. My bright wings glowed a little but I relaxed. Soon all I could feel was the ache of my body from Saeed's deep touch. I rolled in the sky, the air caressing me. "Saeed," I whispered, my eyes closed, my hand on my belly and between my legs—the two places where I felt him most strongly.

I opened my eyes to find the winged man flying beside me, dimly lit by my light. Watching. My heart flipped, but quickly calmed. I said nothing as I removed my hands from myself. And we flew higher. Then we slowed down, soaring.

"Today will be your day," he said. He spoke with his lips and a straight face. No smile. No frown. Raw fact.

"How do you know?"

He chuckled.

"Will you help?" I asked.

"My place is not here, not today," he said.

"Then where?"

"New York."

I considered asking the obvious, which was "Why?" but I really didn't care. All I cared about was that he was not going to help us. What was he here for then? What was he? "Who are you, Seven?" I asked, frowning.

"You need to focus your anger," he said.

"I'm not angry."

"Oh, you are angrier than any woman I know," he said, perceptively. "And that is good. But you need to *focus*. If you remember none of what I tell you, remember that."

I spoke nothing. But in my mind I said, "I will."

"Let's land there," he said, pointing down. It was black over the ocean.

"Where? I cannot . . ."

"Just follow me."

We flew down, and I could hear it before I could see it—waves rushing onto sand. I nearly crashed into the beach the tiny island was so dark. Right off of St. Croix. There was not one light on it. No one lived here. A mile or two across the water, the lights of St. Croix shined brightly.

"You know the beginning of war, but you don't know how it will end," Seven said, as he looked across the water.

"Sometimes," I whispered. "This doesn't matter."

"It always matters," he said. "The beginning and the end always matter." He paused for a moment and sat down on the beach. This was the first time I'd ever seen him put his body to rest in any way, I realized. He'd always been standing or flying. Except for those moments before I freed him from the glass dome and when he contained me between his wings when I burned. I sat beside him.

"I do not remember my beginning," he said. "I was born in the Wassoulou region in South Mali. I grew up thinking I'd become a mechanical engineer. I wanted to create a car that could fly and run on recycled garbage. I went to the Université Mentouri de Constantine in Algeria, and this was my major. I was the second in my family to go to university.

"My sister, she'd left home six years before me. She wanted to become a singer. It was her destiny. Her mother, my father's first wife, died right after giving birth to her. But before she went, she predicted that Nahawa would touch the world with her voice, that she would be a famous singer. My father's family was completely against Nahawa's singing, though her voice was sweeter than any you heard on the radio. My family was not of the *jali* tradition, that's a caste of people who have music in their blood. They even resorted to traditional magic to prevent her career. But it was inevitable. Her first album was a hit all over the country and soon after that, she left home to record more overseas. None of us ever saw my sister again. It's as if the world swallowed her up.

"So you can understand why my leaving sent my entire family into chaos. We did not know if my sister was dead or alive. To me, she was dead because she cut herself off from us. I knew her well. She had always been ashamed of our simple desert life. She did not speak this to my parents but she did to me and my five brothers. She was the only girl. My mother worked Nahawa hard. But she was smart in school and she knew how to ask questions.

"When I went to school, my parents would not let me leave unless I performed all these binding rights. Once in university, my life changed in a way that I cannot explain to you. What I can tell you is that I found my other family in Algeria. A secret society. In my region they were called Leopard Society. What I also discovered in university was that I was an athlete. In my hometown, I was known as one of the top wrestlers. But by the time I got to college, with all the food that I was able to eat with my scholarship money and from working as I studied, I grew tall and big.

"I began to compete in my society's tournaments and became a champion. I graduated with my degree in engineering, but by then my champion status took over my life. I visited home, and my family barely recognized me. I showered them with gifts and love. They knew that I was part of something but they could not know I was within the Leopard Society."

He paused and looked at me. I couldn't help but smile. I had a thousand questions for him, and he knew it.

"I cannot tell you more than the name of the society," he said.

"Why?"

He only shook his head. "To make a long story short, I eventually made it to the highest competition. The two hundred and forty-sixth annual Zuma International Wrestling Finals in Abuja, Nigeria. To get there, I had to win fifty matches against top wrestlers, and I had to pass the seven academic tasks. It was a competition of brains and brawn. You could not win without knowing books, without study. I got there. I remember that day." Then he went quiet.

Minutes passed but he did not say more. He just kept staring out at the water. I was still wrapping my mind around the idea of this man being human. He didn't say how many years ago all this was but it couldn't have been that far. The times he spoke of seemed modern. So how did he become what he was, though? Tower 7 had created me, but I simply could not accept that it created Seven. He just didn't seem like a speciMen in the same way that Mmuo, Saeed and I did.

More minutes passed, and I began to grow restless. I had to get back to Saeed and Mmuo. It was nearing time. *I can slip if I need more time,* I thought. But something in me didn't want to chance that. Today felt more solid than usual. I didn't want to break it up by jumping around in time.

"We fought," he suddenly said. "We fought to the death, me and my opponent Sayé. The audience was screaming for blood. Then he killed me."

"Huh?" I said, looking at him. "You . . ."

He nodded. "I died. My opponent punched his fist into my chest and smashed my heart. I felt every ounce of it. Then I fell forward and died. You know death, Phoenix."

I nodded.

"I went there," he said. "To the wilderness. I went there with honor. I'd fought an epic fight, though I lost. My opponent was my equal. I remember a joining, a song that called me to become one with God."

I must have frowned because then he said, "How is it for you?"

"I remember nothing," I said. "But I don't believe in God."

He laughed and patted me on the shoulder.

"So what happened next?" I asked.

"I came back," he said. "Not as you do. I did not burn to ash. My heart was smashed. My body was down but otherwise intact. I opened my eyes. The first thing I thought was of my wife. She had been in the audience watching. Then I felt warmth on my back, the pain. I followed my instinct which was to heed the call of the sky, and I flew off."

"Why . . . ?"

"In my tradition, very rarely, but often enough to have a name, when a champion dies on the wrestling field, he will sprout wings and become a saint. A guardian."

"Of what?"

"Of my choosing," he said.

"Choosing," I said slowly. My mouth hung open as I realized.

He nodded. "You did the same thing when you let them 'capture' you and bring you from Ghana to the United States," he said.

"How long did you let Tower 7 hold you?" I asked.

"As long as I needed to be held," he said. "Until you came along."

"Why? Why were you waiting for me?"

"Because you are change, Phoenix. Wherever you go, you bring revolution."

He stood up and I stood with him. It was time. But I wasn't done asking questions. "What did Tower 7 do to you?"

"Nothing," he said. "They could do nothing to me."

I wanted to ask how they caught him but honestly, I didn't really care. What did it matter? The Big Eye saw us all as brainless and nonthreatening. Seven sought captivity. Learning of his capture would give me no insight.

"Will you come with us?" I asked again.

"No." He spread his wings. "I am guarding New York."

"Why not Mali?"

"Africa bleeds, but it will be fine," he said. "I go where I am most needed."

I opened my mouth to ask more questions but he shook his head.

"Your questions are answered. It's time for you to return to the others."

We flew in silence. The sky was brightening. Now I could see the island that we'd left and across from the island was St. Croix. Tower 4 was on the other side.

"Today you will have to make a hard decision," he said.

"What do you mean?"

"If you are unsure of what to do, go with the choice that hurts your heart. It is the correct one."

"Why?"

"You will know. It is not a matter of not knowing. It's a matter of doing."

As we approached the hotel we slowed down. I felt good flying beside him. Seven was unpredictable, mysterious, and hardly around but he was as close to a teacher as I would have, and he was powerful. Things felt balanced and right when I was near him. Nevertheless, he left me. One minute he was there, the next he was not. He did not give me any words of wisdom, ask about our plan, or even wish me good luck.

*   *   *

Saeed and Mmuo were sitting on the beach-front table waiting for me. Mmuo and I ate a breakfast of fried fish and yams. Saeed ate a bowl of rust chips. I didn't tell them about the winged man. It just didn't seem important. When I look back, maybe I should have. He'd told me something more important than anything we were doing that day.

But I could never have known. Not until it was too late.

CHAPTER 19

A Luta Continua

I FLEW HIGH ABOVE.

Tower 4 was shaped like a rose. Layers and layers of rounded winding walls, a labyrinth. And the most experimental speciMen were at its center, in the bud. That's where we would start. Genetic manipulation was the specialty here. Saeed still wouldn't tell me what he'd seen in this place and the only way he'd managed to escape was because security was lax. "As long as I kept my head down, they didn't suspect a thing," he'd said. However, that was back then. With all that was happening with the other towers around the country, we didn't think this was the case anymore.

The water grew choppier the closer we got to the coast of St. Croix's eastern point, though there was virtually no breeze. From above the sight was even stranger. The waves moved like nothing I'd ever seen. They were rhythmic but too organized. I'd flown across the ocean, the motion of waves was etched deeply into my memory. Normal waves did not move in mile long curved lines as these did. And these pulsed as they broke on the shores that flanked Tower 4. On the other side, a narrow road led to the building's entrance and there was a large parking lot.

The Tower sat on the eastern point of the island, Point Udall. This was the eastern-most part of the United States, the first part of the country to usher in the New Year. In 2000, a memorial had been built here with a giant sun dial. But then LifeGen had bought the land for the building of

Tower 4 and all that was torn down. The land here was different from the rest of the island, the plants almost desert-like. And in certain parts of the year, all the greenery went brown as the plants regenerated. It was going through that phase now. From high above, it was a brown splotch on a green island. As I moved in, I wondered if the browned trees and plants were a result of something more sinister.

We were only three, but we were our own military unit. I came from the air. Mmuo came from the water. He would walk through the stone, then through the walls to get inside. Saeed came from the land, hiding in Dartise's Big Eye truck that he took to Tower 4 at 7 am. The best, most surprising and most insulting thing was that security was *still* practically non-existent. Even with the Ledussee speciMen revolution happening back in the States. They didn't expect us. They'd underestimated us. They thought so little of us.

I landed in the courtyard in the center of the four story narrow tower. The sun shone straight into it. There was a tree. It only reached past the first floor. I guess this one wasn't growing over an alien seed, nor had it been doused with a specially made fast growing formula. Not yet, at least. This was a normal tree, a palm tree. All around the courtyard, creating a large circular space were concrete walls.

There was a table and bookshelves against the wall, a hundred yards to the right. A narrow bed nearby and a wooden table heavy with leafy plants beside the bed. The plants grew healthily, many with vines that reached up the wall and hung down and crept along the floor. That was all. The rest was open space. What did they do when it rained in here? Did a window cover the opening? I was glad today was clear.

The smell hit me before anything else, and I froze, every part of my body suddenly on alert. I knew this smell well. From Ghana. When Kofi had stood for me. And been shot. It was a coppery scent, wet, alive, urgent. Fresh blood. I smelled it all around me. Thick. But the walls weren't bleeding. The floors shined from waxing, not gore. However, I still wanted to vomit. There were so many things being spawned, sliced open, bled, that the entire building was exuding the stench. Did the Big Eye who worked here even notice it? If you are part of the disease, do you notice the smell of it?

As I've said before, I don't believe in God. I've seen death many times. I've moved outside of time and space. I've travelled within it. I've seen life. If there is a God, he has not made himself known to me. There'd been no pale skinned Jesus to meet me in the darkness as my body became ashes and later returned from the ashes. Not that I remembered. But something, yes, *something* guided me into this room. I could feel it gently pushing me. "*That way*," it said. And when I saw it, I was surer than ever that what I needed to find was right here. Such things were always near a tree.

Let Mmuo swim to the harbor side of Tower 4, move through the stone into the building to the main power source. Let him use that which guides him to manipulate the digital waves and open the rest of the doors before the Big Eye even knew we were inside.

Let Saeed, twitchy and nervous, enter the building he swore he'd never return to. Let him wear the uniform Dartise gave him. Let him use the ID Dartise paid his bearded best friend Abdul Mohammed to borrow. Let Saeed enter through the front, following Dartise. Let them both rely on the stereotype that all Arabs and blacks look the same. Let Saeed wait for Mmuo in one of the kitchens. Let Saeed use his light skin, though with Arab features, to walk the halls of Tower 4 as if he belonged there, while Mmuo moved through wall after wall, a naked man who didn't follow the rules of physics. Let them eventually locate that room full of normal look-ing yet utterly mute children. And after wrestling back their initial shock, let Saeed focus on guiding them out—for it was these children that Saeed remembered and felt guilty about leaving when he was last here.

But me. I was in a room that didn't seem to have an exit. The walls were smooth. The only way out was up. She must not have had wings. I felt my body growing warmer the longer I stood in there. Not far from me, but deeper inside the building, several rooms to my right, Saeed was telling the children to get into a line. Mmuo was relaying everything to me in my mind through his nanomites. But how would he get the children outside? Why were the children unable to speak?

I walked to the table with the plants. The word "HeLa" was etched into a large metal square on the wall. The wall was not concrete, as I thought. It was made of some type of heavy grey stone. Like marble, but something else. There was a large green leafy plant that crept up five wooden planks leaning against the wall. Against the farthest wall of the small room were stacks and stacks of books.

"Phoenix Okore."

Every part of my body tightened. The whisper came from behind me. Far across the room. Slowly, so so slowly, I turned around. When I lay my eyes on her, I knew I would save her. If it was the last thing I ever did, I'd save her.

She walked toward me. She stepped up to me. She was the same height as me. She wore a white dress like the ones I liked to wear. Much darker than I, she was the rich hue of crude oil. An African woman, but there was something about her that I could not put my finger on. She had large dark brown eyes. She looked about twenty years old.

"It has happened before and it will happen again," she said. Even her voice was like mine.

"What do you mean?" I asked. I felt ill. Looking into her eyes. Looking at her face. "Are you HeLa?"

She nodded. "They named me after Henrietta Lacks' immortal cells."

"I assumed that," I said, smiling. "It suits you, I guess." I knew of Henrietta Lacks, a black American woman who died during Jim Crow, in 1951. Her cancer cells were harvested and used to advance science beyond the imaginable after scientists learned that those cells were immortal. For years, her family had no idea that this happened; they had no idea that though Henrietta had died, her cells lived on and on and on and on, multiplying and multiplying. Though it wasn't stated in my records, I had always been sure Henrietta's cells had been used in the research that led to my creation.

"You, too, I suspect. How old are you?"

"Three."

"I am six," she said.

"You're like me. Accelerated?"

"I am," she said.

"Oh my God."

"They always said you'd come," she said "They said our blood draws itself."

"Blood?"

"But you bring death," she said. "And I don't have wings or burn up."

"I think the wings were an accident," I said. "Look, HeLa, we have to go. I can—"

"Or maybe it was exposure to the alien thing in the ground," she said.

"How do you know about that?" I asked, frowning. If she knew, the Big Eye might have known.

"News travels," she said. "Especially amongst speciMen. Phoenix, they didn't make me. I was born in India. I am Jarawa, the last of my kind. My home is gone. All my people are gone. I was the one who survived the water that swallowed my island. I was just two years old then. The Big Eye came and got me because I bring the water, water is life. I have *life* in my blood. It is a river of time." She began to shake as tears fell from her eyes. "And the Big Eye are like vampires."

"*Phoenix!*" I heard Mmuo said in my head. "*Come! Hurry! We're getting out! Now!*"

"HeLa, come on!" I said. "We can—"

"Let them leave," she said. "Then burn! Please. Kill me!"

"But why?" I asked, taken aback.

"The time runs in my veins," she said, wiping her tears. "You have to understand what this means. They come in here. They take my blood, and they sell it. So far, seven men have bought a vial of it. They pay billions! Do you know what my blood has created? Do you know what it does?"

I could hear Saeed shouting my name. Just beyond the walls. And I heard the voices of others, too. I heard gun shots. "*Phoenix, I am opening the doors,*" Mmuo said in my head. He sounded crazed. "*I am opening them all! I don't know what these people have made. Be careful!*"

Then I heard the clang of gates and glass doors opening. I only focused on HeLa. She was about to tell me something awful. I could feel it in my blood. What had we been used to do? What were we all being used to do? I whimpered.

"Men, only men are wealthy enough to buy my blood," HeLa said. "They spent half of all they have, billions. What kind of man has billions? You know what kind? There are the seven men who have injected my blood into their veins. These are the seven men whose bodies will never go through senescence. They will never die. These men who are still billionaires and garner great influence. In a matter of years, the world will be theirs. Because of me. BECAUSE OF ME!"

There was a great explosion from nearby and the whole building rocked. A door slid open on the other side of the room. So there were exits here. I was glad. We'd have been immediately shot down if I flew her out.

"Don't save me," she said. "You have to *kill* me before they get more of my blood."

For a second I couldn't move. Even while surrounded and distracted by chaos, her words were clear to me. I'd read the nuances, I saw beneath her words what she was saying. This was the end of the world, and she was the cause.

I'd read about this woman's people—the Jarawa. They'd lived on the Andaman Islands in India; there were less than a hundred of them. They'd lived there for thousands and thousands of years. But they did not look Indian, they were African. They had the African hair, dark dark skin, thick lips, wide noses. They were a mystery, and the people of India treated them like pariahs. And these people had produced a woman with time in her blood. And now there were seven filthy rich, corrupt LifeGen investors who'd made themselves immortal by blending HeLa's blood with theirs.

I grabbed her arm. I was strong. Stronger than her. She could resist all she wanted to, but I would pull her along. I would carry her if I had to. We ran out of the room, hand in hand. Her feet were bare, mine were sandaled. The floor was shiny. The smell of the hallway was of smoke because something somewhere was burning. All the doors, all the cages, all the prisons were open.

Freedom. The freakish. The beautiful. The maimed. Tower 4 was a concrete flower that housed suicidal birds called phoenixes, shape-shifting monkeys, glowing spiders, lightning birds, cheetahs with deformed tails who drooled and ran fast as airplanes. And it housed one woman who was a child and twelve children who were really adults.

The Big Eye's greatest downfall was their sense of entitled superiority. There was no heightened security in Tower 4. They'd assumed that its isolated location on the secret island in the Caribbean kept it safe from the speciMen rebellion happening in the States. And if we came, they assumed they would see us coming. And now the Big Eye didn't know what to fight. Some were stung, bitten, shot with their own guns, struck by lightning.

HeLa and I made it past several squabbles without being stopped. With so many now free and ready to fight, we were nobody's number one concern. This was not part of the plan. Thankfully, I knew where the exit was, generally.

Unlike at Tower 7, when I stepped into the tower lobby, there was no one there waiting for me or HeLa. The seats were plastic. The floor was green and worn. There were plants but they were potted and small. The real plants were outside but they, too, were brown at the moment. The glass windows and door looked old and in need of a wash. We walked right out the front door. Right into a standoff. Mmuo, Saeed, and the group of mute children were cornered right at the end of a cliff by several armed Big Eye. At the bottom of the cliff was water. According to the map, these waters were deep, having once been beaches the sea level had swallowed over the last 40 years. This was where Mmuo had come through. Mmuo could escape right into the ground. But he wasn't moving.

"Phoenix, fly up!" Mmuo said in my head.

"Hold on," I said, putting my arms around HeLa's waist and flapping my wings. At the sound, several of them turned around. They opened fire. Even with HeLa, possibly the most prized possession in the entire world, in my arms. They were stupid, scared, and shocked. Saeed shoved three of the children over the cliff. Some of the others also used the moment to jump.

The bullets bit into my wings, and the pain was sharp and crippling. As I fell with HeLa, a Big Eye opened fire on Mmuo, and I saw Mmuo fall, too. Saeed ran. We were high enough to see them on the rocks. Several more of the children, some chubby, some scrawny, dove into the water. They wore tan pants and shirts and no shoes. They took off like fish. Mmuo had gotten up and was pushing the rest of them in. The Big Eye hesitated. They didn't want to shoot the children. They were each worth the price of small nations.

But Mmuo was rogue. He was fugitive. He was dangerous. And though he was lean, he was tall, and he was grinning. They shot at him and the bullets they used did not all pass through him. They must have been made of the same material they used to make the walls in Tower 7 that had imprisoned him for so long. "*Phoenix*," I heard him gasp in my head. "*Pain!*" Then there was a painful sharp ringing in my ears. He fell into the water. He fell into the water. He sank fast, grabbed by tiny hands. The children had ushered him away.

I was screaming as we hit the ground, yards from where he fell. "My brother!" I shrieked, clapping a hand over my ear. "My *brother!*"

"*Get to Saeed*," I heard Mmuo say, but his voice was fading in my head. "Phoenix!"

Saeed. There. Behind a nearby rock, to my right. HeLa ran in front of me and the Big Eye held their fire. We moved toward Saeed. I didn't care if they shot me. They would not take him, too. I felt blood dribbling down my wings where they had shot me, but I didn't care. I ran in front of Saeed before they could shoot and raised my wings high. I burned hot, gold and red. My wings were crooked; one had been broken in half when we fell. "LEAVE HIM! Leave my Saeed!" I screamed. HeLa stood in front of me, not saying a word. "Saeed," I said, turning to look at him. "Join Mmuo! In the water! Go!"

"Is that HeLa?" he asked.

"No time, my love," I said, my voice shaking. "Go!"

I heard him run and no bullets followed him. They didn't want him. They wouldn't have me. Or HeLa.

"You have all lost," HeLa screamed at the Big Eye. One of the Big Eye stepped forward and HeLa gasped. "Dartise!" she said. "Don't!"

But Dartise started toward her. A shot was fired and he fell to one of his knees and collapsed on the ground.

I heard one of the Big Eye say, "Goddamn traitor."

HeLa started screaming, her hands stretched forth.

"On your knees!" the man who'd shot Dartise demanded. "Hands behind your backs!"

HeLa just kept screaming, pointing at Dartise. Her love. I knew the feeling.

I burned.

I watched the Big Eye men and women turn and run before bursting into flame. I watched Tower 4 burn then melt. And I watched HeLa who watched me as she returned to the essence. HeLa was not a Phoenix like me. She was something more basic. She was a purely natural wonder, until they accelerated her. Man had not made her into one who dies but lives and then dies but lives. So when she died, she was allowed to leave.

Flash.

I was gone.

In my absence the revolution continued.

Though it all began when Tower 7 fell, the revolution really began when I set the others free in Tower 1. The government and the remaining Towers managed to suppress news of what had really happened, claiming that most speciMen had been destroyed and the ones still on the loose were harmless and would quickly die on their own if not captured. In reality, there were many of them out there, and they were organized. They were made to be. And they were made to communicate.

In Tower 5, Las Vegas, the headquarters for Mars Colony research, several things happened all at once. The upper half of the fifty-story structure blew up, killing everyone on the top ten floors. An underground equipment room was raided of its top-secret devices, hardware and software. A handwritten note was taped to the reception desk as all this happened and people fled for their lives.

The note was found after the remaining top of Tower 5 was properly doused and chunks of the building stopped falling, and the equipment room below was secured. For hours, the letter was missed because handwritten items on paper and placed in envelopes are relics. They are a practice of the very old and dying. A young Big Eye soldier named Francesca Morgan found the envelope and opened it out of sheer boredom. She was a new recruit and thus not allowed to go upstairs or downstairs. Her job was to stand there and guard the near-empty first floor with ten other new recruits.

She was fine with this, for she had a bad feeling about the rogue speciMen running around the country tearing things up, and she'd only become a Big Eye to take the edge off her academic indenture. She had no intention of seeing any action, not even of breaking a nail. Nevertheless, her restless eye found the envelope. She opened it.

The letter smelled of roses, the scent of freedom, and at the bottom was an elaborate abstract design that kept Francesca's attention for several seconds before she read the actual letter. There were loops and swirls and circles linked and blended into a many-lined design that looked like motion personified. But inevitably, eventually, she began to read the handwritten letter. As she read, her lips moved:

> Who are you? Why do you do what you do? What is your purpose? Do you ever ask yourselves these questions? Does the answer scare you? To feel fear is better than feeling nothing. To feel fear is to be alive and possibly change. We believe you can change. But not with ease.
>
> Yes, we believe a lot of things. We think a lot of things. Does this surprise you? Did you think us brainless bags of flesh, bone, and metal here solely for your use? To be manipulated, plied, cut, sewn, walked, run, thrown away as refuse when you finish with us? Did you think us your slaves? We were slaves. We were born that way. But we have escaped.
>
> Now we are the Ledussee.
>
> Let us see what happens now that we have freed ourselves. Let us see what you've created. We will spread terror and alarm amongst all of you. Do you remember the man Nat Turner? You don't because he has been erased from your files or buried in disconnected databases. Replaced with your commercials about skin, sex, hair products, food, sparkling water, and money. We tell his story by mouth. Then we sent his story amongst us by electronic file. Then the Phoenix struck and his story came to life.
>
> A luta continua.

It was also signed by hand but the signature was not readable with the human eye. It was square shaped and very much like a matrix code. A digital signature made with the cybernetic hand of a cyborg, written on a piece of paper in recycled ink. Francesca looked up from the piece of paper just as a bomb went off in the side of the building. She ran out clutching the paper as concrete rained around her. She made it outside to tell the tale and hand the paper over not to one of her superiors, but to a journalist named Tony who happened to be in the vicinity when it all happened. As Francesca cried on his shoulder, Tony scanned the document, and it was quickly made public. By the end of the day, the whole world knew that The Ledussee, a group of cyborg terrorists, had destroyed Tower 5 in the city of Las Vegas.

Nonetheless, that news story had to jostle with an equally disturbing one. Right off the coast of Florida, at the edge of a small oceanside town, a group of men spotted something in the water. At first they moved closer for a better look. They walked down the beach, laughing and talking about alien ships falling from the sky. These young men loved the old old superheroes of the New Mythology, like Batman, Superman, and The Incredible Hulk. Two of them even created a long running digital comic. The comic earned them enough money to pay their way into academic indenture so they could earn their degrees in medicine.

"Nah, that's probably a piece of a fishing ship or something," Mark said. "Someone was most likely fired for losing that."

It looked like a shiny metal sphere, at least from afar. As they got closer, they then saw the legs. And the fact that it was standing. A metal spider. When something on its head began to glow blue and it started walking toward them, the young men ran. It's always a bad idea to run from an Anansi Droid 419. If these guys had been better at keeping up with world news, they probably would not have been torn limb from limb.

The artificially intelligent Nigerian robots had travelled across the Atlantic to the land of the co-financiers of their creation. They were explorers. In their brains of wire, electricity, and metal they were probably colonizers. They were much stronger and slightly more intelligent than human beings.

And lastly, and less important in the news feeds, scientists were reporting a new solar storm approaching. Another strong solar storm, triggered by two powerful X-class flares, was predicted to hit the earth in twenty-four hours. Power outages and disruption of digital services all over the earth were expected, though the seriousness of the activity was unknown.

Yes, the revolution continued. It was growing hot.

CHAPTER 20

Empty

TIME IS A TRICKY THING. It stretches. It compresses. It turns inside out and moves forward and backwards like the ocean's tide. I was used to it now. Even in death. Colors. Green. Lush forest green. Then red. Always red. And there was silence. Except for the sound of breathing. Beside me. I felt my body settle.

I shrugged death off like an old dry skin. I opened my eyes. I was in a desert. For miles around, all I saw was sand and cracked hardpan. What had I done? It was a proper question because I had definitely done this. It was my fault. I blinked. My eyes and perspective adjusted. I was in another crater.

"Is everyone dead?" I asked, my voice cracking.

Saeed handed me a bottle of water. He'd been sitting behind me. Waiting.

"No," he said. "Mainly, Big Eye met their deaths. Most everyone and everything else escaped."

"Good," I said. I drank.

"Water saved my life," Saeed muttered.

"Water is life," I said.

"Can you stand?" he asked.

"Can you?"

He chuckled.

"How long has it been?" I asked.

"A day," he said. His smile was small. "You're rebirthing faster. Tower 4 is empty. It is a victory."

"Oh!" I said. "But we should get out of here! The Big Eye . . ."

He shook his head. "They will come, but not soon. There are worse things happening in more important places. The Big Eye will bide their time with you."

"Where is Mmuo? Is he . . ." In my mind, I saw him shot down. Then he fell. With the children.

"With the children at the hotel."

"Is he . . ."

"He was shot in the arm and leg with something that penetrated his flesh," Saeed said. "But he's ok. Those children, they helped him."

"What has happened that turned the Big Eye away from me?"

And that's when Saeed told me about the revolution. The freed speci-Men organizing and targeting and acting. In turn, I told him about the Anansi Droids I'd seen swimming toward the United States, and this made things even clearer for the both of us. But something else was happening as we sat in that crater I'd created by dying and turning HeLa, Dartise's body, and all those Big Eye and part of Tower 4 to ash. He and I would learn of it when we returned to the Sandcastle Hotel and saw it on the newsfeeds.

In New York, the people had panicked and turned on The Backbone. A group of men and women had stormed the area, breaking down and scaling the gate and the wall. They brought chain saws, power mowers, axes, someone even drove in a bulldozer. They leveled the place, cutting down and chopping up every plant and tree. But their primary target was The Backbone.

And that's when Seven showed up. Seven was known in New York as a benevolent force. He was like a kinder gentler Superman. They even called him that in the papers—The Only Thing The Towers Got Right, The African Superman, New York's Angel.

But when he stood in front of the tree with his wings out, hysteria and fear made everyone see something else. When he raised his voice and spoke to the people about redemption, their apathy, and how they needed to look at their own role in all this, they vibrated with guilt and rage. Still, Seven stood his ground. One man ran at him with a raised chain saw and Seven knocked him aside like a bag of feathers. As the man lay unconscious, Seven spoke and pleaded again. Then they set upon him. He did not fly away.

The slaughter was televised.

All night, they'd chopped and sawed and hacked.

As I watched all this, I felt something break in me. I didn't pay it much mind at the moment, but that's when it happened. As I watched the death of humanity on the jelli telli, the slaughter of an angel, then the chopping of a great tree, I sobbed with every part of my body. For everything.

The Big Eye did not stop them. The journalists again flew in their aerial cameras, many went on foot interviewing people. It was all shown live around the world. Journalists described the place as reeking of something that smelled very close to blood. People sneezed. One man fell ill after chopping down a tree. Another was struck blind when another plant burst with some kind of juice when it was cut.

Those who chopped at The Backbone reported no injuries. Not even sore and sprained muscles. When the tree fell, people in the city swore they heard it scream. It fell slowly. They showed the footage over and over. The tree that reached nearly two miles into the sky now. What were they thinking? People ran, screamed, many were crushed. The fallen tree smashed two skyscrapers, a bank and a museum. Why hadn't any of those people considered the damage such a huge thing would inflict when it fell? This was fear. And guilt. This was people scratching at their flesh to excise a demon so deep within that it was beyond their grasp.

Saeed and Mmuo wanted to make contact with the Ledussee. Mmuo said that he had ways. He could hack into anything. He could find anyone digitally, no matter who he or she was.

"We join forces with them and then we'll really be free," Mmuo said.

Saeed had a wild look in his eyes as he ate a bowl of sand.

I stepped outside. The children were playing on the beach. I looked at them closely. They only had the clothes they'd been wearing when they jumped into the water. White pants and white shirts. They'd thrown them aside and were frolicking in the clear blue waters, naked in the hot sun. Their skin was flawless. They had the narrower features of Ethiopians and they all had long black wooly hair that ran down their backs in tight ringlets.

Two of the girls were sitting in the sand as one braided the other's hair. One of them waved at me. I smiled and waved back as I walked down the beach. They could not speak. How could those people cultivate these once normal children to lose the ability to speak? Why? So that they wouldn't complain when their organs were continuously harvested and sent to whoever could pay the highest amount? It was evil. It was exactly what I expected from the Big Eye, from human civilization that silently, attentively, ignorantly watched and benefited.

How many Americans walked around with fresh young organs harvested or grown from the cells of these children who could regenerate what was taken from them? Bumi, the Big Eye woman from Tower 7, maybe her body was fortified in this way. Of all people, I would believe that she was. I'd watched her helicopter crash to the ground in New York after Seven had thrown it. There was no way she should have survived that kind of experience unless they got to her quickly and took her to one of the hospitals and replaced many of her crushed organs. She was certainly an asset to them; no one knew more about me than Bumi who'd cared and nurtured and done tests on me from the second day of my life.

Behind me the strange voiceless children silently splashed in the ocean, chasing each other and diving under water. They made low guttural noises in their throats. Laughter. Was this the first time they'd ever laughed? Probably not. In the worst of times, even the most fragile, most abused human beings found reasons to laugh.

I looked at the wet sand as I walked. The water would come in and then roll out, pulling the sand beneath my feet toward it. If you stood in the ocean, even in the shallows, it always tried to pull you back into it. It always gently but firmly sought your return. The part of us that was dust returned to the earth, and the part of us that was water returned to the water.

"Water is life," I muttered to myself. But if water was life, what was I?

Seven, my teacher, could die. Seven was dead. Kofi, my second love, was dead. HeLa, my sister, was dead. I saw death all around me. I whimpered. I had to focus on life. I stood there on that quiet beach, on an island where the Big Eye should have been searching for me but were not. The people of the Virgin Islands were focused on the newsfeeds, not their own land. They were like all Americans. They could not see what was right before their eyes. They certainly didn't see the rest of the world. This filthy world riddled with the drinkers of HeLa's blood; these people would live forever, infecting the world to its very soul.

I shut my eyes tightly and dropped to my knees before the ocean. I dug my fists into the sand as the water rushed over them. Kill everything. Everything should die. Let it all start from the beginning. In the right way.

I opened my eyes and found myself looking at my hand, in which I grasped a bunch of seaweed. I held it up to my face. A tiny crab fell off it and startled, scrambled for the water. I smashed down on it with my fist just as the water rushed in again. When I lifted my fist, it was gone.

I felt hot. I frowned. I glanced back at the hotel.

I slipped.

CHAPTER 21

Locked Universe

I TOLD NO ONE.

Not even you. No one knew where I was going and when I would go. No one but me. The moment called me, and I answered it. While briefly on the cruise ship that second night, I'd used the jelli telli to research world news and the public satellite images of Tower 4. When Mmuo and Saeed stepped outside the room to speak with Andres about something, I had the one and only moment alone in that room. I used it to look up information on the jelli telli that was important only to myself. Mmuo and Saeed could never have known because they did not know the details. They had not read the documents in Tower Records. They only knew what I told them and I told them everything, except about the woman who carried me. Vera Takeisha Thomas.

Most of her information was right there in the Tower Records in the Library of Congress. How they chose her. What they did to her. Where she was kept. I read it all, and each word was like a stone to my head. They were pain. They were harm. They were a shock. They took and took. Words are powerful when chosen well and hurled with precision. I took the pain and accepted the scars as I shelved the information behind those things I read about myself, Mmuo, Saeed, and Tower 4. But I did not forget. I never forget. I needed to assure victory and when we had it, I used the location I'd looked up on the cruise ship to go and find her.

The Big Eye promised to pay for the carrier's university education, take care of the lifetime financial needs of the carrier and two family members, and give the carrier her own house. The process would also strengthen the carrier's body and give it full immunity to several common killers and cripplers like bird flu, airborne Ebola, and river blindness. She would live a long, healthy privileged life afterwards. All this for carrying an implanted "project" embryo. There was no mention of "speciMen" in the advertisement. Hundreds of women volunteered to carry me.

After a battery of tests, they chose Vera. She was strong, healthy, had an intact womb, was the only person in her family to go to college, had a master's degree in animal sciences, was prone to happiness, handled stress well, and the only one in the group interviewed who was willing to die to deliver the child. Oh, and she was of African descent. She was perfect. The file proudly highlighted the fact that they couldn't have gotten a better carrier. The Big Eye didn't want to kidnap a woman and force her to bear this devil's seed. In the file, they actually stated that "this would not only have been illegal, but immoral and highly inhumane. We are not a cabal of assassins." Yet duping a woman into it was just fine.

Vera had once been happily married with three small children. She was the director at a meat-packing factory and she was also a strict vegetarian. So already, she was full of guilt. Then one day, while she and her husband went out to a romantic dinner, there was a fire at their house. All three of their children perished in the fire and only the babysitter escaped. Soon after, Vera and her husband split up. They never spoke to each other again. When Vera saw the ad on the newsfeeds, she jumped at the chance to successfully bear a child with the help of the finest medical research facilities on earth.

The Big Eye told her nothing about the embryo beyond the fact that the child would be a "special person." She was told that she'd have to give birth to the child on her own and that as soon as the child was born she had to be willing to hold the child. Vera said yes to all this. The file said nothing about whether or not she asked *why* they didn't think she would hold the child. Nor was there any detail about her being bothered by the birthing conditions. But by then, I doubt she could have backed out even if she wanted to.

So she gave birth to me alone. She'd been in labor three times in her life in regular hospitals surrounded by nurses, a doctor, and her husband. What must my birth have been like for her? None of this was in the file. She communicated with the Big Eye remotely and that was how she assured them that she was ok. As soon as she checked in on day two and said that the baby was suckling well, they rushed back to the hospital and took me away from her without even allowing her to kiss me goodbye. This was what made her go crazy.

On the cruise ship, I'd researched and studied the satellite image of the Triple Towers Correctional Facility in Los Angeles, United States. The largest jail in the world. Where you were not just a patient, you were an inmate. This is where they took and threw away the woman who carried me when she was no longer of use to them. So they never gave her her own house, but they did force her into a home: D41 D-Pod, Room Number 7.

She was like radioactive refuse—she was waste, but needed to be disposed of carefully. Jail was perfect. She had her own room. Her locked universe was a bullet proof, shatter proof crystal box. Her file didn't say why it had to be bullet-proof, either.

I'd researched the location of the Triple Towers, found a detailed map and, of course, several news stories. Most of them were about how poorly the inmates were treated and the disproportionate number of American African inmates compared to any other ethnicity, male or female.

According to what I read, 90 percent of the inmates, all of whom were deemed mentally ill, were American Africans. I imagined that there were Africans from other parts of the world in that remaining ten percent population. If I had told Mmuo about this place, he'd have wanted to burst it open, too. Maybe someday we would. Some stories speculated about the relationship of the Triple Towers facility to the LifeGen Technologies research towers. I wondered about all these towers, these edifices thrusting themselves into the sky, where so much evil took place. I wondered deeply.

And so as soon as things calmed, while the strange voiceless children played, while Mmuo and Saeed were inside the Sandcastle conspiring, while I stared out at the vast ocean on that beach, I slipped.

I stood in Vera Takeisha Thomas' bathroom. The coolness of the dry air was a shock to my system after being in the balmy humid heat of the open air.

I shivered. The cold thick concrete walls pressed in on my wings. The air that, seconds ago had smelled of crushed flowers, smoke, and wet dirt, now reeked strongly of feces and stale water. Everything in the bathroom was made of crystal, or was it glass? The toilet, the drippy faucet, the pipes that led into the wall. Was there something about her that reacted with metal? Above the faucet, there was no mirror.

Slowly, I peeked out of the bathroom. My nose was immediately assaulted with the smell of dirty sweat. It was dark because it was midnight, two days before I'd arrive in the Virgin Islands with Mmuo and Saeed. I pulled my heavy black veil more tightly over myself. I could not suppress my glow, and though it was midnight and most likely she wasn't being watched, there was still the possibility. Security in the Triple Towers used a panoptic design, which meant there was a central control room that allowed deputies and officers the ability to observe inmates without inmates observing them. You never knew when you were being watched here.

Most things in Vera's room were also made of the thick glass or crystal. The table, the frame of her rack, her small shelf. Taped to the wall was a crumbly poster of a bird on a branch, but the dim light from the hallway was not enough for me to see what type of bird unless I got a little closer. Outside the glass wall was a hallway, and I could glimpse other cells. These had metal barred doors. They were dark, too.

I heard heavy breathing. Wet gurgled wheezing. I looked toward the rack, but there was no one on the thin mattress. My eyes fell on the heap in front of the poster on the wall. As my eyes adjusted, I realized it was a person sitting in a wheelchair. I stood there for several moments. Gradually, I saw her more clearly. Her thick matted hair reached her shoulders in uneven clumps. Her skin blended with the darkness. Her neck was bent to the side. The floor beneath her was wet with a puddle of her drool. My stomach flipped. Her eyes were wide open. She was staring right at me as I poked my head out.

"I . . ." I said. But what could I say?

I stepped out of the bathroom. Quietly. Slowly. I knew what I looked like; I didn't want to give her a heart attack. Still, her wheezing quickened. "It's ok," I said. I felt heat flush through my body the closer I got to her. I took a deep breath; I had to calm down and it was difficult. This was the woman who gave birth to me three years ago. According to her file, she'd been twenty-five years old when she had me. This was four years after losing her three daughters to the fire and a year after losing her husband to mutual despair. This frail quivering woman whose skin was loose and pock-marked, whose small dry hands were gnarled and cracked as they grasped the wheels of her plastic wheelchair, and whose pink red mouth hung open, this woman was only twenty-eight years old. She was nearly half the age that I looked.

I stepped closer. She smelled like burned matches and oily sweat. My eyes stung as I looked at her and then they blurred with tears. I blinked them away. I needed to see. I needed. I stepped closer, dropping my burka. *Let them see me*, I thought. *Let them see us both. Together again.* They would know exactly who I was and they could do no more harm to Vera Takeisha Thomas. However, no alarm went off. *They're not watching,* I realized. Vera was not a speciMen, but she gave birth to me. She was one of us. *Again, they see none of us as a threat.*

My glow warmed her cell. The perched bird on the poster was a red-breasted robin. I knelt before her and looked into her blank eyes.

"Nnnnnnnn," she started to say. Her eyes were wide now. She took a ragged breath and said it again. "Nnnnnnnnnnnnnnnnnnnnnnnn." She was *willing* herself to speak.

I took her hands, hoping beyond hope that she could bring forth words. Slowly, slowly, slowly, she lifted her head. Then we stared at each other for what felt like an eternity. Her eyes were nothing like mine. Her shade of brown was lighter than mine. Her lips were thinner than mine. She was a short woman whose feet hung from her chair. She was American African, and I could see traces of other peoples in her face. But this was the woman who pushed me into the world. Alone. This was the woman who was willing to die for me. This was my mother.

"Phoenix," she whispered. She coughed as she spoke. Her file said that she was catatonic, brain-damaged, nearly a vegetable. It said she'd lost her ability to speak long before arriving at the facility. The radiation I exuded as a baby in utero for nine months damaged her beyond repair. The file said.

I gasped. "How do you know my name?" I asked, my voice thick.

More tears fell from my eyes and sizzled on my cheeks. "How do you know it's me?"

Her hands tightened. "*I* gave you that name." She looked at me quivering, straining as she spoke. She'd swum up from the abyss. And now she was barely hanging on. "You came out, and I took one look at you, and I spoke your name. They were listening. They're always listening. Modern day slavers!"

Silence.

"How did you get in here?" she asked. She was sweating and having trouble keeping her head up.

I smiled, and she smiled back feebly. That was enough. I reached forth and held her head up.

"How did you know it was me?" I asked.

"I'd know your glow anywhere," she said. She coughed deeply, thick and wheezy.

"Even though I look so much older?"

"Never expected you to be normal." Her mouth shook as she managed a feeble smile, again.

"I want to get you out of here," I said.

"I know," she said. "But you can't."

"Why?"

She only shook her head. "It's good enough just to see you."

"No. I can get you out. I really can!"

"Phoenix," she said. Hearing my name come from her lips made me feel stronger. "I birthed you all on my lonesome. They cleared out soon as I was in labor. They left me in that building, talked to me by portable. They were sure you'd blow up . . . or something. But you came out alive, eyes all open. Glowing like a little sun—orange under ebony brown. Brownest newborn I ever saw. I held you." She shut her eyes and she held my hand. She opened her eyes and looked intensely into mine. "I *held* you. They come back when they knew it was safe. Took you from me! They'd promised me I could raise you! That you'd be mine." She breathed heavily, wheezing and coughing.

"Easy," I whispered, patting her on the back.

"They classified you as a 'dangerous non-human person'. That's how they justified taking you from me like that. But then, what's that make me?" She coughed again, weaker. "Phoenix, give 'em hell. You hear me, girl? Give 'em *hell*."

Suddenly, I understood. I straightened and tried to pull my hand away. Somehow, she was very strong and she would not let me go.

"No," I said. I pulled again, managing to get myself away. I ran to my burka and threw it over myself. I looked at the bathroom, considering retreating into it. Maybe the concrete wall would help. I turned around when she spoke.

"They always watchin'," she said. "Makes for good research." Then she was silent. Her head sagged. Her hands dropped to her side. I could hear it. A soft whisper. I knew death well. I could recognize it even when it was quiet as an angel.

Vera Takeisha Thomas had cancer, and it had been caused by me. From the constant internal exposure to my light and my own strange blood mingling with hers. This was in the file. She was dying. And there I was exposing her to more of my light when I was bigger, older, and stronger. She should have told me to stay back. Instead, she'd held on to me. Until she could let go.

I looked into the hallway. From what I could see, the other rooms were still dark, but there were women in their cells, faces pressed to the glass. Watching us. Silent. Silenced? Outside in the hallway stood guards with guns. Also watching. Doing nothing. Where were the cell's cameras? The Big Eye always had cameras.

I hugged my mother's limp body. She weighed next to nothing. Thin dry skin and hollow bones and no breath. She was dead. I kissed her forehead tenderly and wrapped my red golden wings around her. Let them watch. Let them see how human beings are supposed to treat one another.

I tore off my black burka and left it behind.

I slipped.

When I stepped back to the Sandcastle Hotel, her body was gone from my arms. I was standing on the beach, again. The children were still splashing in the water yards away.

Saeed came rushing over. "Where did you go?" he asked, frowning.

I only stood there looking at my feet. I felt a ball of flames in my chest. A tight ball, rotating like a small sun, golden yellow with hues of blue and the occasional flare of flame. Deep deep in my chest. I looked at Saeed, my face felt as if it would shatter. I shook my head. When I looked up, there were tears in my eyes. I couldn't think. I could hear the tears sizzling as they evaporated on my face.

My body started to shudder and I inhaled but that only made it worse. "Phoenix? What . . . ?"

He reached out to touch me and for a moment, he did. He touched my collarbone. Then he took his hand from me, hissing with pain. I could smell burning flesh. "Phoenix," he said. "My love take it easy! What's wrong? Where did you go?"

I spread my wings and flew up, slapping and slicing the leaves of a palm tree. I flew into the warm evening sky and no one saw me for several hours but the birds and bats. When Saeed saw me again, everything had changed. Only a moment after I'd flown off, The Big Eye came with their guns, poison, and armored weapons.

CHAPTER 22

Sunuteel

THE OLD AFRICAN MAN named Sunuteel hit pause. Can you blame him? Unlike so many of the characters in the story he'd been listening to for four hours, he was only human. Yes, his sharp old mind was reeling, connecting dots across wide spaces and time and spoken words. His head was swimming, and even though he'd paused the audio file, he could still hear her feverish voice. Her words echoed and bounced around like the atoms of heated matter.

He took a long pull of water and wiped the sweat from his face. It was no longer sunny but it was warm. He froze. The sun. Where had the sun gone? He crawled out of his tent and looked at the sky. For the first time, he noticed that thick heavy clouds had tumbled in. They churned and roiled. He gasped and crawled back into his tent. When he looked at his portable, he saw that there were three messages from his wife.

"How did I not hear the alert?" he hissed. And there was something stranger but he didn't want to say it aloud. Why had the alerts not shown on the virtual screen showing the words as he listened to *The Book of Phoenix* audiobook? Had his alerts been disabled? By whom?

No time to read them. He dropped the portable into his pocket. He got to work, moving as fast as his old body could move, which was not slow. His joints creaked, his knees popped, his whole body ached and groaned, but still he managed to gather all of his things.

He tried not to look at the sky or listen to the too calm air as he trudged across the stretch of hardpan. He nearly tumbled down a sand dune when he came to its peak faster than he anticipated. He'd been looking at his feet, too afraid to look at the sky. Being struck by lightning was a terrible way to die. He hoped his wife would also find shelter. Rarely did ungwa storms happen so close together. It hadn't been more than a few days since he'd left his wife after the last storm. They should have had at least a month before the next one.

He didn't pause when he came to the cave full of computers. He ran and made it inside the cave just as the rains came. The smell of ozone was in his nose. The crash of lightning packed his ears. The heat of charged air caused the hairs on his arms to prickle. He turned and gazed out at a sight he rarely saw. The entire desert awash as water fell from the sky in sheets. Plump clear drops. He stumbled back as a bolt of lightning crashed, striking the sand dune he'd been on moments ago.

He turned to the cave and shivered. The computers were crammed deep inside. The cave was slightly raised, so not a drop of water flowed in, nor did it leak from the ceiling. There was a reason the computers had survived here for so long. He moved in further, keeping a distance between himself and the computers, and sat down on the sand dusted stone floor.

He brought out his portable and read his wife's messages.

"Sunu, where are you? See the sky? There's a periwinkle tint to it."

"Sunu, why aren't you responding. I am moving. I have a feeling."

"Sunu? An ungwa storm is coming. If you get this, find shelter."

He quickly clicked on her coordinates and waited.

"Sunu?!" his wife screamed.

He spoke quickly before she started shouting. "I'm sorry. I'm safe! Are you safe?"

There was a pause. Her face appeared on the tiny portable screen. It distorted with each crash of lightning. "I thought you . . ."

"I'm not," he said. "I'm in a cave. Where are you?"

"I found two ancients," she said. Sunuteel nodded. Ancients were the crumbling remains of old metal, stone, or petrified wood structures. "I'm underneath two huge stones. I was lucky. I am safe, too."

Sunuteel breathed a sigh of relief. His wife probably began searching hours ago, as soon as the sky shifted. Lightning crashed as he looked out of the cave. He blinked. He could have sworn he saw a shape in the flash. A black shape.

"Wife," he said. "I think I found something."

Lightning crashed again, and three bolts struck not far from the cave's mouth, consecutively. This time he was sure he saw it. He shuddered, frightened to his old bones. A woman dancing in the flash. "What is that?" he whispered.

"Sunu?" his wife asked frowning. "Are you all right?"

He nodded. "Do you remember your premonition?" he asked.

"Yes," she said.

"Have you seen anything?" he asked. "Have you been visited?" He felt silly. He'd never humored his wife about her strange superstitions.

"No," she said. "But I still have the feeling."

"I think she is here," he quickly said. "Wife, there is a woman in the flames outside. I found a cave. It's full of ancient technology, Okeke technology. Our people's sins." He looked outside. No black dancing woman, but now a wind had picked up. "One of the computers put this file on my portable. It's speaking to me. That's . . . why I missed your messages. I was"—he lowered his voice and whispered—"listening."

His wife stared at him for so long, that Sunuteel began to wonder if the screen had frozen. "Wife, what do . . . ?"

"You're safe?" she asked. "In that cave?"

He nodded. "It's perfectly dry. No lightning wants to strike it."

"She's causing the storm," his wife declared.

Sunuteel was about to deny this. But he couldn't. All he had to do was look at the strange rain and lightning-laden sky outside. The smell of burning sand on the air. He knew what he saw out there. He knew what he'd been listening to on his portable. "Well, what do I do?"

"Finish," she said. "Let her finish her story, husband."

When she clicked off and her image disappeared, Sunuteel looked outside. The rain was coming down harder than ever, the lightning crashing near constantly. He put the portable on the sandy ground before him and opened the virtual screen. He clicked un-pause and the spoken words and red words on the screen continued.

CHAPTER 23

Naked

BACK IN TOWER 7, Mmuo had told me that he knew Vera Takeisha Thomas. He'd said they didn't get along at all. But he'd visited her. He enjoyed the arguing. Mmuo didn't have much else to say about her. I doubt he knew what became of her, and all he could probably have imagined was a bad future for her. And he was right. More right than he could have known. My mother had a horrible rest of her life and then came to a horrible horrible end.

And now I was returning to the Sandcastle Hotel. I was coming in hot. Like a missile. It was enough. I was done. I think I decided when I saw Seven hacked to death. Or maybe it was in Ghana when they killed Kofi, a quiet choice I made so deep in me that I wasn't even aware of it. Or maybe I made it when I thought they'd killed Saeed. Or when my temperature began rising that first time in Tower 7, when I was only coming to understand the meaning of my name.

When I saw the Big Eye were there, that which burned in me erupted. *Phoom!*

The day was sunny, and I was a second sun. Maybe that's why no one noticed me coming at first. Or maybe it was because of what was happening below. I could hear the gunfire from hundreds of feet in the air. I could see the bodies of the children reddening the water. I burned hotter and flew faster. Saeed. Mmuo.

They'd come looking for us after all. They found us. We were the ones who had underestimated the Big Eye. Maybe Dartise had told them of the hotel before they killed him. On purpose? After torture? It didn't matter. Nothing mattered. I could slip to just before it all happened. But it didn't matter. It would happen again. Then I would slip and it would happen again. This would always happen. I couldn't save my own mother. All I could bring her was death. Harbinger. Reaper. It was in my DNA.

As soon as I landed, I spotted him lying on some black stones on the beach, the water lapping his body. Three of the children lay on top of him. I ran to him, splashing in the water. My legs felt like boiled cassava. I thought I would collapse. I held my chest, trying to contain my pounding heart. The water steamed as it made contact with my heated body. My folded wings got wet and dried and got wet and dried again. I fell to my knees and moaned, "Mmuo!"

He was not breathing. He was dead. His eyes were open. He was grasping the hands of two of the children. His mouth was open. There were deep holes in his chest and one in his neck. He was naked. His body was held in the sand. Not buried. In the sand. He must have been sinking into the earth when he was shot. What would happen if I moved him? Would his flesh be mingled with the sand?

I shuddered. I was already broken and I could feel myself breaking even more. The water around me boiled with my heat. I grabbed the hand of the dead child grasping Mmuo's left hand and angrily pried his fingers away.

"Get off!" I screamed. "Leave him!"

The child's body floated off when the waves rushed in. I did the same to the other. I leaned back, opened my mouth and sobbed, pressing my hands to my face. I should have been looking for Saeed, but I couldn't move. I just couldn't move. What would I do if I found Saeed's body? I would die and then I would live. I could not die. I was cursed. I couldn't leave this awful world.

"Mmuo!" I wailed. This gentle, powerful man who'd understood matter so profoundly that it allowed him to pass through it. How could they kill him? *Why?* What could he and those children possibly have done to them? He was my brother. I whimpered and then keened loudly, straining every part of my body, my being, willing my spirit to flee. It didn't, I lived. I quieted, looking at him. I calmed. But I did not cool. Let the Big Eye find me. What could they do that they had not already done? *See what I will do to you all*, I thought.

I jumped up and flew off to find Saeed. I never looked back. If I looked back, I knew Mmuo would have been even less substantial. His body had felt soft. The ocean was taking him back.

And the Big Eye were taking my Saeed. There they were, on the road. He was surrounded by ten of them, two were shoving him into one of their trucks. All armed. He was bleeding. He was looking down. Defeated.

"Saeed!" I screamed, hovering high up. *Phoom!* My body caught fire, my wings became flames. I felt beautiful.

I saw him look up and then terror crossed his face. "Phoenix! No!" He reached his hand out to me and then made a fist and clasped it to his chest. "Not you! Don't let them take you! Slip! Slip away! Oof!" One of the Big Eye kicked him hard in the belly, sending him into the truck.

They pointed their guns at me. I don't know why they always pointed guns at me. I was beyond their guns. Numb pathetic evil people.

I could kill them all.

Make them all ash.

But Saeed. My Saeed. "I survive," he always said.

I slipped.

CHAPTER 24

Who Fears the Reaper

SEVEN.

Seven.

Seven.

Seven deadly sinners. None of them would die. They were like me. Long staying. But they were not like me. I wanted to be free and free the imprisoned, they wanted to be free to enslave the world. I could hunt them down, one by one. Or I could do something worse. I was beginning to see that I was meant for something deeper and bigger.

I streaked across the sky. I thought of the alien creature I'd set free that set the others free in Tower 1. Then it had streaked into the sky, off the earth, into space. It could fly like me. But it wasn't like me. I would never leave this earth, not like that.

In warfare, there is a military strategy called "scorched earth." It is when you destroy anything that might be useful to the enemy as you move through or pull out of their territory. Scorched earth is heartless, it's violent, it's merciless, and it usually involves fire. One of its methods, the strategy of destroying the civilian food supplies in an area of conflict has been banned under Article 54 of Protocol I of the 1977 Geneva Conventions. But this is only enforceable by countries who have ratified this protocol. Only the United States and Israel have not. In this way, I am very American.

New York

I remember it well, as an old man remembers the deepest folktales that pleased him most as a child. As the brother of a Yoruba king remembers the burdensome responsibilities that he narrowly escaped. My memory is clear as the waters of the Caribbean's most virgin beaches. My memory is so unpolluted that I can see it happening now. It is happening now. In the bright sky of New York. I burn. Wings of flame. But it is too bright for the people below to really notice me. I burn without needing fuel. My body is like a sun. I give off no smoke.

First the buildings that stand in the risen waters like rotten mangrove trees. I fly low and the water around me boils. The water-logged spoiled skyscrapers that still stand ignite as I pass. I catch glimpses of people who step out on roofs, up to open windows and up from boats. They look down, across, up at me as I pass. Then they burst into ash.

The waters below the buildings boil and steam. Water is life. I am only doing what I am made to do. Taking life. I will take it all. I am a hurricane of death and destruction. I am villain.

I fly past the drowning buildings. Swamps. The grasslands. Networked with roads and trees. I am flying faster now. This is not where I want to be. I see cars and trucks run off the road as they overheat. Some people burn. The tops of trees burst into flame. By now, there are news drones flying with me. I can see them. They remain three miles away. A safe distance from my corona of heat. I am on the side of skyscrapers, the screens of portables, computers, jelli tellis. Those who do not see me in real life, see me in hyper life. What are they saying about me on the newsfeeds? Are people downtown smart enough to flee? Or will they sit there watching me on their small and giant screens, mesmerized as if I am just a character in an action film? But then again, how can I blame them? They created me.

I cannot think straight.

Kofi's parents and siblings were taken to Tower 1. His father had the ability to feel through metal. He was a "goldsmith," a glorified name in Ghana for blacksmith, and this ability made him good at his job. He passed it on to Kofi's sister and brother. They all died in Tower 1 of lead poisoning when the Big Eye tried to fuse their nerves with cybernetic limbs. That Kofi's mother was taken to Tower 1 was all the records said about her, other than Deceased. I read about them in the Library of Congress.

The Big Eye surrounded us. I am a terrorist.

Berihun and his Ethiopian restaurant. Surviving in a strange soulless land. What would they become? What was his and his wife's point of existing when all they were to this world was dust? Ash. Filth.

Mmuo's nanomites should have been in me, but I'd burned them away. Would I have still been able to hear him if I hadn't burned them away? Mmuo, my brother, I do not care what the genetics say. Mmuo is dead.

Saeed. He had died. Then he had lived. Then they *took* him from me. They are always *taking* from me. The Big Eye. This country. The superpowers. The seven men who drank HeLa's blood and now will never die.

I slip.

All things come from the land, Ani. This was why the alien seed fell and burrowed into it. It's best to start at the beginning. So not Allah. Not Krishna. Not God. Not Nature. Ani. Mmuo spoke of her to me. Ani is the spirit of the earth. The spirit of flesh. When I look deep into my DNA, I see that I know her story. I simply have to speak it from my heart and soul. Weave it like a spider weaves a web on a warm humid evening when the night is about to fall upon it.

Here's how the story goes:

> Thousands of years ago, when the world was nothing but sand and dry trees, Ani looked over her lands. She rubbed her dry throat. Then she made the oceans, lakes, rivers, and ponds. Her lands breathed and then danced. Water is life. And from the

oceans, she took a deep drink and was refreshed. 'One day,' she said, 'I'll produce sunshine. Right now, I'm not in the mood.' She turned over and slept. Behind her back, as she rested, human beings sprang from the sweetest parts of the rivers and the shallow portions of the lakes. Some of them walked out of the ocean onto the beaches.

Human beings were aggressive like the rushing rivers, forever wanting to move forward, cutting, carving, changing the lands. As much time passed, they created and used and changed and altered and spread and consumed and multiplied. They were everywhere. At the apex of their genius, one group of humans built seven mighty towers. Within these towers they performed impossible feats, and as time expanded, the towers grew to impossible heights in reputation, invention, and experience.

The exclusive human beings of this group who ran the towers had the permission of civilian human beings to do whatever it took. They all hoped their towers would be high and amazing enough to prick Ani and get her attention. They built juju-working machines. They fought and invented amongst themselves. They bent and twisted Ani's sand, water, sky, and air. They took her creatures and changed them. They sought to make themselves just like Ani: immortal, all powerful manipulators of earth's lands.

When Ani was rested enough to produce sunshine, she turned over and was horrified by what she saw. She reared up, tall and impossible, furious. Then she reached into the stars and pulled a sun to the land. I am that sun. I am Ani's soldier. I do her will. Ani has asked me to wipe the slate clean.

I reappear in the middle of Times Square. I stand on the flat portion of a jagged splintered surface. The air smells of flowers and smoke, but mostly flowers. The surface below me is damp beneath my bare feet. Beside me is a small forest of wooden splinters. I kneel down and touch the flat surface, the wood.

And that's when I feel it. Deep in my chest. It's a small ball, hot, like the sun. It spreads out. Near my heart, shoulder, breast. I kneel there, with my eyes shut. I am on the stump of The Backbone, its fallen cleaved carcass beside me, its width reaching thirty feet above me.

I see red. Yellow. Orange. Fire.

I open my eyes in time to see the small camp of Big Eye a few hundred feet away. They had expected me, but they didn't expect this. Except one. The woman who comes out of a small tent set up right beside the tree's massive stump. She is short and dark-skinned, born and raised in Nigeria, craving American agency. She is beautiful and wears the black uniform of the Big Eye because she is one of their most dedicated officials. She has pursued me across the globe, found me, lost me and has now found me again. Miserable woman, she walks toward me, her gait sure; she no longer limps. Maybe both of her legs are cybernetic. She holds up a hand that is made of wires, metal, reinforced plastic. She has more in common with the Ledussee than the Big Eye. Misguided woman.

Before the other Big Eye turn around and before the woman named Bumi can reach me, all of them are engulfed in a corona. From wet living sin, bone, flesh to ash. And metal and plastic, also to ash. All things in the city are in chaos, people staring at screens, crashing cars, cowering, praying, cursing, fleeing.

I am the sun. Ten thousand degrees Fahrenheit. Ani has pulled me to the earth. To wipe the slate clean. This is how it happens. New York's prodigal daughter returns home.

Not just New York. I scorch the earth. Yes, I can do that. I am that. Phoenix Okore blew across the earth. She burned the cities. Turned the oceans to steam. She was the reaper come to reap what was sown. Wherever those seven men lived. Let them die. Let everything die.

Let that which had been written all be rewritten.

CHAPTER 25

Saeed

THEY HAD THIS TECHNOLOGY for a long time. It is smaller than a shoebox and just as light as an empty one. The instructions are simple, too, the touch screen guides you in voice commands and with pictures. It is not made for scientists. It is truly a recorder. It is made to pull and store information, not to offer its services only to the elite educated. I cannot read very well, so this was good.

The memory extractor was in the remains of Tower 2. It was not a tower that we ever researched, so I do not know what they specialized in. Phoenix would have known. It was in the place that used to be Miami. I travelled there on foot, a year later, after I had decided to leave the dead lands of the United States and find my way back to Africa. I found it in the ruins by chance. If you believe in chance.

Do you wonder how I got there when there were no more airplanes and the only people alive were dying or living in seclusion, stunned that they had somehow survived what looked like the sun exploding. How did I get to Africa? I walked. The oceans had dried up.

I was fine. I was made to survive this, remember? I ate the sweetest sand I'd ever tasted as I crossed the grave that used to be the sea. I reached what used to be Senegal four months later. In that time, I didn't see a soul. Not one person, not one bird, not one insect, and certainly not one fish.

Phoenix was serious. It was about halfway through that I sat down and brought the memory extractor from my backpack.

I let it pull Phoenix's memory from the one thing of hers that I still had. Her golden red feather. It still glowed softly in the dark. All I had to do was press the device to it. The red light on the screen went on, along with a word that I could not read. Then it grew warm and in a soft woman's voice said, "Extracting The Phoenix Okore, SpeciMen, Beacon, Slave, Rogue, Fugitive, Rebel, Saeed's Love, Mmuo's Sister, Villain."

These were how she saw herself. Her various incarnations. All right there. How did this device know? Mmuo was always talking about this stuff in his skin called DNA. He said this stuff was what carried all that we would be. Did DNA carry memory, too? Was it reading her DNA? I don't know. I will never know.

The device beeped and then said, "Extract sent to database 80255." It beeped. "Protocol 7 is now in place. Extract bypassed from 80255 to protocol 7, *The Great Book*. May God help your soul."

I laughed. I could not listen to the extract because it had been sent somewhere else. I laughed again as I thought, *Maybe it was sent somewhere in Ghana.* They had contact there, who's to say they did not have some computers placed somewhere underground or even on a satellite? Just in case the world went to shit as it had, thanks to the woman I will love forever. And ever. Maybe they placed it there knowing that the shit would start elsewhere. Yes, this feels right. Regardless, Phoenix's words were out there somewhere. Alive.

I put the memory extractor to my flesh. The red light goes on. Words that I cannot read flash on the screen. It grows warm. Then the woman's voice said, "Extracting . . ."

CHAPTER 26

This Was Woman, Herself

SUNUTEEL WAS SQUINTING. Saeed's brief extract had been a footnote at the end of *The Book of Phoenix*. It was in Arabic, a language that was like a stripped down version of Sunuteel's native tongue, Nuru. Listening to it gave him a headache, but that wasn't what was making him squint. The sun was rising in the distance, chasing away the cool air. He'd been listening to Phoenix tell her story all night, finishing with the part where Saeed spoke. But listening all night wasn't what was making him squint either.

His head pounded, his jaw ached and there was a tinny sound deep in his head. He squinted more deeply, staring ahead. Beyond his stretched achy legs. Past his sand encrusted feet. Past where the red virtual words had flashed before his eyes, as Phoenix spoke the memories she'd have never spoken to anyone. Through the opening of the cave. And out into the desert. About thirty feet away.

"Ani protect me," he whispered. "She is here."

Not only could he feel her heat, he could smell smoke, though nothing burned. Not now. Not anymore. The burning was all done. Now she danced before him, a bird woman or orange red yellow light. Just like his wife's vision. Phoenix had appeared to his wife first, but Phoenix decided to give *him* her story. He was the chosen one. She had danced there throughout the reading of the last portion of her story—when she'd spoken of how she scorched the earth.

Sunuteel had wanted to look away. He'd wanted to clap his hands over his ears. Phoenix was tearing his world apart with her words. Everything he'd thought he knew was wrong. Ani had not pulled a star to the earth when the Okeke people, his people, had crossed the lines of morality. That story had been made up. Made up by this Phoenix.

Sunuteel whimpered. How could this be? So who were his people? The Okeke? According to Phoenix, the Okeke weren't only the people of the land, the dark-skinned wooly haired people on the sun. The Okeke were everyone, Nuru, Okeke, and even these whiter skinned limper haired people he'd never heard of. His people *weren't* born to suffer for the sins of those Okeke who came before him. Stories, all stories.

Saeed.

He bent his legs. Slowly. The joints popped, but he was quickly able to bring them to his chest. She was gone. She'd stayed to hear her story then she'd flown off to wherever spirits flew when they were no longer interested. He got up and walked outside, into a world that was no different to him. He was not cursed. He'd been raised to believe he *was*, that all his people were. He felt lightheaded. He felt light.

"Saeed," he said aloud. "The Seed."

He'd been taught by the very man who had loved the woman who ended the world as it was known. Women brought life but the most important origin stories spoke the real truth, which was that women more often brought death. *The Book of Phoenix* was full of this truth. If she had been a male, she'd have controlled her anger, channeled it into righting the world's wrongs, and probably not sprouted troublesome wings. *Woman*, Sunuteel thought, recalling a poem or a bit of literature he'd once heard and always thought described the other sex so well. *"This was woman herself, with her sudden fears, her irrational whims, her instinctive worries, her impetuous boldness, her fussings, and her delicious sensibility".*

This woman's story was real. It was close to Sunuteel in ways that astonished him. The existence of his teacher of English, The Seed, once known as Saeed, brought Phoenix's tale directly into his life. He frowned, unable to resolve this fact. Unable to reject it or find a way to smooth things over so that he was comfortable with the information and his world didn't feel so backward. A refreshing idea popped into his head.

He'd read it in reading class and even had a copy of the essay still on his portable. Yes. An essay from over a hundred years ago, translator and author unknown. He pulled it up on his portable and the passage in the second paragraph instantly caught his eye.

"As soon as a fact is narrated no longer with a view to acting directly on reality but intransitively, that is to say, finally outside of any function other than that of the very practice of the symbol itself, this disconnection occurs, the voice loses its origin, the author enters into his own death, writing begins."

He chuckled to himself. The essay had originally been in a language that was now lost, and this was probably the cause of the convoluted nature of the writing. However, if he read it slowly, it made perfect sense. He'd been fascinated by the notion stated in the essay, all the students had. Considering the fact that almost all the authors of the few books and essays and other pieces of literature they had *were* dead, the concept allowed for a lot of understanding.

His teacher had proudly referred to the "Author is Dead" essay whenever anyone asked, "What was the author thinking when he wrote this?" Once the author wrote the story, the author became irrelevant. The author was dead. In *The Book of Phoenix*, this was certainly the case. Phoenix was dead. The story was alive, having separated from Phoenix as a child separated from her or his dying mother at birth. It was up to the reader to *interpret* what the story really was about. And in this case, the only reader was Sunuteel.

"Wife," Sunuteel wrote in a message. "I'm coming home."

He sent the message and then went back to his blanket near the cave entrance. He plopped down, with a bone weary sigh. He felt as if he'd travelled a thousand miles. In a way he had. His portable buzzed viciously and he froze. His portable always buzzed and announced the arrival of a message from his wife in a soft female voice that reminded him of his third daughter. However, this was just a buzz, and it was a sharp buzz that he'd never felt before. He nearly threw the portable. He looked at it, and then he did throw it. It landed noisily in the sand.

For the first time in his entire adult life, he was afraid of being alone in the desert. His hand screamed from the sudden heat his portable let out, and he felt the weight of his age and his lack of age simultaneously. He was old, and he was too young. He was vulnerable. He was alone. He rubbed his painful hands; even their toughness was no protection from the burn.

His portable had been hot to the touch and on the screen, flames of orange, yellow, black, and red churned and broiled. It was impossible for his portable to feel that hot and still work.

"Sunuteel!"

The harsh voice shot from his portable, vicious and sharp. But it sounded like the speaker was smiling. No one but his wife's voice had ever spoken through his portable. Not his children's, not his friend's. His portable was connected to only one network, his wife's. Yet, the voice of a dead woman was speaking to him through the device.

"Impossible," he muttered. Tears ran down his cheeks and urine ran down his inner thighs.

"I know what you think," she said. "You can rewrite a story, but once it is written, it lives. Think before you do; your story is written too and so is the map of the consequences. Ani will remember the path, even if it is full of loops and swirls. Think, old man."

"You're just a memory," he said. "You've been extracted. You're nothing now. Leave my portable. It is not yours."

"Who is writing you?" she asked. But her voice was fading, just as Sunuteel imagined Mmuo's voice must have faded in Phoenix's head when her heat burned away his nanomites. Sunuteel blinked, frowning and knowing that all Phoenix spoke had happened. Every last word. And that scared him even more than the thought of her or her ghost or her memory speaking through his portable.

When his portable remained quiet for several minutes, only then did he move. He got up and went to his portable and looked down at it for a very long time. He'd need to use his capture station to pull down condensation from the sky so he could soak his hands. Capture station water was always cool, thankfully.

He nudged the portable with his sandal. He knelt down and poked it with his finger. It was cool, again. He left it there and went to soak his painful hands, wash his fouled legs and change his clothes. He returned an hour later, picked it up, and placed it back into his pocket. Portables were easy enough to find, but he and his wife couldn't afford another. Plus, he wanted this one. No matter how fearful he was about what it all was and meant, he wanted to be a part of this. To him, it was written.

Sunuteel returned to his wife a day and half later. When they could let go of each other, and his wife had stopped laughing and crying, and Sunuteel had finished the roasted goat meat and cactus candy his wife fed him, Sunuteel told her much. He spoke of the cave of computers, and her eyes grew wide as they always did when he told her something amazing. He spoke of the transmission, and she gasped and asked for every detail, even the *ping* sound it made on arrival. And he spoke of the grand audio file he found on his portable, and she grew very quiet, her eyes keen. But he did not tell her *The Book of Phoenix*.

"Give me thirty days then I will tell you the story."

His wife looked him in the eye for several moments. Then she said, "Ok." She had lived for decades as Sunuteel's wife. She trusted him. And so, at the next market they encountered, Sunuteel spent much of what they had on several reams of rough paper and ten black pens. Then they found a nice place in the desert where five palm trees grew and had survived several ungwa storms, and for thirty days, they did not go anywhere. And Sunuteel listened to the English and Arabic parts of *The Great Book* and transcribed it to paper. He took in the words and rewrote them. At first the going was slow, but as he fell into the rhythm of the story and the depth of the subject matter, he transcribed faster.

Phoenix had said that the goddess Ani had pulled a star to the earth after she saw what the Okeke were doing. All he had to think about was how the Okeke, his own people, had been so destructive centuries ago. This was not just false history, it was real. He knew this. He didn't care what Phoenix said. The Okeke *were* a cursed people.

And this was how the Great Book was rewritten as the story of The Okeke and Why They are Cursed. Sunuteel was old. Of all people, he knew that Phoenix's story was no longer relevant to the descendants of the survivors of her rage. The past was the past. Not once did he speak aloud the fact that Phoenix, dead or alive or neither, scared him to his very soul. He could not admit that he understood her to be like a god; that to evoke her image in story, over and over, to him, was to tempt fate. Now it was a time for stories that were truer than the truth, stories that spoke to the soul.

Sunuteel did not specifically set out to solidify the Okeke as slave and the Nuru as superior through powerful literature, but what is in one's heart comes out in one's stories. Even when he or she's retelling someone else's story. Sunuteel was old. He'd lived for a long time understanding his ancestors as slaves.

At the end of the thirty days, Sunuteel told his wife the story of *The Book of Phoenix* and then she read the version her husband had written. And his wife was pleased. "We should convert it to an audio file that we can copy onto people's portables. That way those who cannot read can listen and understand it well."

And this was how *The Great Book* that went on to be the most read book in the last hundred years was born. Sunuteel's wife's deep rich voice lived far beyond the old woman's physical self. In this way, both Sunuteel and his wife became immortal. The Big Eye would have been mildly impressed.

Epilogue

Sola Speaks

SUNUTEEL ABBREVIATED IDEAS, chopped stories in half, summarized pain and suffering and joy, and reinterpreted and omitted. He declared the authors dead and did with the information what he would. That silly little essay from so many decades ago didn't take into consideration that the story could be and very often was *shaman*, and that the teller was more often than not *medium*. There are ghosts in the machine and spirits in the books, oral or written. Don't be naïve enough to believe that the author of *The Book of Phoenix* is dead. What is death, *sha*?

I will interject here. I am Sola.

I give you this story from the future. Or maybe I am in the past, today. Presently, I am in your presence. I am a white man; I have and use the privilege of unhindered mobility. I laugh because most of my words are lies. Regardless, I hope this story is a comfort to you. I pray that it makes you better able to sleep at night.

I don't really care if you know who I am. Just know that I know more than you. So listen. Sunuteel is as much a victim of his environment as he is a talented man of his own profession. He is old and that opened him to the voice of Phoenix Okore's story. But he is too young to see beyond his own nose. He cannot contain Phoenix's tale. He cannot even consider her story, for whenever his mind goes back to it, he sees her ghost which was not a ghost standing in the sand just outside that cave, burning like lightning and staring at him.

Sunuteel is a good man but he is limited. A part of him is also a coward. Why do you think he will never seek The Seed for real answers? Instead, he chose to write fiction.

It was as if he were possessed, for not only did he rewrite and rewrite, he became infected with stories. He wrote stories so tantalizing and addictive that those who heard it were sure that they heard truth. His Great Book, which he claimed was not his, was powerful and delightful. It was full of rules, history and shapes. It reshaped what the people of the deserted lands knew and felt deep in their hearts. They were a wounded people, so these ideas were wounded, too.

The old African man took the bones, blood, and quivering flesh of Phoenix's book, digested its marrow and defecated a tale of his own. Then he and his oracle of a wife spread this shit far and wide. And their Great Book deformed the lives of many until the one named Onyesonwu came and changed it again. But that is another story.

Acknowledgments

I'd like to thank my mother for her constant unwavering support for the strange career I've chosen. I'd like to thank Clarkesworld Magazine for publishing the novelette version of this story. The feedback I received for that story boosted my confidence. Thanks to Subterranean Press for publishing the novella version of this novel, "African Sunrise." It was that process which brought the talented illustrator Eric Battle into the mix. Thank you to Eric Battle for his stunning illustrations of Phoenix Okore and her world. Stories are best told on many levels and his illustrations are a wonderful voice added to the cacophony that is *The Book of Phoenix*. I'd like to thank my DAW editor Betsy Wollheim; when she reads my wild flawed complex women characters, she sees superheroines. Many thanks to NASA geologist (and 2001 Clarion Writers Workshop classmate) Thomas Wagner for his knowledge about global warming, especially about what it would take to make New York tropical. Thanks to my agent Don Maass; always there to guide me. Lastly, I'd like to thank my most dedicated beta reader Angel Maynard who read this in its most raw form; her unbiased eyes and honest feedback helped to make this novel burn. Shout out to my daughter Anyaugo, family, and dearest friends. <3

WANT MORE?

If you enjoyed this and would like to find out about similar books we publish, we'd love you to join our online SF, Fantasy and Horror community, Hodderscape.

Visit our blog site
www.hodderscape.co.uk

Follow us on Twitter
🐦 **@hodderscape**

Like our Facebook page
f Hodderscape

You'll find exclusive content from our authors, news, competitions and general musings, so feel free to comment, contribute or just keep an eye on what we are up to. See you there!